AMERICAN SCHOOL TEXTBOOK

VOCABULARY KEY

GRADE 3

Michael A. Putlack

FUN學美國英語課本

各學科關鍵英單 二版+ Workbook

MP3

學好美國學生課堂上常用的各學科詞彙，就能輕鬆看懂英語課本、用英文上課啦！

FÜN學美國英語課本

各學科關鍵英單 GRADE 3

AMERICAN SCHOOL TEXTBOOK
VOCABULARY KEY

二版

作者簡介

Michael A. Putlack

專攻歷史與英文，擁有美國麻州 Tufts University 碩士學位。

作　　者　Michael A. Putlack
　　　　　Zachary Fillingham / Shara Dupuis (Workbook B 大題)
編　　輯　丁宥榆／歐寶妮
翻　　譯　歐寶妮
校　　對　丁宥暄
封面設計　林書玉
內頁排版　丁宥榆／林書玉
製程管理　洪巧玲
出 版 者　寂天文化事業股份有限公司
電　　話　+886-(0)2-2365-9739
傳　　真　+886-(0)2-2365-9835
網　　址　www.icosmos.com.tw
讀者服務　onlineservice@icosmos.com.tw
出版日期　2021 年 2 月　二版二刷

郵撥帳號　1998620-0 寂天文化事業股份有限公司
‧劃撥金額 600 元（含）以上者，郵資免費。
‧訂購金額 600 元以下者，請外加郵資 65 元。
〔若有破損，請寄回更換，謝謝。〕

國家圖書館出版品預行編目資料

Fun 學美國英語課本：各學科關鍵英單 (寂天雲隨身聽 APP 版)
Grade. 3 / Michael A. Putlack 著 ; 歐寶妮譯 . -- 二版 . -- [臺北市]
: 寂天文化 , 民 110.02
　　面；　公分

ISBN 978-986-318-975-6(菊 8K 平裝)

1. 英語 2. 詞彙

805.12　　　　　　　　　　　110001031

FUN學美國英語課本：各學科關鍵英單

進入明星學校必備的英文單字

　　用美國教科書學英文是最道地的學習方式，有越來越多的學校選擇以美國教科書作為教材，用**全英語授課（immersion）**的方式教學，讓學生把英語當成母語學習。在一些語言學校裡，也掀起了一波「用美國教科書學英文」的風潮。

　　同時，108 課綱強調跨領域學習，本套書以 STEAM（Science, Technology, Engineering, Art, and Math）元素的學習內容，讓孩子能把英語當作工具學習數學、科學、藝術等別的學科，實踐跨領域學習。另外，還有越來越多的父母優先考慮讓子女用美國教科書來學習英文，讓孩子將來能夠進入明星學校或國際學校就讀。

　　為什麼要使用美國教科書呢？TOEFL 等國際英語能力測驗都是以各學科知識為基礎，使用美國教科書不但能**大幅提升英文能力，也可以增加數學、社會、科學等方面的知識**，因此非常適合用來準備考試。即使不到國外留學，也可以像在美國上課一樣，而這也是使用美國教科書最吸引人的地方。

以多樣化的照片、插圖和例句來熟悉跨科學習中的英文單字

　　到底該使用何種美國教科書呢？還有如何才能讀懂美國教科書呢？美國各州、各學校的課程都不盡相同，而學生也有選擇教科書的權利，所以單單是教科書的種類就多達數十種。若不小心選擇到程度不適合的教科書，就很容易造成孩子對學英語的興趣大減。

　　因此，正確的作法應該要先累積字彙和相關知識背景。我國學生的學習能力很強，只需要**培養對不熟悉的用語和跨科學習（Cross-Curricular Study）**的適應能力。

　　本系列網羅了在以**全英語教授社會、科學、數學、語言、藝術、音樂**等學科時，所有會出現的必備英文單字。只要搭配書中真實的照片、插圖和例句，就能夠把這些在美國小學課本中會出現的各學科核心單字記起來，同時還可以熟悉相關的背景知識。

四種使用頻率最高的美國教科書的字彙分析

　　本系列套書規畫了 6 個階段的字彙學習課程，搜羅了 McGraw Hill、Harcourt、Pearson 和 Core Knowledge 等四大教科書中的主要字彙，並且整理出各科目、各主題的核心單字，然後依照學年分為 Grade 1 到 Grade 6。

　　本套書的適讀對象為「準備大學學測的學生」和「準備參加 TOEFL 等國際英語能力測驗的學生」。對於「準備赴美唸高中的學生」和「想要看懂美國教科書的學生」，本套書亦是最佳的先修教材。

《FUN學美國英語課本：各學科關鍵英單》系列的結構與特色

1. 本套書中所收錄的英文單字都是美國學生在上課時會學到的字彙和用法。

2. 將美國小學教科書中會出現的各學科核心單字，搭配多樣化照片、插圖和例句，讓讀者更容易熟記。

3. 藉由閱讀教科書式的題目，來強化讀、聽、寫的能力。透過各式各樣的練習與題目，不僅能夠全盤吸收與各主題有關的字彙，也能夠熟悉相關的知識背景。

4. 每一冊的教學大綱（syllabus）皆涵蓋了社會、歷史、地理、科學、數學、語言、美術和音樂等學科，以循序漸進的方式，學習從基礎到高級的各科核心字彙，不僅能夠擴增各科目的字彙量，同時還提升了運用句子的能力。（教學大綱請參考第 8 頁）

5. 可學到社會、科學等的相關背景知識和用語，也有助於準備 TOEFL 等國際英語能力測驗。

6. 對於「英語程度有限，但想看懂美國教科書的學生」來說，本套書是很好的先修教材。

7. 全系列 6 階段共分為 6 冊，可依照個人英語程度，選擇合適的分冊。

   Grade 1 美國學校 1 年級課程　　**Grade 2** 美國學校 2 年級課程

   Grade 3 美國學校 3 年級課程　　**Grade 4** 美國學校 4 年級課程

   Grade 5 美國學校 5 年級課程　　**Grade 6** 美國學校 6 年級課程

8. 書末附有關鍵字彙的中英文索引，方便讀者搜尋與查照（請參考第 141 頁）。

強烈建議下列學生使用本套書：

1. 準備大學學測的學生

2. 「準備參加以全英語授課的課程，想熟悉美國學生上課時會用到的各科核心字彙」的學生

3. 「對美國小學各科必備英文字彙已相當熟悉，想朝高級單字邁進」美國學校的七年級生

4. 「準備赴美唸高中」的學生

MP3

收錄了本書的「Key Words」、「Power Verbs」、「Word Families」單元中的所有單字和例句，和「Checkup」中 E 大題的文章，以及 Workbook 中 A 大題聽寫練習文章。

How to Use This Book

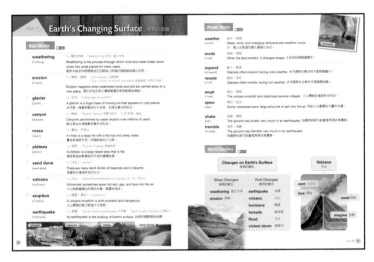

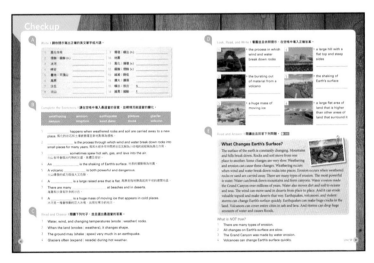

Table of Contents

Workbook 聽力閱讀試題本

Syllabus Vol.3

Subject	Topic & Area	Title
Social Studies ● **History and Geography**	Citizenship	Laws and Rules
	Economics	Earning, Spending, and Saving
	Economics	Goods and Resources
	Science, Technology, and Society	Technology Changes the World
	Geography and Culture	Living in Different Climates
	Geography	Geography Skills
	The Government	The Government
	World History	Ancient Egypt
	World History	Ancient Greece
	World History	Ancient Rome
Science	Plants	A World of Plants
	Animals	A World of Animals
	A World of Living Things	Food Chains
	Ecosystems	Ecosystems
	Our Earth	Earth's Rocks and Soil
	Earth's Resources	Conserving Our Resources
	Our Earth	Earth's Changing Surface
	Weather and Climate	Weather and the Water Cycle
	The Universe	The Universe
	The Human Body	The Senses
Mathematics	Fractions	Fractions
	Geometry	Geometry
	Computation	Multiplication and Division
	Measurement	Measurement
Language and Literature	Mythology	Myths From Ancient Greece
	Language Arts	Learning About Language
Visual Arts	Visual Arts	Appreciating Artwork
	Visual Arts	Creating Designs
Music	A World of Music	Elements of Music
	A World of Music	A World of Music

CHAPTER 1

Social Studies • History and Geography ①

Laws and Rules 法律與規範

Key Words ● 001

| 01 | **court** [kort] | (n.) 法院；法庭；球場 | *go to court over sth. 為某事打官司
 *high/supreme court 高等／最高法院 |

People with legal problems go to **court** to solve their problems.
人們碰到法律問題會訴諸法院解決。

| 02 | **judge** [dʒʌdʒ] | (n.) 法官 | *judge sb./sth. by . . . 根據……判斷某人／某事物 |

Judges and juries decide if laws have been broken.
法官和陪審團負責裁定違法與否。

| 03 | **jury** [ˈdʒʊrɪ] | (n.) 陪審團；評審委員會 | *serve/sit on a jury 作為陪審團成員
 *trial by jury 陪審團審判 |

The **jury** decides on the guilt or innocence of an accused person.
陪審團對被告的有罪與否做出裁定。

| 04 | **lawyer** [ˈlɔjɚ] | (n.) 律師 | *lawsuit 訴訟 *consult a lawyer 諮詢律師 |

Lawyers try to help their clients get decisions in their favor.
律師試圖為他的當事人爭取有利的判決。

| 05 | **defendant** [dɪˈfɛndənt] | (n.) 被告（人） | *plaintiff 原告；起訴人 *defend 進行辯護 |

The **defendant** is a person who is accused of a crime. 被告是指涉嫌犯罪的人。

| 06 | **legal** [ˈligl] | (a.) 合法的；法定的 | *take legal action 提出訴訟 *legal right 合法權利 |

Something **legal** is allowed to be done. 合法的事是可以做的。

| 07 | **illegal** [ɪˈligl] | (a.) 不合法的；非法的 | *illegal immigrant 非法移民 *illegal drugs 非法毒品 |

Something **illegal** is against the law and cannot be done.
非法的事是違法並且不可以做的。

| 08 | **punishment** [ˈpʌnɪʃmənt] | (n.) 懲罰；處罰；刑罰 | *physical punishment 體罰
 *inflict a punishment on sb. 對某人施以處罰 |

A guilty person often receives some kind of **punishment**.
犯罪的人通常會受到一些懲罰。

| 09 | **guilty** [ˈgɪltɪ] | (a.) 有罪的；犯……罪的 (n.) guilt 有罪
 *be guilty of sth. 犯有某罪 *be found guilty/not guilty 被判決有罪／無罪 |

A person found **guilty** of a crime must be punished.
人一旦被裁定為有罪，就必須受到懲罰。

| 10 | **innocent** [ˈɪnəsn̩t] | (a.) 無罪的；清白的 (n.) innocence 無罪 *be innocent of 未犯有某罪 |

An **innocent** person did not commit a crime. 沒有犯罪的人即為無罪清白。

Court

judge   jury

defendant   prosecutor

commit a crime

break the law 違法；違反法律
People should not break the law. 人們不可犯法。

obey the law 守法；遵守法律
People should always obey the law. 人們應該要守法。

sue
[su]
提出訴訟；控告
A person can sue someone else for causing him or her harm.
一個人可以對傷害他人者提出訴訟。

accuse
[ə`kjuz]
指控；控告
The government might accuse someone of a crime. 政府可以指控某人犯罪。

prosecute
[`prɑsɪ,kjut]
起訴；告發
The prosecutor can prosecute a person for committing a crime.
檢察官可以犯下罪行為由，起訴一個人。

commit
[kə`mɪt]
犯（罪）；做（錯事等）
A person may commit crimes like murder or theft. 一個人可能犯下謀殺或偷竊的罪行。

punish
[`pʌnɪʃ]
懲罰；罰
The judge decides how criminals should be punished. 法官判決罪犯應受到何種懲罰。

Word Families
◉ 003

sentence	判決；宣判；課刑 A sentence is the punishment a person receives. 判決是指一個人所受到的處罰。
term	期；期限 A guilty person may receive a prison term. 犯罪的人可能要服刑。
prosecution	起訴方；原告及其律師 The prosecution tries to prove the guilt of a person. 起訴方試圖證明對方有罪。
defense	辯護方；被告及其律師 The defense tries to prove the innocence of a person. 辯護方試圖證明己方的清白。
prosecutor	檢察官 The prosecutor acts as a lawyer against the defendant. 檢察官擔任律師與被告抗衡。

Kinds of Punishments
刑罰的種類

fine 罰金　　　**jail term** 刑期

community service 社會服務

suspended prison sentence 緩刑

lifetime prison sentence 無期徒刑

death penalty 死刑
[`pɛnḷtɪ]

Kinds of Courts
法院的種類

municipal court 地方法院　**superior court** 高等法院
[mju`nɪsəpḷ]

tax court 稅務法庭　　**family court** 家事法庭

appeals court 上訴法院　**supreme court** 最高法院

Checkup

A

Write I 請依提示寫出正確的英文單字或片語。

1	法院；法庭；球場	_____	9 有罪的	_____
2	法官	_____	10 無罪的；清白的	_____
3	陪審團；評審委員會	_____	11 違反法律	_____
4	律師	_____	12 罰金	_____
5	被告（人）	_____	13 指控；控告	a _____
6	合法的；法定的	_____	14 檢察官	_____
7	不合法的；非法的	_____	15 犯（罪）；做（錯事等）	_____
8	懲罰；處罰 (n.)	_____	16 判決；宣判；課刑	_____

B

Complete the Sentences I 請在空格中填入最適當的答案，並視情況做適當的變化。

punishment	jury	legal	judge	guilty
innocent	court	illegal	lawyer	prosecution

1   _____ and juries decide if laws have been broken.
    法官和陪審團負責裁定違法與否。

2   People with legal problems go to _____ to solve their problems.
    人們碰到法律問題會訴諸於法院裁決。

3   The _____ decides on the guilt or innocence of an accused person.
    陪審團對被告的有罪與否做出裁定。

4   A guilty person often receives some kind of _____.
    犯罪的人通常會受到某種懲罰。

5   A person found _____ of a crime must be punished.
    人一旦被裁定為有罪，就必須受到懲罰。

6   An _____ person did not commit a crime. 沒有犯罪的人即為無罪清白。

7   Something _____ is allowed to be done. 合法的事是可以做的。

8   The _____ tries to prove the guilt of a person.
    起訴方試圖證明對方有罪。

C

Read and Choose I 閱讀下列句子，並且選出最適當的答案。

1   People should not (obey | break) the law.

2   The prosecutor can (sue | prosecute) a person for committing a crime.

3   The (defense | prosecution) tries to prove the innocence of a person.

4   The government might (sue | accuse) someone of a crime.

Look, Read, and Write | 看圖並且依照提示，在空格中填入正確答案。

1 ▶ a group of people who decide if someone is guilty or not in court

_____

4 ▶ a sum of money to be paid as a punishment

_____

2 ▶ the person who listens to a case and decides how criminals should be punished

_____

5 ▶ a person who acts as a lawyer against the defendant

_____

3 ▶ a person who is accused of a crime

_____

6 ▶ a place where trials take place and legal cases are decided

_____

E

Read and Answer | 閱讀並且回答下列問題。 ◎ 004

The Jury System

Most criminal cases in the United States are done in a trial by jury. Jury trials are an important part of the justice system. A jury is made up of regular citizens. There are two kinds of juries: a grand jury and a petit jury. A grand jury has between 12 and 23 members. The prosecutor presents his or her evidence to the grand jury. Then, the grand jury decides if there is enough evidence to have a trial. If the jury says yes, then there will be a trial. If the jury says no, there will be no trial. A petit jury is also called a trial jury. This jury has usually 12 members. The members listen to actual court cases. They hear all of the evidence. Then, at the end of the trial, they must make a decision. They decide if the defendant is innocent or guilty.

Answer the questions.

1 How many kinds of juries are there? _____

2 How many people serve on a grand jury? _____

3 What is another name for a trial jury? _____

4 What does a trial jury do? _____

Key Words
🔊 005

| 01 | **income** [ˈɪnˌkʌm] | (n.) 收入　　*annual income 年收益　　*source of income 收入來源 |
| | | Income is the money you earn from working. 收入是指工作的所得。 |

| 02 | **spending** [ˈspɛndɪŋ] | (n.) 開銷；花費　　*public spending 公用事業支出　　*spending money 零用錢 |
| | | People must be careful that their spending is not more than their earnings. 人們一定要小心，勿使入不敷出。 |

| 03 | **savings** [ˈsevɪŋz] | (n.) 積蓄；儲金　　*life savings 畢生積蓄　　*live off/on one's savings 靠存款生活 |
| | | Many people put their savings in the bank. 很多人將他們的積蓄放在銀行裡。 |

| 04 | **budget** [ˈbʌdʒɪt] | (n.) 預算；經費　　*go over budget 超出預算　　*balance the budget 量入為出 |
| | | A budget is a plan that shows income, spending, and savings. 預算是一個顯示收入、開銷與儲蓄的計畫。 |

| 05 | **profit** [ˈprɑfɪt] | (n.) 利潤；盈利　　*nonprofit 非營利的　　*profit from/by 得益於某事物 |
| | | The goal of every company is to make a profit. 每間公司的目標都是要獲利。 |

| 06 | **demand** [dɪˈmænd] | (n.) 要求；需要　(v.) 要求；需要　　*demand sth. from sb. 向某人索討某物　　*be in demand 需求量大 |
| | | The demand for a product is how much people want it. 產品的需求是指人們對產品的渴求度。 |

| 07 | **supply** [səˈplaɪ] | (n.) 庫存　(v.) 供應　　*supply and demand 供需　　*supplies 補給品（medical supplies 醫療用品） |
| | | The supply is the amount of a certain product that is available. 庫存是指特定產品的存量。 |

| 08 | **goods** [gʊdz] | (n.) 商品　　*goods and services 商品與服務　　*stolen goods 贓物 |
| | | Goods are products like food, cars, and appliances that people buy. 商品是指人們購買的食物、汽車以及電器等產品。 |

| 09 | **service** [ˈsɝvɪs] | (n.) 服務業；服務　　*service industry 服務業　　*at sb.'s service 聽候某人吩咐 |
| | | Services are jobs that one person provides for another. 服務業是為他人提供服務的職業。 |

| 10 | **product** [ˈprɑdəkt] | (n.) 產品；產物；產量　　*consumer product 消費品　　*by-product 副產品 |
| | | Goods and services are all products. 商品和服務都是產品。 |

Budget

My Budget

Week	Income	Spending	Savings
Week 1	$5	$1	$4
Week 2	$5	$1	$4
Week 3	$5	$2	$3
Week 4	$5	$2.5	$2.5
Total	$20	$6.5	$13.5

savings

balance
[ˈbæləns]

使收支平衡；結算

You must **balance** your income and expenses. 你必須要使收支平衡。

make a budget

編制預算

It is important to **make a budget** to control your spending.
編制一個預算來控制你的開銷是很重要的。

manage
[ˈmænɪdʒ]

設法做到；勉力完成

Some people cannot **manage** to balance their income and expenses.
有些人無法使收支取得平衡。

earn
[ɝn]

賺得

People **earn**, spend, and save money. 人們賺錢、花錢以及存錢。

make a profit

賺錢；獲利

Most businesses try to **make a profit** every year. 大部分公司每年都嘗試獲利。

deposit
[dɪˈpɑzɪt]

把（錢）儲存；存放（銀行）等

A lot of people **deposit** their money in a bank. 很多人把他們的錢存在銀行裡。

invest
[ɪnˈvɛst]

投（資）[（+ in）]

A lot of people **invest** their money in the stock market.
很多人把他們的錢投資在股票市場。

needs

必要之物；需求

Needs are things that people need to live. 必需品是指人們生活中不可或缺的東西。

wants

需求品；需要的東西

Wants are things that people would like to have. 需求品是指人們想要的東西。

Budget Items
預算項目

rent 租金
food 食物
clothing 衣服
insurance 保險
education 教育

transportation costs 交通費
entertainment 娛樂
taxes 稅金

Types of Services
服務的種類

consulting 諮詢
repair work 維修工作
delivery 運輸
catering 外燴服務
transportation 交通

Checkup

A

Write l 請依提示寫出正確的英文單字或片語。

1	收入	_____	9	服務業;服務	_____
2	開銷;花費	_____	10	產品;產物;結果	_____
3	存款;儲金	_____	11	使收支平衡;結算	_____
4	預算;經費	_____	12	設法做到;勉力完成	_____
5	利潤;利益	_____	13	編制預算	_____
6	要求;需要	_____	14	賺錢;獲利	_____
7	庫存	_____	15	把錢存放（銀行等）	_____
8	商品	_____	16	投（資）	_____

B

Complete the Sentences l 請在空格中填入最適當的答案，並視情況做適當的變化。

spending	profit	income	demand	product
goods	budget	supply	balance	savings

1 _____ is the money you earn from working. 收入是指工作的所得。

2 Many people put their _____ in the bank. 很多人將他們的儲蓄放在銀行裡。

3 People must be careful that their _____ is not more than their earnings.
   人們一定要小心，勿使入不敷出。

4 A _____ is a plan that shows income, spending, and savings.
   預算是一個顯示收入、開銷與儲蓄的計畫。

5 The _____ for a product is how much people want it.
   產品的需求是指人們對產品的渴求度。

6 The _____ is the amount of a certain product that is available.
   庫存是指特定產品的存量。

7 _____ are products like food, cars, and appliances that people buy.
   商品是指人們購買的食物、汽車以及電器等產品。

8 Goods and services are all _____. 商品和服務都是產品。

C

Read and Choose l 閱讀下列句子，並且選出最適當的答案。

1 You must (balance | invest) your income and expenses.

2 It is important to make a (profit | budget) to control your spending.

3 The goal of every company is to make a (profit | budget).

4 A lot of people (provide | deposit) their money in a bank.

Look, Read, and Write | 看圖並且依照提示，在空格中填入正確答案。

 ▶ a plan that shows income, spending, and savings

_____

 ▶ products like food, cars, and appliances that people buy

_____

 ▶ to put money in a bank account

_____

 ▶ the money you earn from working

_____

 ▶ things that people need to live

_____

 ▶ to use your money with the goal of making a profit from it

_____

E

Read and Answer | 閱讀並且回答下列問題。 ⊙ 008

Money Management

When people work, they get paid. This money is called earnings. With their earnings, they can do two things: spend or save their money. Most people do a combination of these two. First, they have to spend their money on many things. They have to pay for their home. They have to pay for food and clothes. And they have to pay for insurance, transportation, and even entertainment costs. Usually, there is some money left over. People often save this money. They might put it in the bank. Or they might invest in the stock market. Unfortunately, some people spend too much money. They spend more than they earn. So they go into debt. Debt is a big problem for many people. People can plan to buy something if they budget their income, spending, and savings. A budget helps people to manage money and to save it.

What is NOT true?

1 The money people make from working is their savings.

2 People usually spend or save their earnings.

3 Some people put their savings in the bank.

4 Budgets help people manage their money.

Key Words ● 009

01	**renewable** [rɪˋnjuəbļ]	*(a.)* 可更新的；可恢復的　　*renew 使更新　　*renewable energy 可再生能源 Renewable resources like water and solar energy can be used again. 水和太陽能之類的可再生資源可以重複利用。
02	**nonrenewable** [ˏnɑnrɪˋnjuəbļ]	*(a.)* 不可更新的；不可再生的 Nonrenewable resources like coal, oil, and gas cannot be used again. 煤、石油和天然氣之類的不可再生資源無法重複利用。
03	**human resource** [ˋhjumən rɪˋsors]	*(n.)* 人力資源 The people who make products or provide services are called **human resources**. 製造產品或提供服務的人稱為人力資源。
04	**producer** [prəˋdjusɚ]	*(n.)* 生產者　　*wine producer 葡萄酒生產商　　*film producer 電影製片 A **producer** makes various kinds of products. 生產者製造各種不同的產品。
05	**assembly line** [əˋsɛmblɪ laɪn]	*(n.)* 生產線；裝配線　　*assemble (v.) assembly (n.) 裝配；組裝 People can make cars, computers, and other products quickly because of **assembly lines**. 生產線的出現使人們得以快速製造汽車、電腦以及其他產品。
06	**international trade** [ˏɪntɚˋnæʃənļ tred]	*(n.)* 國際貿易　　*foreign trade 外貿；對外貿易　　*trade agreement 貿易協定 **International trade** is trade between two or more countries. 國際貿易是指兩國或多國之間的貿易。
07	**free trade** [fri tred]	*(n.)* 自由貿易　　*trade barrier 貿易壁壘　　*fair trade 公平交易 **Free trade** is trade that has no taxes or government interference. 自由貿易是指免除關稅和政府干預的貿易。
08	**tariff** [ˋtærɪf]	*(n.)* 關稅　　*tariff barrier 關稅壁壘 A **tariff** is a tax on imported or exported products. 關稅是指對進出口貨物所徵收的稅。
09	**interdependence** [ˏɪntɚdɪˋpɛndəns]	*(n.)* 互相依賴　　*dependence 依賴　　*economic interdependence 經濟相依 The **interdependence** of countries on each other is increasing nowadays. 當今國與國之間的互賴性日益升高。
10	**scarcity** [ˋskɛrsətɪ]	*(n.)* 匱乏；不足　　*scarcity of food 食物短缺 A **scarcity** of some items means that there is not enough of them. 某產品的匱乏是指該產品的產量不足。

renewable resources

nonrenewable resources

assembly line

mass-produce

produce
[prə`djus]

生產

The company can produce many items in one day.
公司可以在一天之內製造出許多產品。

mass-produce
[`mæsprə`djus]

大量生產

Companies can mass-produce items like cars on assembly lines.
公司可以利用生產線來大量生產像車子這樣的產品。

specialize in

專門從事；專門經營

Most companies specialize in making certain products.
大部分的公司專門製造特定的產品。

take advantage of

利用；趁……之機

A good company takes advantage of its human resources.
一間好的公司會善用人力資源。

import
[ɪm`port]

進口

That company imports products from other countries.
那家公司從其他國家進口產品。

export
[ɪks`port]

出口

That company exports products to other countries.
那家公司把產品出口至其他國家。

collect
[kə`lɛkt]

收（租、稅、帳等）

The government collects taxes from everyone. 政府向人民收稅。

duty	關稅；責任 A duty is a kind of import or export tax. 關稅是一種進出口的稅。
tariff	關稅 A tariff is a kind of import or export tax. 關稅是一種進出口的稅。
tax	稅金；稅 People have to pay many different kinds of taxes. 人們需要繳納各種不同的稅金。

free market	自由市場 People can choose what to produce and what to buy in a free market. 在自由市場中，人們可以選擇要製造以及購買的項目。
producer	製造者 Producers can choose what to produce in a free market. 在自由市場中，生產者可以選擇生產的項目。
consumer	消費者 Consumers can choose what to buy in a free market. 在自由市場中，消費者可以選擇要購買的項目。

Checkup

A

Write | 請依提示寫出正確的英文單字或片語。

1	可更新的；可恢復的 _____	9	關稅 t_____
2	不可更新的 _____	10	匱乏；不足 _____
3	人力資源 _____	11	大量生產 _____
4	生產者 _____	12	消費者 _____
5	生產線；裝配線 _____	13	專門從事、經營 _____
6	國際貿易 _____	14	利用；趁……之機 _____
7	自由貿易 _____	15	出口 _____
8	互相依賴 _____	16	收（租、稅、帳等） _____

B

Complete the Sentences | 請在空格中填入最適當的答案，並視情況做適當的變化。

| renewable | nonrenewable | scarcity | assembly line | tariff |
| consumer | interdependence | producer | free market | human |

1 A _____ makes various kinds of products. 生產者製造各種不同的產品。

2 _____ resources like water and solar energy can be used again.
水和太陽能等可再生資源可以重複利用。

3 _____ resources like coal, oil, and gas cannot be used again.
煤、石油和天然氣等不可再生資源無法重複利用。

4 People can make products quickly because of _____.
生產線的出現使人們得以快速製造產品。

5 A _____ of some items means that there is not enough of them.
某產品的匱乏是指該產品的產量不足。

6 _____ can choose what to buy in a free market.
在自由市場中，消費者可以選擇要購買的項目。

7 The people who make products or provide services are called _____
resources. 製造產品和提供服務的人稱為人力資源。

8 The _____ of countries on each other is increasing nowadays.
當今國與國之間的互賴性日益升高。

C

Read and Choose | 閱讀下列句子，並且選出最適當的答案。

1 Companies can (choose | mass-produce) items like cars on assembly lines.

2 Most companies (specialize | produce) in making certain products.

3 That company (exports | imports) products from other countries.

4 A (trade | tariff) is a tax on imported or exported products.

Look, Read, and Write | 看圖並且依照提示，在空格中填入正確答案。

1
▶ to send a product to be sold in another country

_____

2
▶ a resource that can be used again

_____

3
▶ a person who makes products or provides services

_____

4
▶ a line of machines and workers in a factory that builds a product by passing work from one station to the next

_____

E

Read and Answer | 閱讀並且回答下列問題。 ⊙ 012

All Kinds of Resources

There are many kinds of resources on the earth. Four of them are very important. They are renewable, nonrenewable, human, and capital resources. Renewable resources can be used again and again. They can be replaced within a short time. Some energy resources are renewable. The energy from the sun, tides, water, and wind is renewable. Also, trees and animals are renewable. But humans still need to take good care of them. We should not waste them at all. Nonrenewable resources are limited in supply.

Once we use them, they disappear forever. They can't be replaced. Many energy resources are like this. Coal, gas, and oil are all nonrenewable. Human resources are people and the skills they have. This also includes the knowledge and information that humans have. People make products using renewable and nonrenewable resources. Machines are often used to produce goods. The machines and tools that are used to produce goods are called capital resources.

Answer the questions.

1 What are the four important kinds of resources? _____

2 What are some renewable energy resources? _____

3 What kind of resources are coal, gas, and oil? _____

4 What are capital resources? _____

Key Words ● 013

01 communication
[kə,mjunəˋkeʃən]

(*n.*) 傳達；交流；通訊　　*a mean of communication 通訊方式
*communications satellite 通訊衛星

New forms of **communication** help people to communicate faster and easier. 新的通訊方式使人們之間的溝通更加快速便利。

02 postal service
[ˋpostl̩ ˋsɝvɪs]

(*n.*) 郵遞服務；郵局服務處　　*postal address 郵寄地址

The **postal service** sends letters and packages all around the world.
郵遞服務將信件和包裹寄送到全世界。

03 telegraph
[ˋtɛlə,græf]

(*n.*) 電報；電信　　*telegraph operator 電報員

The **telegraph** sent electronic signals called Morse code over the wires.
電報透過電線來傳送稱作摩斯密碼的電子信號。

04 invention
[ɪnˋvɛnʃən]

(*n.*) 發明　　*Necessity is the mother of invention. 需要為發明之母。

The **invention** of the lightbulb changed the way people lived.
燈泡的發明改變了人們的生活方式。

05 wireless
[ˋwaɪrlɪs]

(*a.*) 無線的　　*wire 電線　　*wireless Internet access 無線上網

Cell phones operate with **wireless** communication.
手機是透過無線通訊的方式來運作。

06 transportation
[,trænspəˋteʃən]

(*n.*) 運輸；運輸工具；運輸業　　*air/ground transportation 航空／地面運輸

The inventing of new forms of **transportation** like cars and airplanes changed the world. 車子及飛機等新式交通工具的發明改變了世界。

07 railroad
[ˋrel,rod]

(*n.*) 鐵路；鐵路公司　　*transcontinental railroad 橫貫大陸鐵路
*railroad crossing 鐵路平交道

Railroads made travel safer and faster. 鐵路使旅行變得更加安全快速。

08 automobile
[ˋɔtəmə,bɪl]

(*n.*) 汽車　　*automobile insurance 汽車保險
*automobile manufacturer 汽車製造商

The **automobile** became popular in the twentieth century.
汽車在 20 世紀開始普及。

09 technology
[tɛkˋnɑlədʒɪ]

(*n.*) 技術　　*technology park 科技園區　　*high technology 高科技

New **technology** is created almost every day. 幾乎每天都有新的技術產生。

10 vaccination
[,væksn̩ˋeʃən]

(*n.*) 疫苗接種　　*vaccination against/for sth. 某疫苗的接種

A **vaccination** protects a person from a certain disease.
疫苗接種能預防人們得到某種疾病。

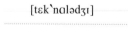

old telegraph

invention

vaccination

communicate
[kə`mjunə,ket]

傳達；傳播；通訊
People use phones, computers, and the Internet to **communicate** with others around the world. 人們利用手機、電腦及網路來和世界上的其他人溝通。

transmit
[træns`mɪt]

傳送
People can **transmit** messages on the Internet. 人們可以利用網路來傳送訊息。

transport
[træns`pɔrt]

運輸；傳送
Ships can **transport** huge amounts of goods. 船隻可以運輸非常大量的貨物。

broadcast
[`brɔd,kæst]

播放；廣播
TV stations **broadcast** many shows all day long. 電視台一整天都播放著許多節目。

air
[ɛr]

播送；廣播
TV stations **air** many shows all day long. 電視台一整天都播送著許多節目。

send out

發送；放出
TV stations **send out** signals to air their shows. 電視台發送訊號來播送他們的節目。

advance
[əd`væns]

推進；促進
Scientific knowledge is **advancing** all the time. 科學知識日新月異。

prevent
[prɪ`vɛnt]

防止；預防
A vaccine **prevents** people from getting a disease. 疫苗能預防人們得到疾病。

invention

發明；發明物
The automobile has been a very important invention.
汽車一直是一項很重大的發明。

invent

發明
Samuel Morse invented the telegraph. 山姆・摩斯發明了電報。

inventor

發明家
Thomas Edison was one of the world's greatest inventors.
湯瑪斯・愛迪生是世上最偉大的發明家之一。

vaccine
[`væksin]

疫苗
The polio vaccine has saved millions of people's lives.
小兒麻痺症的疫苗拯救了數百萬人的生命。

vaccination

疫苗接種
The polio vaccination has prevented people from getting polio.
小兒麻痺症的疫苗避免人們得到此症。

vaccinate
[`væksn̩,et]

接種疫苗
Doctors often vaccinate babies for various diseases.
醫生常為嬰兒接種不同的疫苗。

vaccine

Checkup

A Write I 請依提示寫出正確的英文單字或片語。

1	傳達；交流；通訊	_____	9	技術 _____
2	郵遞服務；郵局服務處	_____	10	疫苗接種 (n.) _____
3	電報；電信	_____	11	運輸；傳送 _____
4	發明	_____	12	播放；廣播 b_____
5	無線的	_____	13	發送；放出 s_____
6	運輸；運輸工具；運輸業	_____	14	推進；促進 _____
7	鐵路；鐵路公司	_____	15	防止；預防 _____
8	汽車	_____	16	接種疫苗 (v.) _____

B Complete the Sentences I 請在空格中填入最適當的答案，並視情況做適當的變化。

invention	technology	telegraph	communication	vaccinate
railroad	wireless	advance	automobile	vaccine

1 New _____ is created almost every day. 幾乎每天都有新的技術產生。

2 The _____ of the lightbulb changed the way people lived.
燈泡的發明改變了人們的生活方式。

3 New forms of _____ help people to communicate faster and easier.
新的通訊方式使人們之間的溝通更加快速便利。

4 Cell phones operate with _____ communication.
手機是透過無線通訊的方式來運作。

5 _____ made travel safer and faster. 鐵路使旅行變得更加安全快速。

6 The _____ became popular in the twentieth century.
汽車業在 20 世紀蓬勃發展。

7 Scientific knowledge is _____ all the time. 科學知識日新月異。

8 A _____ prevents people from getting a disease. 疫苗能預防人們得到疾病。

C Read and Choose I 閱讀下列句子，並且選出最適當的答案。

1 People can (transport | transmit) messages on the Internet.

2 The polio (vaccinate | vaccine) has saved millions of people's lives.

3 Thomas Edison was one of the world's greatest (inventors | inventions).

4 TV stations (advance | broadcast) many shows all day long.

D

Look, Read, and Write | 看圖並且依照提示，在空格中填入正確答案。

 ▸ a method of sending messages using electronic signals called Morse code

_____

 ▸ not using wires to send and receive electronic signals

_____

 ▸ the giving of a vaccine to prevent someone from getting a disease

_____

 ▸ to send out messages or programs by radios or televisions

_____

E

Read and Answer | 閱讀並且回答下列問題。 ● 016

How Technology Helps People

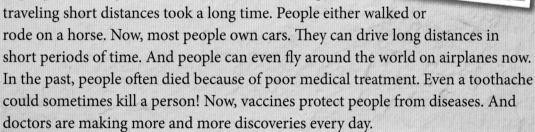

Nowadays, we live in an advanced world. We use many new inventions that people long ago never imagined. In the past, people could not regularly communicate with others. It took days, weeks, or even months just to send a letter. There were no telephones. So people had to talk face to face. Nowadays, we use cell phones to call anyone anywhere in the world. And we send email to people instantly thanks to the Internet. In the past, traveling short distances took a long time. People either walked or rode on a horse. Now, most people own cars. They can drive long distances in short periods of time. And people can even fly around the world on airplanes now. In the past, people often died because of poor medical treatment. Even a toothache could sometimes kill a person! Now, vaccines protect people from diseases. And doctors are making more and more discoveries every day.

Fill in the blanks.

1   We live in an _____ world today.

2   People nowadays use _____ phones to call others.

3   People can _____ around the world on airplanes.

4   _____ protect people from diseases.

Living in Different Climates

在不同的氣候中生活

Key Words 🔊 017

01	**tropical** [ˋtrɑpɪk!]	(a.) 熱帶的；位居熱帶的　　*subtropical 亞熱帶的　　*tropical climate 熱帶氣候 A tropical region has hot weather all year long. 熱帶地區終年炎熱。
02	**temperate** [ˋtɛmprɪt]	(a.) 溫帶的；溫暖的　　*temperate zone 溫帶　　*temperate forest 溫帶森林 Temperate regions can be both hot and cold. 溫帶地區時冷時熱。
03	**Mediterranean** [ˌmɛdətəˋrenɪən]	(a.) 地中海的　　*Mediterranean cuisine 地中海式飲食 The Mediterranean climate can be very mild. 地中海的氣候非常溫暖。
04	**arctic** [ˋɑrktɪk]	(a.) 北極的；北極地區的　　*Arctic Circle 北極圈　　*arctic coast 北極海岸 An arctic region has very cold weather all year long. 北極地區終年寒冷。
05	**rain forest** [ren ˋfɔrɪst]	(n.) (熱帶) 雨林　　*tropical rain forest 熱帶雨林 　　*Amazon rain forest 亞馬遜熱帶雨林 A rain forest has very many trees and plants and gets lots of rain. 熱帶雨林擁有非常多的樹木與植物，而且雨量充沛。
06	**woodland** [ˋwʊdˌlænd]	(n.) 森林地帶；林地　　*woodland creature/plant/animal 林地生物／植物／動物 A woodland is a place with a lot of trees. 森林地帶是指充滿樹木的地方。
07	**tundra** [ˋtʌndrə]	(n.) 凍原；苔原　　*arctic tundra 極地凍原 A treeless area in an arctic region is called tundra. 北極地區的無樹地帶稱為凍原。
08	**drought** [draʊt]	(n.) 乾旱 When there is a drought, it doesn't rain for a long period of time. 乾旱的時候，會有好長一段時間不下雨。
09	**flood** [flʌd]	(n.) 洪水　　*in (full) flood 氾濫　　*flood tide 滿潮；漲潮 A flood can happen when an area gets too much rain. 當一個區域下太多雨，就有可能引發洪水。
10	**tropical storm** [ˋtrɑpɪk! stɔrm]	(n.) 熱帶風暴 Tropical storms bring huge amounts of rain in a short time. 熱帶風暴會在短時間內帶來豪雨。

tropical region　　　arctic region　　　rain forest　　　tundra

affect [əˈfɛkt]　影響
Climate **affects** people in many ways. 氣候在許多方面影響著人類。

be affected by　被……影響
People **are affected by** climate in many ways.　人類在許多方面受到氣候的影響。

vary [ˈvɛrɪ]　變更；多元化
The temperature may **vary** in different places. 氣溫在不同的地方會有所差異。

depend on　依……而異；依靠
The climate of a place **depends on** where it is located.
一個地方的氣候依它的位置而異。

be found in　分佈於
Tundra **is found in** the Arctic region.　凍原分佈於北極地區。

needleleaf forest

extreme　極端的；極度的；最大的
Tropical storms can be **extreme** forms of weather.
熱帶風暴是極端的氣候型態。

hazardous [ˈhæzədəs]　有危險的；冒險的
Tornadoes can be **hazardous** to many people.
龍捲風會對許多人造成危險。

hurricane [ˈhɝɪˌken]　颶風；暴風雨
A **hurricane** is a powerful storm that happens in the North Atlantic Ocean.
颶風是發生在北大西洋的強大暴風雨。

typhoon　颱風
A **typhoon** is a powerful storm that happens in the West Pacific Ocean.
颱風是發生在西太平洋的強大暴風雨。

cyclone　氣旋；暴風；龍捲風
A **cyclone** is a powerful storm that happens in the Indian Ocean.
氣旋是發生在印度洋的強大暴風雨。

broadleaf forest　闊葉林
A **broadleaf forest** has trees like oaks and maples.
闊葉林是像橡樹和楓樹這樣的樹林。

needleleaf forest　針葉林
A **needleleaf forest** has trees that do not lose their needles all year long.
針葉林是指終年不會掉落針葉的樹林。

Checkup

A

Write I 請依提示寫出正確的英文單字或片語。

1	熱帶的;位居熱帶的	_____	9 洪水 _____
2	溫帶的;溫暖的	_____	10 熱帶風暴 _____
3	地中海的	_____	11 影響;發生作用 _____
4	北極的;北極地區的	_____	12 被……影響 _____
5	(熱帶)雨林	_____	13 變更;多元化 _____
6	森林地帶;林地	_____	14 依……而異;依靠 _____
7	凍原;苔原	_____	15 分佈於 _____
8	乾旱	_____	16 極端的;極度的 _____

B

Complete the Sentences I 請在空格中填入最適當的答案,並視情況做適當的變化。

extreme	Mediterranean	tropical	arctic	rain forest
temperate	tropical storm	drought	flood	hazardous

1 The _____ climate can be very mild. 地中海的氣候非常溫暖。

2 A _____ region has hot weather all year long. 熱帶地區終年炎熱。

3 _____ regions can be both hot and cold. 溫帶地區時冷時熱。

4 A _____ has very many trees and plants and gets lots of rain.
熱帶雨林擁有非常多的樹木與植物,而且雨量充沛。

5 When there is a _____, it doesn't rain for a long period of time.
乾旱的時候,會有好長一段時間不下雨。

6 _____ bring huge amounts of rain in a short time.
熱帶風暴會在短時間內帶來豪雨。

7 Tornadoes can be _____ to many people. 龍捲風會對許多人造成危險。

8 Tropical storms can be _____ forms of weather. 熱帶風暴是極端的氣候型態。

C

Read and Choose I 閱讀下列句子,並且選出最適當的答案。

1 People are (found | affected) by climate in many ways.

2 The temperature may (vary | depend) in different places.

3 The climate of a place (affects | depends) on where it is located.

4 Tundra is (found | happened) in the Arctic region.

Look, Read, and Write | 看圖並且依照提示，在空格中填入正確答案。

1 ▶ a powerful storm that happens in the West Pacific Ocean

_____

4 ▶ a long period of dry weather when there is no rain

_____

2 ▶ a climate that is very cold all year long

_____

5 ▶ land covered with trees and bushes

_____

3 ▶ a treeless area in an arctic region

_____

6 ▶ a forest that has trees like oaks and maples

_____

E

Read and Answer | 閱讀並且回答下列問題。 020

Extreme Weather Conditions

Many people live in areas with four seasons. It's hot in summer and cold in winter. The weather in spring and fall is either warm or cool. These are very normal weather conditions. But sometimes there are extreme weather conditions. These can cause many problems for people. Sometimes, it might not rain somewhere for a long time. Lakes, rivers, and streams have less water in them. Trees and grasses die. People and animals become very thirsty. This is called a drought. Other times, it rains constantly for many days. Water levels become much higher than normal. Water often goes on the ground and even onto city streets. These are called floods. In many warm places near the water, there are tropical storms. These storms drop heavy rains and have very strong winds. Tropical storms can drop several inches of rain in a few hours. Some places might get two or three tropical storms every year.

Answer the questions.

1   How many seasons are there where many people live?   _____

2   What happens during a drought?   _____

3   What is it called when the water level becomes too high?   _____

4   What do tropical storms do?   _____

A

Write | 請依提示寫出正確的英文單字或片語。

1	法院;法庭;球場	11	陪審團;評審委員會
2	法官	12	違反法律　b___
3	收入	13	使收支平衡;結算
4	開銷;花費	14	編制預算
5	可更新的;可恢復的	15	大量生產
6	不可更新的	16	匱乏;不足
7	發明	17	技術
8	無線的	18	疫苗接種 (n.)
9	溫帶的;溫暖的	19	熱帶風暴
10	地中海的	20	影響;發生作用

B

Choose the Correct Word | 請選出與鋪底字意思相近的答案。

1　The company can produce many items in one day.

　a. mass-produce　　　b. make　　　c. spend

2　TV stations broadcast many shows all day long.

　a. air　　　b. send　　　c. transmit

3　Ships can transport huge amounts of goods.

　a. transmit　　　b. export　　　c. carry

C

Complete the Sentences | 請在空格中填入最適當的答案,並視情況做適當的變化。

communication	illegal	budget	needs	assembly line

1　Something _____ is against the law and cannot be done.
　人們不能做違反法律的事。

2　A _____ is a plan that shows income, spending, and savings.
　預算是一個顯示收入、開銷與儲蓄的計畫。

3　People can make cars, computers, and other products quickly because of
　_____.
　生產線的出現使人們得以快速製造汽車、電腦以及其他產品。

4　New forms of _____ help people to communicate faster and easier.
　新的通訊方式使人們之間的溝通更加快速便利。

5　_____ are things that people need to live. 必需品是指人們生活中不可或缺的東西。

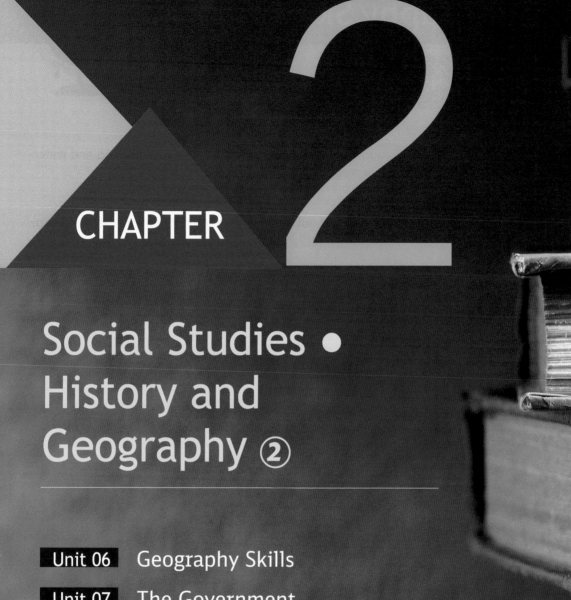

CHAPTER 2

Social Studies •
History and
Geography ②

Geography Skills 地理技能

Key Words ● 021

01 globe
[glob]

(n.) 地球儀；地球　*the globe 地球

A **globe** is a model of Earth that shows all of the planet's land and water.
地球儀是顯示地球水陸的模型。

02 map scale
[mæp skel]

(n.) 比例尺

Use a **map scale** to find out the real distance between places on a map.
利用比例尺將圖上地點的實際距離找出來。

03 feature
[ˈfitʃɚ]

(n.) 特色；特徵　*featureless 無特色的　*feature writer 專欄作家

A map has many **features**, like a map key, symbols, and a compass rose.
地圖有很多特色，像是地標、符號和羅盤方位。

04 grid
[grɪd]

(n.) 網格；方格

A **grid** is a pattern of lines that forms squares on a map.
網格是在地圖上構成正方形的線條形式。

05 border
[ˈbɔrdɚ]

(n.) 邊界；國界　*cross the border 穿越邊界　*border dispute 邊界糾紛

This line shows the **border** between two countries.
這條線顯示了兩國之間的邊界。

06 equator
[ɪˈkwetɚ]

(n.) 赤道　*the equator 赤道（與 the 連用）

The **equator** is an imaginary line that lies halfway between the North Pole and the South Pole. 赤道是介於南北極中間的假想線。

07 hemisphere
[ˈhɛməsˌfɪr]

(n.) 半球　*the Eastern/Western Hemisphere 東／西半球

The earth is divided into the Northern **Hemisphere** and the Southern **Hemisphere** by the equator. 赤道將地球分為北半球以及南半球。

08 latitude
[ˈlætəˌtjud]

(n.) 緯度　*be located at a latitude of . . . degrees north/south
= be located at . . . degrees north/south latitude 位於北／南緯……度

Lines of **latitude** are the horizontal lines running east to west on the map.
緯線是指地圖上東西向的水平線。

09 longitude
[ˈlɑndʒəˈtjud]

(n.) 經度　*be located at a longitude of . . . degrees east/west
= be located at . . . degrees east/west latitude 位於東／西經……度

Lines of **longitude** run from the North Pole to the South Pole.
經線從北極向南極延伸。

10 prime meridian
[praɪm məˈrɪdɪən]

(n.) 本初子午線

The **prime meridian** divides the Western Hemisphere from the Eastern Hemisphere. 本初子午線將東西半球劃分開來。

Globe

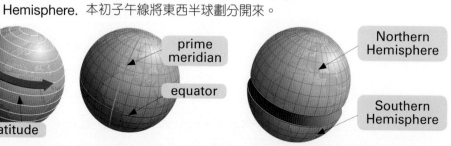

longitude

latitude
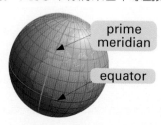
prime meridian
equator
Northern Hemisphere
Southern Hemisphere

divide (from) 把……分開
[dəˈvaɪd]
The Mediterranean Sea divides Europe from Africa. 地中海將歐洲和非洲分開來。

be divided into 被分成；被分為
The earth is divided into two hemispheres. 地球被分成兩個半球。

border 與……接壤；與……有共同邊界
[ˈbɔrdə]
The two countries border one another. 這兩個國家彼此接壤。

be connected to 與……相連
The two countries are connected to one another. 這兩個國家彼此相連。

run 延伸；伸展
[rʌn]
The equator runs around the entire world. 赤道環繞整個世界。

intersect 相交；交叉
[ˌɪntəˈsɛkt]
Lines of latitude and longitude intersect with each other. 緯線與經線彼此相交。

Word Families ⊙ 023

Western Hemisphere

Eastern Hemisphere

North Pole 北極
The North Pole is the northernmost place on the planet.
北極是地球的最北端。

South Pole 南極
The South Pole is the southernmost place on the planet.
南極是地球的最南端。

Northern Hemisphere 北半球
The Northern Hemisphere is the half of the earth north of the equator. 北半球是指赤道以北的半個地球。

Southern Hemisphere 南半球
The Southern Hemisphere is the half of the earth south of the equator. 南半球是指赤道以南的半個地球。

Eastern Hemisphere 東半球
The Eastern Hemisphere includes Europe, Africa, and Asia. 東半球涵蓋了歐洲、非洲以及亞洲。

Western Hemisphere 西半球
The Western Hemisphere includes North and South America. 西半球涵蓋了北美以及南美洲。

Directions
方位

Cardinal Directions
基本方位

north 北方 **south** 南方

east 東方 **west** 西方

Intermediate Directions
複合方位

northwest 西北方 **southeast** 東南方

southwest 西南方 **northeast** 東北方

Checkup

A

Write | 請依提示寫出正確的英文單字或片語。

1 地球儀；地球 _____	9 經度 _____
2 比例尺 _____	10 本初子午線 _____
3 特色；特徵 _____	11 被分為 _____
4 網格；方格 _____	12 與……相連 _____
5 邊界；國界 _____	13 延伸；伸展 _____
6 赤道 _____	14 相交；交叉 _____
7 半球 _____	15 基本方位 _____
8 緯度 _____	16 複合方位 _____

B

Complete the Sentences | 請在空格中填入最適當的答案，並視情況做適當的變化。

globe	map scale	hemisphere	equator	feature
grid	prime meridian	latitude	border	longitude

1 A _____ is a model of Earth that shows all of the planet's land and water.
地球儀是顯示地球水陸的模型。

2 A map has many _____, like a map key, symbols, and a compass rose.
地圖有很多特色，像是地標、符號和羅盤方位。

3 A _____ is a pattern of lines that forms squares on a map.
網格是在地圖上構成正方形的線條形式。

4 Use a _____ to find out the real distance between places on a map.
利用比例尺將圖上地點的實際距離找出來。

5 The Earth is divided into the Northern Hemisphere and the Southern _____ by the equator. 赤道將地球分為北半球以及南半球。

6 The _____ is an imaginary line that lies halfway between the North Pole and the South Pole. 赤道是南北極中間的假想線。

7 Lines of _____ run from the North Pole to the South Pole.
經線從北極向南極延伸。

8 Lines of _____ are the horizontal lines running east to west on the map.
緯線是指地圖上東西向的水平線。

C

Read and Choose | 閱讀下列句子，並且選出最適當的答案。

1 Earth is (divide | divided) into two hemispheres.

2 The two countries (border | connected) one another.

3 Lines of latitude and longitude (run | intersect) with each other.

4 The (South | North) Pole is the northernmost place on the planet.

Look, Read, and Write | 看圖並且依照提示，在空格中填入正確答案。

1 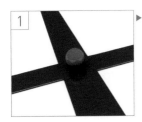 ▶ to divide (something) by passing through or across it

_____

4 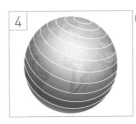 ▶ horizontal lines running east to west

_____

2  ▶ an imaginary line that lies halfway between the North and South Poles

_____

5 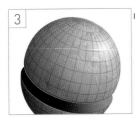 ▶ lines running from the North Pole to the South Pole

_____

3  ▶ a half of the earth

_____

6 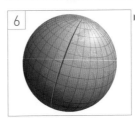 ▶ It divides the Western Hemisphere from the Eastern Hemisphere.

_____

E

Read and Answer | 閱讀並且回答下列問題。　⊙ 024

Understanding Hemispheres

Earth is a big planet. But we can make it smaller by dividing it into sections. We call these sections hemispheres. One hemisphere is half of the earth. There is an imaginary line that runs from east to west all around the earth. It is in the center of the earth. We call it the equator. The equator divides the Northern Hemisphere from the Southern Hemisphere. The Northern Hemisphere includes Asia and Europe. North America is also in it. Below the equator is the Southern Hemisphere. Australia and Antarctica are in it. So are most of South America and Africa. We can also divide Earth into the Eastern and Western hemispheres. The line that does this is the prime meridian. It runs from north to south. It goes directly through Greenwich, England. The Eastern Hemisphere includes Europe, Africa, and Asia. The Western Hemisphere includes North and South America.

What is NOT true?

1 The equator runs from east to west.

2 Australia is in the Northern Hemisphere.

3 Earth has an Eastern Hemisphere and a Western Hemisphere.

4 North and South America are in the Western Hemisphere.

The Government 政府部門

Key Words ⊙ 025

| 01 | **executive branch** | (n.) 行政部門　　*chief executive 政府最高首長；州長 |
| | [ɪgˋzɛkjʊtɪv bræntʃ] | The president, governors, and mayors belong to the executive branch.
總統、州長及市長隸屬於行政部門。 |

| 02 | **legislative branch** | (n.) 立法部門　　*legislative body/assembly 立法機關 |
| | [ˋlɛdʒɪsˏletɪv bræntʃ] | Congress and state legislatures belong to the legislative branch.
國會及州議會隸屬於立法部門。 |

| 03 | **judicial branch** | (n.) 司法部門　　*the judicial system 司法系統　　*judicial power 司法權 |
| | [dʒuˋdɪʃəl bræntʃ] | All of the courts and judges belong to the judicial branch.
所有的法院及法官隸屬於司法部門。 |

| 04 | **candidate** | (n.) 候選人；應試者　　*a candidate for 某職位的候選人
*select sb. as a candidate 推舉某人作為參選人 |
| | [ˋkændədet] | A candidate for a political office tries to get elected.
公職的參選人盡力拚當選。 |

| 05 | **consent** | (n.) 同意；贊成　(v.) 同意；贊成
*by common/mutual consent 經一致／雙方同意　　*written consent 書面同意 |
| | [kənˋsɛnt] | People give their consent to the elected leaders to make and carry out the laws. 人們同意當選的領導人來制訂及執行法律。 |

| 06 | **bill** | (n.) 法案；議案　　*pass/reject the bill 通過／否決議案
*paying the telephone/water bill 付電話費／水費 |
| | [bɪl] | Legislatures vote on bills and pass them to become laws.
立法機關表決通過法案並使其成為法律。 |

| 07 | **veto** | (n.) 否決權　　*have the veto over sth. 對某事物有否決權
*use or exercise one's veto 行使否決權 |
| | [ˋvito] | The right of a president or a governor to reject bills is called the veto.
總統或州長否決議案的權力稱為否決權。 |

| 08 | **enforcement** | (n.) 執行；強制　　*the enforcement of sth. 執行某事物 |
| | [ɪnˋforsmənt] | The executive branch is responsible for the enforcement of the law.
行政部門負責執行法律。 |

| 09 | **taxation** | (n.) 稅收；稅金　　*increase/reduce taxation 增／減稅 |
| | [tæksˋeʃən] | Taxation is how the government collects money. 政府靠稅收來募集資金。 |

| 10 | **community service** | (n.) 社區服務；社會服務 |
| | [kəˋmjunətɪ ˋsɝvɪs] | Local governments provide community services like security and education. 地方政府提供安全和教育等社區服務。 |

The Government in the USA

the executive branch

the legislative branch

the judicial branch

enforce
[ɪnˈfors]

執行；實施

The executive branch enforces laws. 行政部門執行法律。

carry out

實行；完成

The executive branch carries out laws. 行政部門實行法律。

apply
[əˈplaɪ]

實施

The executive branch applies laws. 行政部門實施法律。

---

veto
[ˈvito]

否決；反對

A governor or the president may veto a bill. 州長或是總統可能會否決法案。

reject
[rɪˈdʒɛkt]

駁回；拒絕

A governor or the president may reject a bill. 州長或是總統可能會駁回法案。

refuse
[rɪˈfjuz]

拒絕；不准

A governor or the president may refuse a bill. 州長或是總統可能會拒絕法案。

---

approve
[əˈpruv]

同意；贊成

A bill must be approved by the state legislature. 法案需經過州議會的同意。

make	制訂 The legislative branch makes laws. 立法部門制訂法律。
carry out	實行 The executive branch carries out laws. 行政部門實行法律。
determine	決定 The judicial branch determines if laws have been broken. 司法部門決定違法與否。

elect	選舉；推選 The people in a community elect the candidates they want. 社區的人民選出他們想要的候選人。
vote for	投票支持 The people in a community vote for the candidates they want. 社區的人民投票支持他們想要的候選人。
be elected by	被……所選 A mayor is elected by the citizens of the community. 市長由社區的公民所選出。

candidate

vote

Checkup

A

Write | 請依提示寫出正確的英文單字或片語。

1	行政部門	_____	
2	立法部門	_____	
3	司法部門	_____	
4	候選人；應試者	_____	
5	同意；贊成	c_____	
6	法案；議案	_____	
7	否決權	_____	
8	執行；強制 (n.)	_____	
9	稅收；稅金	_____
10	社區服務；社會服務	_____
11	決定	_____
12	實行；完成	c_____
13	應用	_____
14	贊成；同意	a_____
15	投票支持	_____
16	駁回；拒絕	r_____

B

Complete the Sentences | 請在空格中填入最適當的答案，並視情況做適當的變化。

legislative	apply	executive	consent	bill
determine	judicial	enforcement	taxation	veto

1 Congress and state legislatures belong to the _____ branch.
國會及州議會隸屬於立法部門。

2 The president, governors, and mayors belong to the _____ branch.
總統、州長及市長隸屬於行政部門。

3 All of the courts and judges belong to the _____ branch.
所有的法院及法官隸屬於司法部門。

4 Legislatures vote on _____ and pass them to become laws.
立法機關表決通過法案並使其成為法律。

5 People give their _____ to the elected leaders to make and carry out the laws. 人們同意當選的領導人來制訂及執行法律。

6 The executive branch is responsible for the _____ of the law.
行政部門負責執行法律。

7 _____ is how the government collects money. 政府靠稅收來募集資金。

8 The judicial branch _____ if laws have been broken. 司法部門決定違法與否。

C

Read and Choose | 請選出與鋪底字意思相近的答案。

1 The executive branch enforces laws.

a. approves   b. carries out   c. decides

2 A governor or the president may reject a bill.

a. veto   b. reuse   c. consent

3 The people in a community vote for the candidates they want.

a. serve   b. elect   c. decide

D Look, Read, and Write I 看圖並且依照提示，在空格中填入正確答案。

1		▶ a service that is performed for the benefit of the public _____	4		▶ a person who runs for office _____
2		▶ the branch of government that decides if laws have been broken _____	5		▶ the right of a president or a governor to reject bills _____
3		▶ the branch of government responsible for making laws _____	6		▶ permission to do something _____

E Read and Answer I 閱讀並且回答下列問題。　🔊 028

The Three Branches of Government

The government is made up of three branches. They are the executive, legislative, and judicial branches. These three branches of the government make and enforce laws. All three of them have their own duties and responsibilities.

The legislative branch is Congress. Congress proposes bills and discusses them. Then Congress votes on the bills. If the bills pass and the president signs them, then they become laws. After a law has been passed, it must be carried out, or enforced. The executive branch enforces laws. The executive branch is the president and everyone who works for him. The judicial branch is the court system. The judicial branch determines if laws have been broken. When people break the law, the judicial branch takes care of their cases.

Fill in the blanks.

1 The three branches of the government make and enforce _____.

2 Congress is a part of the _____ branch.

3 The president _____ a bill to make it become a law.

4 The _____ system is the judicial branch.

Ancient Egypt 古埃及

Key Words ● 029

01	**pharaoh**
	[ˈfɛro]

(n.) 法老

A pharaoh was an Egyptian king. 法老是埃及的國王。

02	**god-king**
	[ˈɡɑdkɪŋ]

(n.) 神王

The pharaohs were like god-kings in Egypt. 法老在埃及就像神王一般。

03	**pyramid**
	[ˈpɪrəmɪd]

(n.) 金字塔

The pharaohs built huge pyramids to be their tombs.
法老建造龐大的金字塔來當作他們的墓地。

04	**Sphinx**
	[sfɪŋks]

(n.) 獅身人面像　　*the Great Sphinx of Giza = the Sphinx 獅身人面像

The Sphinx is an enormous statue that stands near the pyramids in Egypt.
獅身人面像是一座巨大的雕像，座落於埃及金字塔的旁邊。

05	**hieroglyphics**
	[haɪərəˈɡlɪfɪks]

(n.) 象形文字

The Egyptians used a form of picture writing called hieroglyphics.
埃及人使用的圖畫書寫形式稱為象形文字。

06	**mummy**
	[ˈmʌmɪ]

(n.) 木乃伊

After a pharaoh died, he or she was preserved as a mummy.
法老死後會被保存為木乃伊。

07	**tomb**
	[tum]

(n.) 墳墓 (= grave)

There are many tombs of pharaohs in the Valley of the Kings.
許多法老的墳墓位於帝王谷。

08	**Nile River**
	[naɪl ˈrɪvɚ]

(n.) 尼羅河

The Nile River provided life for Egyptian civilization. 尼羅河是埃及文明之母。

09	**cuneiform**
	[ˈkjunɪəˌfɔrm]

(n.) 楔形文字

Cuneiform was the form of writing used in ancient Mesopotamia.
楔形文字是古美索不達米亞地區的書寫形式。

10	**ziggurat**
	[ˈzɪɡʊˌræt]

(n.) 金字形神塔

pharaoh

A ziggurat was a kind of temple in Mesopotamia.
金字形神塔是美索不達米亞地區的一種神殿。

pyramid

Sphinx

Egyptian hieroglyphics

Nile River

erect
[ɪˋrɛkt]
建立；樹立
The Egyptians erected huge pyramids throughout the land.
埃及人建立的龐大金字塔遍及了整個國家。

construct
[kənˋstrʌkt]
建造
The Egyptians constructed huge pyramids throughout the land.
埃及人建造的龐大金字塔遍及了整個國家。

flood
[flʌd]
淹沒；使氾濫
Every year, the Nile River flooded the land around it. 尼羅河年年氾濫周遭土地。

overflow
[ˌovɚˋflo]
氾濫；溢出來
Every year, the Nile River overflowed its banks. 尼羅河年年溢流出河堤之外。

regard
[rɪˋgɑrd]
看作；尊重
The Egyptians regarded their gods as great. 埃及人視他們的神為至高無上。

honor
[ˋɑnɚ]
崇敬；使光榮
The Egyptians honored their gods. 埃及人崇敬他們的神。

enormous
巨大的；龐大的
The Egyptians built enormous stone temples and pyramids.
埃及人建造了巨大的石殿和金字塔。

gigantic
[dʒaɪˋgæntɪk]
巨大的；龐大的
The Egyptians carved gigantic statues in stone. 埃及人利用石頭雕刻出巨大的雕像。

huge
巨大的；龐大的
The Sphinx in Egypt is huge. 埃及的獅身人面像非常巨大。

Egyptian
埃及的
Ancient Egyptian culture was centered on the Nile River.
古埃及文化以尼羅河為中心。

Mesopotamian
[ˌmɛsəpəˋtemɪən]
美索不達米亞的
Mesopotamian culture was centered on the Tigris and Euphrates rivers.
美索不達米亞文化以底格里斯河和幼發拉底河為中心。

Egyptian Gods
埃及眾神

Famous Pharaohs
著名的法老

Horus 荷魯斯（太陽神）　**Set** 賽特（邪惡之神）

Isis 伊西斯（諸神之后）　**Anubis** 阿奴比斯（死神）

Osiris 奧西里斯（陰間之神）

Tutankhamen 圖坦卡門

Ramses 拉美西斯

Amenhotep 阿蒙霍特普

Hatshepsut 哈特謝普蘇特

Checkup

A

Write | 請依提示寫出正確的英文單字或片語。

1 法老	_____	9 象形文字	_____
2 金字塔	_____	10 楔形文字	_____
3 獅身人面像	_____	11 金字形神塔	_____
4 木乃伊	_____	12 建立；樹立	e_____
5 墳墓	_____	13 淹沒；使氾濫	_____
6 尼羅河	_____	14 氾濫；溢出來	_____
7 埃及的	_____	15 看作；尊重	_____
8 神王	_____	16 巨大的；龐大的	e_____

B

Complete the Sentences | 請在空格中填入最適當的答案，並視情況做適當的變化。

hieroglyphics	tomb	Nile River	god-king	ziggurat
cuneiform	pharaoh	Egyptian	pyramid	mummy

1 The pharaohs were like _____ in Egypt. 法老在埃及就像神王一般。

2 The pharaohs built huge _____ to be their tombs.
法老建造龐大的金字塔來當作他們的墓地。

3 There are many _____ of pharaohs in the Valley of the Kings.
許多法老的墳墓位於帝王谷。

4 The _____ provided life for Egyptian civilization. 尼羅河是埃及文明之母。

5 The Egyptians used a form of picture writing called _____.
埃及人使用的圖畫書寫形式稱為象形文字。

6 _____ was the form of writing used in ancient Mesopotamia.
楔形文字是古美索不達米亞地區的書寫形式。

7 Ancient _____ culture was centered on the Nile River.
古埃及文化以尼羅河為中心。

8 After a pharaoh died, he or she was preserved as a _____.
法老死後會被保存為木乃伊。

C

Read and Choose | 請選出與鋪底字意思相近的答案。

1 Every year, the Nile River flooded the land around it.

a. flowed　　　　　　b. centered　　　　　　c. overflowed

2 The Egyptians erected huge pyramids throughout the land.

a. honored　　　　　　b. constructed　　　　　　c. preserved

3 The Egyptians built enormous stone temples and pyramids.

a. god-king　　　　　　b. huge　　　　　　c. mummy

D

Look, Read, and Write | 看圖並且依照提示，在空格中填入正確答案。

 ► the wedge-shaped characters used in the ancient writing systems

_____

 ► a huge stone building used as a pharaoh's tomb

_____

 ► an enormous statue that stands near the pyramids in Egypt

_____

 ► a dead body that has been preserved for a long time

_____

 ► a form of picture writing used in Egypt

_____

 ► a chamber in which a dead body is kept

_____

E

Read and Answer | 閱讀並且回答下列問題。　⊙ 032

Ancient Egyptian Civilization

Over 5,000 years ago, Egyptian civilization began. It was centered on the Nile River. Every year, the Nile flooded. The water from the floods made the land around the Nile very rich. So it was good for farming. This let a civilization start in Egypt.

Egyptian life was centered on the pharaohs. They were god-kings who ruled the entire land. Most Egyptians were slaves. They lived their lives to serve the pharaohs. The pharaohs were very wealthy. They built huge monuments. They also constructed the pyramids and the Sphinx. There are many pyramids all through Egypt. Egypt also had its own form of writing. It was called hieroglyphics. It was a kind of picture writing. It didn't use letters. Instead, it used pictures. They represented different sounds and words.

What is true? Write T(true) or F(false).

1　Egyptian civilization began 500 years ago.　_____

2　The pharaohs were slaves in Egypt.　_____

3　The Egyptians built the pyramids and the Sphinx.　_____

4　Hieroglyphics was a form of picture writing.　_____

Ancient Greece 古希臘

Key Words 🔊 033

01	**democracy** [dɪˈmɑkrəsɪ]	(n.) 民主制度；民主政體；民主國家　*monarchy 君主政體

Democracy was first practiced by the ancient Greeks.
民主制度由古希臘人率先實行。

02	**Olympics** [oˈlɪmpɪks]	(n.) 奧林匹克運動會　*the Olympics = the Olympic Games 奧運

The first Olympics were held in ancient Greece more than 2,500 years ago.
第一屆的奧林匹克運動會於 2,500 多年前由古希臘舉辦。

03	**city-state** [ˈsɪtɪˈstet]	(n.) 城邦

City-states like Athens and Sparta were very powerful.
雅典和斯巴達這樣的城邦非常強大。

04	**Athens** [ˈæθɪnz]	(n.) 雅典

Athens was the greatest of all the Greek city-states.
雅典是希臘的城邦中最壯大的一個。

05	**birthplace** [ˈbɝθˌples]	(n.) 發源地；出生地

Athens was the birthplace of democracy. 雅典是民主的發源地。

06	**tyrant** [ˈtaɪrənt]	(n.) 暴君；專制君主

Tyrants were like kings but were very cruel.　暴君是指非常殘暴的君主。

07	**Sparta** [ˈspɑrtə]	(n.) 斯巴達

Sparta was a warlike city-state. 斯巴達是個好戰的城邦。

08	**philosophy** [fəˈlɑsəfɪ]	(n.) 哲學　*philosophy of life 人生哲學　*Doctor of Philosophy = PhD 博士學位

Many great thinkers lived in Athens and studied philosophy.
許多偉大的思想家居住在雅典研究哲學。

09	**philosopher** [fəˈlɑsəfɚ]	(n.) 哲學家

Socrates, Plato, and Aristotle are the most important Greek philosophers.
蘇格拉底、柏拉圖及亞里斯多德是最有影響力的希臘哲學家。

10	**civilization** [ˌsɪvl̩əˈzeʃən]	(n.) 文明；文明階段；文明國家　*modern civilization 現代文明

Ancient Greek civilization was highly advanced. 古希臘文明非常先進。

the relay race in the ancient Olympics

the Acropolis (the center of ancient Greece)

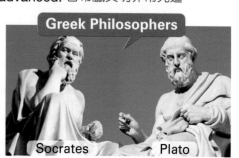
Greek Philosophers
Socrates　　　Plato

train
[tren]
接受訓練;鍛鍊
The men of Sparta constantly **trained** for war. 斯巴達的男人持續地為戰爭而訓練。

prepare
[prɪˋpɛr]
準備;籌備
The men of Sparta constantly **prepared** for war. 斯巴達的男人持續地為戰爭做準備。

take part in
參加
Many Greeks **took part in** the Olympics. 許多希臘人參加奧林匹克運動會。

take charge of
接管
Alexander the Great **took charge of** many different countries.
亞歷山大大帝接管許多不同的國家。

compete
[kəmˋpit]
競爭;對抗
Greek athletes **competed** against each other in the Olympics.
希臘的運動員在奧林匹克運動會上互相競爭。

cooperate
[koˋɑpəˌret]
合作;協作
The Greek city-states sometimes **cooperated** with each other.
希臘的城邦有時會彼此合作。

tough
剛強的;強硬的;冷酷的
The Spartans were very **tough**. 斯巴達人非常剛強。

rough
粗暴的;粗野的
The Spartans were very **rough**. 斯巴達人非常粗暴。

cruel
殘忍的
The Spartans were very **cruel**. 斯巴達人非常殘忍。

Spartan warrior

Greek
希臘人
The Greeks lived in many different city-states. 希臘人居住在許多不同的城邦。

Athenian
雅典人
The Athenians were the people living in Athens. 居住在雅典的人稱為雅典人。

Spartan
斯巴達人
The Spartans were the people living in Sparta. 居住在斯巴達的人稱為斯巴達人。

Persian
[ˋpɝʒən]
波斯人
The Persians were the people living in Persia. 居住在波斯的人稱為波斯人。

Greek City-States
希臘的城邦

| **Athens** 雅典 | **Sparta** 斯巴達 | **Thebes** 底比斯 [θibz] |
| **Corinth** 哥林斯 | **Argos** 阿哥斯 | |

Checkup

A

Write I 請依提示寫出正確的英文單字或片語。

1	民主制度	_____	9	哲學家	_____
2	奧林匹克運動會	_____	10	文明；文明階段	_____
3	城邦	_____	11	參加	_____
4	雅典	_____	12	接管	_____
5	斯巴達	_____	13	競爭；對抗	_____
6	發源地；出生地	_____	14	合作；協作	_____
7	暴君；專制君主	_____	15	剛強的；強硬的	_____
8	哲學	_____	16	粗暴的；粗野的	_____

B

Complete the Sentences I 請在空格中填入最適當的答案，並視情況做適當的變化。

birthplace	Sparta	Olympics	city-state	philosophy
Athens	tyrant	civilization	democracy	philosopher

1 The first _____ were held in ancient Greece more than 2,500 years ago.
第一屆的奧林匹克運動會於 2,500 多年前由古希臘舉辦。

2 _____ like Athens and Sparta were very powerful.
雅典和斯巴達這樣的城邦非常強大。

3 Athens was the _____ of democracy. 雅典是民主的發源地。

4 _____ was a warlike city-state. 斯巴達是個好戰的城邦。

5 _____ was first practiced by the ancient Greeks.
民主制度由古希臘人率先實行。

6 _____ were like kings but were very cruel. 暴君是指非常殘暴的君主。

7 Many great thinkers lived in Athens and studied _____.
許多偉大的思想家居住在雅典研究哲學。

8 Ancient Greek _____ was highly advanced. 古希臘文明非常先進。

C

Read and Choose I 閱讀下列句子，並且選出最適當的答案。

1 Greek athletes (competed | cooperated) against each other in the Olympics.

2 The (Spartans | Athenians) were the people living in Athens.

3 The men of Sparta constantly (trained | studied) for war.

4 Many Greeks (took part | took charge) in the Olympics.

Look, Read, and Write | 看圖並且依照提示，在空格中填入正確答案。

1 ▶ an ancient festival made up of contests of sports, music, and literature

_____

3 ▶ a large community such as Athens or Sparta

_____

2 ▶ causing pain or suffering to others

_____

4 ▶ to work together

_____

E

Read and Answer | 閱讀並且回答下列問題。 ● 036

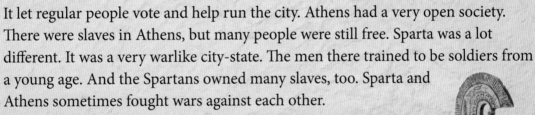

Athens and Sparta

There were many city-states in ancient Greece. They controlled the land around them. Two of the most famous were Athens and Sparta. These two city-states were very different from each other.

First, Athens was the birthplace of democracy. It let regular people vote and help run the city. Athens had a very open society. There were slaves in Athens, but many people were still free. Sparta was a lot different. It was a very warlike city-state. The men there trained to be soldiers from a young age. And the Spartans owned many slaves, too. Sparta and Athens sometimes fought wars against each other.

Athens is also known for its many accomplishments. There were many great thinkers in Athens. Socrates and Plato were two of the world's greatest philosophers. Plato recorded many of his and Socrates's thoughts. People still read his works today.

Fill the blanks.

1　Athens and _____ were the two most famous city-states.

2　_____ was first practiced in Athens.

3　The Spartans owned many _____.

4　Socrates and Plato were two great Athenian _____.

Ancient Rome 古羅馬

Key Words ● 037

---

01 **republic**
[rɪˋpʌblɪk]

(n.) 共和政體;共和國　*Central African Republic 中非共和國

For centuries, Rome was a **republic**. 羅馬在過去的數個世紀都是共和政體。

---

02 **Senate**
[ˋsɛnɪt]

(n.)（古羅馬的）元老院　*senate 參議院　*the Senate 亦指美國等的參議院

The Roman **Senate** had very much power during the republic.
羅馬的元老院在共和政體期間握有很大的權力。

---

03 **citizen**
[ˋsɪtəzn̩]

(n.) 公民;市民　*citizenship 公民的權利與義務　*senior citizen 老人

Many people wanted to be **citizens** of Rome. 很多人都想當羅馬的公民。

---

04 **patrician**
[pəˋtrɪʃən]

(n.)（古羅馬的）貴族

Patricians were wealthy men who owned lots of land.
貴族是指擁有很多土地的富裕人家。

---

05 **plebeian**
[plɪˋbiən]

(n.)（古羅馬的）平民　*plebeian 普通人;普通的（plebeian inhabitant 普通居民）

Plebeians were ordinary citizens in Rome. 平民是指羅馬的普通公民。

---

06 **emperor**
[ˋɛmpərə]

(n.) 皇帝　*empress 皇后;女皇

Augustus Caesar was the first **emperor** of Rome. 奧古斯都是羅馬的第一個皇帝。

---

07 **Latin**
[ˋlætɪn]

(n.) 拉丁語　*(a.)* 拉丁語的;拉丁人的　*Latin America 拉丁美洲

Latin was the language used in ancient Rome. 古羅馬使用的語言為拉丁語。

---

08 **chariot**
[ˋtʃærɪət]

(n.)（古羅馬的）雙輪戰車

Chariots were used in battles and races in ancient Rome.
在古羅馬時期,雙輪戰車被使用在戰爭和競賽中。

---

09 **forum**
[ˋforəm]

(n.)（古羅馬的）公共集會場所
*forum 論壇;討論區（open forum 公開論壇;online forum 線上討論區）

The **forum** was an enormous public space in Rome.
公共集會場所在羅馬時期是指龐大的公共空間。

---

10 **barbarian**
[barˋbɛrɪən]

(n.) 野蠻人;粗野的人　*barbarian tribe 原始部落　*barbarian invasion 蠻族入侵

Germanic **barbarians** defeated Rome in the fifth century.
日耳曼蠻族於五世紀打敗了羅馬。

the ruins of the Roman forum

gladiators

emperor

Colosseum

found
[faʊnd]
建立；創立
Romulus and Remus are said to have **founded** Rome.
傳說中羅馬是由羅慕路斯和雷穆斯所建立。

establish
[əˈstæblɪʃ]
建立；創辦
Romulus and Remus are said to have **established** Rome.
傳說中羅馬是由羅慕路斯和雷穆斯所建立。

expand
[ɪkˈspænd]
擴張；發展
The Roman Empire **expanded** all over Europe. 羅馬帝國擴張到整個歐洲。

take over
接管
The Roman Empire **took over** many places in Europe.
羅馬帝國接管了歐洲許多地方。

enslave
[ɪnˈslev]
奴役
The Romans often **enslaved** people they captured in battle.
羅馬人常常奴役他們在戰爭中俘虜的人。

invade
[ɪnˈved]
侵入；侵略
Germanic barbarians **invaded** and attacked Rome. 日耳曼蠻族侵襲羅馬。

fall
[fɔl]
垮臺
The Roman Empire **fell** in 476. 羅馬帝國於 476 年滅亡。

Word Families 🔊 039

gladiator	（古羅馬）格鬥士 Gladiators fought each other while people watched. 格鬥士在群眾的觀賞下互相搏鬥。
arena	格鬥場；競技場 Gladiators fought each other in arenas. 格鬥士在競技場內互相搏鬥。
senator	元老院議員 Roman senators had very much power during the Roman Republic. 元老院議員在羅馬共和國擁有至高的權力。
consul	執政官 Every year, the Roman Republic selected two leaders, called consuls. 每一年羅馬共和國會選出兩位稱作執政官的領袖。

Famous Romans
著名的羅馬人

Augustus Caesar
奧古斯都
（羅馬帝國開國君主）

Julius Caesar
凱撒大帝
（古羅馬軍事統帥）

Nero
尼祿
（古羅馬暴君）

Checkup

A

Write | 請依提示寫出正確的英文單字或片語。

1	共和政體；共和國	_____	9	（古羅馬的）公共集會場所 _____
2	元老院	_____	10	野蠻人 _____
3	公民；市民	_____	11	接管 _____
4	貴族	_____	12	奴役 _____
5	平民	_____	13	侵入；侵略 _____
6	皇帝	_____	14	垮臺 _____
7	拉丁語	_____	15	元老院議員 _____
8	雙輪戰車	_____	16	執政官 _____

B

Complete the Sentences | 請在空格中填入最適當的答案，並視情況做適當的變化。

plebeian	patrician	Latin	republic	senator
enslave	forum	Senate	chariot	barbarian

1 For centuries, Rome was a _____. 羅馬在過去的數個世紀都是共和政體。

2 The Roman _____ had very much power during the republic.
羅馬的元老院在共和政體期間握有很大的權力。

3 _____ were wealthy men who owned lots of land.
貴族是指擁有很多土地的富裕人家。

4 _____ was the language used in ancient Rome. 古羅馬使用的語言為拉丁語。

5 _____ were used in battles and races in ancient Rome.
在古羅馬時期，雙輪戰車被使用在戰爭和競賽中。

6 The Romans often _____ people they captured in battle.
羅馬人常常奴役他們在戰爭中俘虜的人。

7 The _____ was an enormous public space in Rome.
公共集會場所在羅馬時期是指龐大的公共空間。

8 Germanic _____ defeated Rome in the fifth century.
日耳曼蠻族於五世紀打敗了羅馬。

C

Read and Choose | 閱讀下列句子，並且選出最適當的答案。

1 The Roman Empire (expensed | expanded) all over Europe.

2 The Roman Empire (took over | took care) many places in Europe.

3 Roman (gladiators | senators) had very much power during the Roman Republic.

4 Germanic barbarians (fought | invaded) and attacked Rome.

D Look, Read, and Write | 看圖並且依照提示，在空格中填入正確答案。

 ▶ a political institution that had very much power during the Roman Republic

_____

 ▶ a man who rules an empire

_____

 ▶ ordinary citizens in ancient Rome

_____

 ▶ a two-wheeled carriage used in battles and races in ancient times

_____

 ▶ wealthy men who owned lots of land and became consuls and senators

 ▶ a strong man who fought other men at an event in ancient Rome

_____

E Read and Answer | 閱讀並且回答下列問題。 🔘 040

All Roads Lead to Rome

When it ruled the most land, the Roman Empire was enormous. It covered much of the known world. To the north, it stretched as far as England. To the west, it ruled land in Spain and western Africa. To the south, it covered much land in Africa. And to the east, it stretched far into the Middle East. However, the most important city in the empire was always Rome. There was an important saying: *All roads lead to Rome.* At that time, the emperors were trying to be connected to their provinces far from the capital. So they built many roads. And all of them led back to the capital. When Rome was powerful, the empire was powerful, too. When Rome was weak, the empire was weak. In later years, Rome was defeated by invaders from Germany. How did the invaders get to Rome? They went there on one of the Roman roads!

What is NOT true?

1 The Roman Empire was huge.

2 The Romans built many roads.

3 Rome used to rule land in America.

4 The invaders who conquered Rome traveled on the empire's roads.

A

Write | 請依提示寫出正確的英文單字或片語。

1	地球儀；地球	11	半球
2	赤道	12	緯度
3	行政部門	13	司法部門
4	立法部門	14	否決；反對 v
5	法老	15	象形文字
6	金字塔	16	楔形文字
7	民主制度	17	哲學
8	城邦	18	文明；文明階段
9	共和政體；共和國	19	元老院議員
10	元老院	20	執政官

B

Choose the Correct Word | 請選出與鋪底字意思相近的答案。

1 The executive branch enforces laws.

   a. approves   b. carries out   c. decides

2 A governor or the president may reject a bill.

   a. veto   b. reuse   c. consent

3 Every year, the Nile River flooded the land around it.

   a. flowed   b. centered   c. overflowed

4 The Egyptians erected huge pyramids throughout the land.

   a. honored   b. constructed   c. preserved

C

Complete the Sentences | 請在空格中填入最適當的答案，並視情況做適當的變化。

enforcement	birthplace	Egyptian	prime meridian

1 The _____ divides the Western Hemisphere from the Eastern Hemisphere. 本初子午線將東西半球劃分開來。

2 The executive branch is responsible for the _____ of the law.
行政部門負責執行法律。

3 Ancient _____ culture was centered on the Nile River.
古埃及文化以尼羅河為中心。

4 Athens was the _____ of democracy. 雅典是民主的發源地。

CHAPTER 3

Science ①

A World of Plants 植物的世界

Key Words

● 041

| 01 | **embryo** | (n.) 胚芽;胚胎　*in embryo 在萌芽時期 |
| | [ˈɛmbrɪˌo] | An embryo is a young plant that is just beginning to grow inside a seed. 胚芽是指種子內部新生的幼小植物。 |

| 02 | **seedling** | (n.) 幼苗;秧苗　*seed 種子 |
| | [ˈsidlɪŋ] | A young plant or flower is a seedling. 幼小的植物或花朵稱為幼苗。 |

| 03 | **flowering plant** | (n.) 開花植物 |
| | [ˈflaʊərɪŋ plænt] | Flowering plants produce seeds in flowers. 開花植物會從花朵中結籽。 |

| 04 | **conifer** | (n.) 針葉樹;松柏科植物 |
| | [ˈkɑnəfɚ] | Conifers like pine trees don't have flowers and produce seeds inside of cones. 像松樹這樣的針葉樹無花,並且在毬果中結籽。 |

| 05 | **chlorophyll** | (n.) 葉綠素 |
| | [ˈklɔrəfɪl] | Chlorophyll is a green substance inside leaves that absorbs sunlight. 葉綠素是一種存在於葉片中的綠色物質,負責吸收陽光。 |

| 06 | **photosynthesis** | (n.) 光合作用　*photosynthesize 行光合作用 |
| | [ˌfotəˈsɪnθəsɪs] | Plants use photosynthesis to create food for themselves. 植物利用光合作用為自己製造養分。 |

| 07 | **carbon dioxide** | (n.) 二氧化碳　*carbon monoxide 一氧化碳 |
| | [ˈkɑrbən daɪˈɑksaɪd] | Plants take in carbon dioxide from the air. 植物從空氣中吸收二氧化碳。 |

| 08 | **deciduous** | (a.) 落葉的　*deciduous forest 落葉林 |
| | [dɪˈsɪdʒʊəs] | Deciduous trees lose their leaves in the winter. 落葉樹在冬天落葉。 |

| 09 | **coniferous** | (a.) 針葉的;結毬果的　*coniferous forest 針葉林 |
| | [koˈnɪfərəs] | Coniferous trees have needles and keep them all year long. 針葉樹的針葉終年不落葉。 |

| 10 | **heredity** | (n.) 遺傳(= inheritance) |
| | [həˈrɛdətɪ] | Heredity is the passing of characteristics from parents to their children. 遺傳是指由親代將特徵傳給子代。 |

Germination of a Bean Plant

embryo　　　seedling

Photosynthesis

oxygen

sunlight

carbon dioxide

water　　　minerals

birch

germinate
['dʒɝmə,net]

生長；發芽
A seed needs water, nutrients, and the right temperature to germinate.
種子需要水、養分以及適當的溫度來生長。

produce
[prə'djus]

製造；生產
Plants use photosynthesis to produce energy and oxygen.
植物利用光合作用來製造能量及氧氣。

elm

give off

放出；發出
When leaves make food for a plant, they give off oxygen.
當葉片為植物製造食物時，會放出氧氣。

release
[rɪ'lis]

釋放；解放
When leaves make food for a plant, they release oxygen.
當葉片為植物製造食物時，會釋放氧氣。

maple

take in

吸收；汲取
When leaves make food for a plant, they take in carbon dioxide.
當葉片為植物製造食物時，會吸收二氧化碳。

absorb
[əb'sɔrb]

吸收；汲取
When leaves make food for a plant, they absorb carbon dioxide.
當葉片為植物製造食物時，會吸收二氧化碳。

oak

pass on

傳遞
Plants pass on their characteristics to their offspring. 植物將它們的特徵傳給子代。

be passed from

從……遺傳
The characteristics of plants are passed from the parent plants to their offspring.
植物的特徵會從親代遺傳給它們的子代。

Word Families 🔊 043

annual

一年生的植物
An annual completes its life cycle in one year.
一年生的植物用一年的時間完成生命週期。

biennial
[baɪ'ɛnɪəl]

兩年生的植物
A biennial completes its life cycle in two years.
兩年生的植物用兩年的時間完成生命週期。

fir cones

perennial
[pə'rɛnɪəl]

多年生的植物
A perennial continues to grow year after year. 多年生的植物每年持續生長著。

| **Coniferous Trees** 針葉樹 | **pine** 松樹
fir 冷杉
spruce 雲杉
cedar 西洋杉
['sidɚ] | **Deciduous Trees** 落葉樹 | **oak** 橡樹
maple 楓樹
birch 樺；白樺
[bɝtʃ]
elm 榆樹 |

Checkup

A

Write | 請依提示寫出正確的英文單字或片語。

1	胚芽；胚胎	_____	9	落葉的	_____
2	幼苗；秧苗	_____	10	針葉的；結毬果的	_____
3	開花植物	_____	11	生長；發芽	_____
4	針葉樹；松柏科植物	_____	12	兩年生的植物	_____
5	葉綠素	_____	13	釋放；解放	r_____
6	光合作用	_____	14	樺；白樺	_____
7	二氧化碳	_____	15	吸收；汲取	a_____
8	遺傳	_____	16	傳遞	_____

B

Complete the Sentences | 請在空格中填入最適當的答案，並視情況做適當的變化。

chlorophyll	embryo	flowering	heredity	photosynthesis
coniferous	seedling	germinate	conifer	carbon dioxide

1 An _____ is a young plant that is just beginning to grow inside a seed.
胚芽是指種子內部新生的幼小植物。

2 _____ is a green substance inside leaves that absorbs sunlight.
葉綠素是一種存在於葉片中的綠色物質，負責吸收陽光。

3 Plants use _____ to create food for themselves.
植物利用光合作用為自己製造養分。

4 _____ trees have needles and keep them all year long.
針葉樹的針葉終年不落葉。

5 _____ is the passing of characteristics from parents to their children.
遺傳是指由親代將特徵傳給子代。

6 _____ plants produce seeds in flowers. 開花植物會從花朵中結籽。

7 A young plant or flower is a _____. 幼小的植物或花朵稱為幼苗。

8 A seed needs water, nutrients, and the right temperature to _____.
種子需要水、養分以及適當的溫度來生長。

C

Read and Choose | 閱讀下列句子，並且選出最適當的答案。

1 When leaves make food for a plant, they (take in | give off) oxygen.

2 When leaves make food for a plant, they (take in | give off) carbon dioxide.

3 Plants pass (from | on) their characteristics to their offspring.

4 An (perennial | annual) completes its life cycle in one year.

D

Look, Read, and Write | 看圖並且依照提示，在空格中填入正確答案。

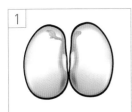 ▶ a young plant that is beginning to grow inside a seed

_____

 ▶ the process that plants use to create food by using sunlight

_____

 ▶ a young plant that is grown from seed

_____

 ▶ a green substance inside leaves that absorbs sunlight

_____

 ▶ a gas that is produced when people and animals breathe out

_____

 ▶ trees that lose their leaves in the winter

_____

E

Read and Answer | 閱讀並且回答下列問題。 044

Photosynthesis

Every living creature needs food and water to survive. Without food and water, a creature would die. Plants are also living creatures. So they need to have these things, too. Plants can create their own food. They do this in a process called photosynthesis. Plants need sunlight in order to make energy. First, when the sun shines, chlorophyll in the plants captures the sunlight. Sunlight is just energy. So the chlorophyll is capturing energy. Then a plant needs two more things: water and carbon dioxide. That is when photosynthesis can take place. In photosynthesis, a plant undergoes a chemical reaction. Thanks to the chlorophyll, it creates sugar. The plant feeds off of the sugar. The reaction also produces oxygen. The plant releases oxygen into the air, and people breathe it. So, without photosynthesis, people could not survive either.

What is true? Write T(true) or F(false).

1 Plants can make their own water. _____

2 Plants need sunlight to live. _____

3 Chlorophyll helps plants go through photosynthesis. _____

4 Plants breathe oxygen. _____

A World of Animals 動物的世界

Key Words 045

01	**warm-blooded** [ˋwɔrmˋblʌdɪd]	(a.) 恆溫的；溫血的　　*hot-blooded 熱血的；激動的 Warm-blooded animals can control their body temperature. 恆溫動物可以控制自己的體溫。
02	**cold-blooded** [ˋkoldˋblʌdɪd]	(a.) 變溫的；冷血的　　*cold-blooded murderer 冷血殺手 　　　　　　　　　　　　*in cold blood 蓄意而殘忍地 Cold-blooded animals depend on the sun for heat. 變溫動物依賴太陽來維持溫度。
03	**vertebrate** [ˋvɝtə͵bret]	(n.) 脊椎動物　(a.) 有脊椎的　　*vertebrate animals 脊椎動物 A vertebrate is an animal with a backbone. 脊椎動物是指有脊骨的動物。
04	**invertebrate** [ɪnˋvɝtəbrɪt]	(n.) 無脊椎動物 (a.) 無脊椎的　　*invertebrate zoology 無脊椎動物學 An invertebrate is an animal with no backbone. 無脊椎動物是指無脊骨的動物。
05	**trait** [tret]	(n.) 特徵；特點；特性　　*personality trait 性格特徵 All animals have different traits or characteristics. 所有的動物都有不同的特徵或特性。
06	**instinct** [ˋɪnstɪŋkt]	(n.) 本能；直覺　　*first instinct 本能的直覺 　　　　　　　　*have an instinct for sth./doing sth. 具有某種／做某事的天性 Many animals react by instinct. 許多動物依本能反應。
07	**migration** [maɪˋgreʃən]	(n.)（候鳥等）遷徙；遷移　　*emigration 移居國外　　*immigration 移居入境 Bird migration to the south takes place every year. 鳥類每年都會南遷。
08	**hibernation** [͵haɪbəˋneʃən]	(n.) 冬眠　　*emerge from/come out of hibernation 結束冬眠 　　　　　　*in hibernation 處於冬眠狀態 In winter, some animals go into hibernation for several weeks. 有一些動物會在冬天冬眠數週。
09	**organism** [ˋɔrgən͵ɪzəm]	(n.) 有機體；生物　　*microscopic organism 微生物 　　　　　　　　　　*economic organism 經濟有機體 An organism is any form of life. 有機體是指生命的任何形式。
10	**reproduction** [͵riprəˋdʌkʃən]	(n.) 生殖；繁育　　*sexual/asexual reproduction 有性／無性生殖 Reproduction is the way organisms make more of their own kind. 生殖是指有機體製造更多本身物種的方式。

warm-blooded animals

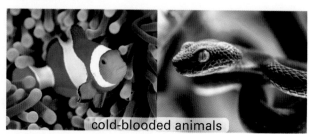

cold-blooded animals

respond to
對……有反應
How do animals **respond to** changes in the environment?
動物如何對環境的變遷作出反應？

react to
對……作出反應
How do animals **react to** changes in the environment?
動物如何對環境的變遷作出反應？

migrate
[ˋmaɪˌgret]
遷移；移居
Birds **migrate** south looking for warmer places in winter.
鳥類在冬天南遷，尋找較溫暖之地。

hibernate
[ˋhaɪbəˌnet]
冬眠；過冬
Bears **hibernate** through the cold winter. 熊會冬眠以度過寒冬。

reproduce
[ˌriprəˋdjus]
繁殖；生殖
Animals must **reproduce** in order to survive. 動物必須繁殖以求生存。

exhibit
[ɪgˋzɪbɪt]
顯現；表示
Most animals **exhibit** the same traits as their parents.
大部分的動物顯現和牠們父母相同的特徵。

bird migration

Word Families 🔊 047

inherited trait 遺傳特質
An animal's color and size are **inherited traits**. 動物的膚色及大小是遺傳特質。

learned trait 後天學習
Using tools is an example of a **learned trait**. 使用工具是一種後天學習。

Vertebrates
脊椎動物

Invertebrates
無脊椎動物

mammals 哺乳動物 **reptiles** 爬行動物

birds 鳥 **fish** 魚

amphibians 兩棲動物

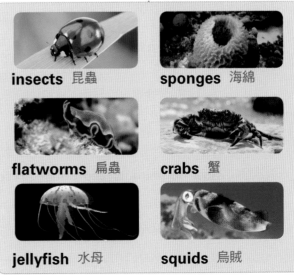

insects 昆蟲 **sponges** 海綿

flatworms 扁蟲 **crabs** 蟹

jellyfish 水母 **squids** 烏賊

Checkup

A

Write | 請依提示寫出正確的英文單字或片語。

1 恆溫的；溫血的 _____	9 特徵；特性 _____
2 變溫的；冷血的 _____	10 生殖；繁育 (n.) _____
3 脊椎動物 _____	11 對⋯⋯有反應 _____
4 無脊椎動物 _____	12 哺乳動物 _____
5 本能；直覺 _____	13 （海中動物）海綿 _____
6 （候鳥等）遷徙；遷移 (n.) _____	14 顯現；表示 _____
7 冬眠 (n.) _____	15 遺傳特質 _____
8 有機體；生物 _____	16 後天學習 _____

B

Complete the Sentences | 請在空格中填入最適當的答案，並視情況做適當的變化。

warm-blooded	organism	hibernation	vertebrate	migration
cold-blooded	instinct	reproduction	trait	invertebrate

1 An _____ is any form of life. 有機體是指生命的任何形式。

2 _____ animals depend on the sun for heat.
變溫動物依賴太陽來維持溫度。

3 _____ animals can control their body temperature.
恆溫動物可以控制自己的體溫。

4 All animals have different _____ or characteristics.
所有的動物都有不同的特徵或特性。

5 An _____ is an animal with no backbone.
無脊椎動物是指無脊骨的動物。

6 A _____ is an animal with a backbone. 脊椎動物是指有脊骨的動物。

7 Many animals react by _____. 許多動物依本能反應。

8 _____ is the way organisms make more of their own kind.
生殖是指有機體製造更多本身物種的方式。

C

Read and Choose | 閱讀下列句子，並且選出最適當的答案。

1 How do animals (reproduce | respond) to changes in the environment?

2 An animal's color and size are (inherited | learned) traits.

3 Birds (hibernate | migrate) south looking for warmer places in winter.

4 Most animals (react | exhibit) the same traits as their parents.

Look, Read, and Write ｜ 看圖並且依照提示，在空格中填入正確答案。

1 ▸ animals that can control their body temperature

_____

2 ▸ animals that depend on the sun for heat

_____

3 ▸ an animal with no backbone

_____

4 ▸ an animal with a backbone

_____

5 ▸ any form of life

_____

6 ▸ a quality passed on through the genes

_____

E

Read and Answer ｜ 閱讀並且回答下列問題。　🔊 048

Warm-Blooded vs. Cold-Blooded Animals

All animals are either warm-blooded or cold-blooded. This refers to how the animals maintain their body temperature. Warm-blooded animals can regulate their body temperature. So, even if it is very cold outside, their bodies will stay warm. But warm-blooded animals have to eat a lot of food. They use the food to produce energy. That helps keep their bodies warm. Mammals are warm-blooded, and so are birds. Cold-blooded animals rely upon the sun for heat. So their internal temperatures can change all the time. These animals often rest in the sun for hours. This lets their bodies soak up heat and become warm. Most cold-blooded animals don't live in cold places. They prefer hot places instead. Reptiles, amphibians, and fish are all cold-blooded.

Fill in the blanks.

1 _____ animals can control their body temperature.

2 Mammals and _____ are both warm-blooded.

3 Cold-blooded animals get their heat from the _____.

4 Reptiles, amphibians, and _____ are cold-blooded animals.

Food Chains 食物鏈

Key Words   ⊙ 049

| 01 | **herbivore**
[ˈhɝbəˌvɔr] | *(n.)* 食草動物（= plant-eating animal）
A **herbivore** is an animal that eats only plants.
食草動物是指以植物為生的動物。 |

| 02 | **carnivore**
[ˈkɑrnəˌvɔr] | *(n.)* 食肉動物（= flesh-eating animal）
A **carnivore** is an animal that only eats other animals.
食肉動物是指以其他動物為生的動物。 |

| 03 | **omnivore**
[ˈɑmnəˌvɔr] | *(n.)* 雜食動物　*insectivore 食蟲動物
Omnivores can eat both plants and animals. 雜食動物吃植物也吃動物。 |

| 04 | **producer**
[prəˈdjusɚ] | *(n.)* 生產者　*produce 生產；出產　*product 產品
Producers are organisms like plants that make their own food.
生產者是指像植物這樣自己製造食物的有機體。 |

| 05 | **consumer**
[kənˈsjumɚ] | *(n.)* 消費者　*consume 消耗；消費　*consumer goods 消費品
Consumers are organisms that get energy by eating other organisms.
消費者是指依靠吃其他有機體獲得能量的有機體。 |

| 06 | **decomposer**
[ˌdikəmˈpozɚ] | *(n.)* 分解者　*decompose 分解；腐爛
Decomposers break down the bodies of dead plants and animals.
分解者分解死亡動植物的屍體。 |

| 07 | **predator**
[ˈprɛdətɚ] | *(n.)* 掠食性動物
Animals like lions that hunt others for food are **predators**.
像獅子這樣獵捕其他動物為生的動物，稱為掠食性動物。 |

| 08 | **prey**
[pre] | *(n.)* 獵物　*be/fall prey to sth. 成為某物的獵物　*prey on sth. 捕食某物
A **prey** animal is one that is hunted for food by other animals.
獵物是指被其他動物捕食的動物。 |

| 09 | **scavenger**
[ˈskævɪndʒɚ] | *(n.)* 食腐動物　*scavenge 覓食；清理垃圾
Scavengers like hyenas eat dead animals.
像鬣狗這樣的食腐動物專門吃死的動物。 |

| 10 | **parasite**
[ˈpærəˌsaɪt] | *(n.)* 寄生生物　*host 寄主；宿主
Parasites live on or inside the bodies of other animals.
寄生生物生活在其他動物的體表或是體內。 |

consumer

producer

predator

prey

🔊 050

hunt [hʌnt]	追獵	Many predators **hunt** prey at night. 許多掠食性動物在夜晚追捕獵物。
prey on	捕食	Many predators **prey on** other animals at night. 許多掠食性動物在夜晚捕食其他動物。
consume [kənˋsjum]	吃完；喝光	A carnivore **consumes** its prey after it catches it. 食肉動物在捕獲獵物後就會將其吃掉。
scavenge [ˋskævɪndʒ]	（從腐物中）覓食	Some animals **scavenge** to get their food. 有些動物吃腐爛的食物。
decompose [ˌdikəmˋpoz]	被分解；腐爛	A dead body will **decompose** and break down. 屍體會腐爛分解。

Word Families 🔊 051

Herbivores
食草動物

rabbit	兔子
horse	馬
cow	母牛
kangaroo	袋鼠
elephant	大象
rhinoceros [raɪˋnɑsərəs]	犀牛

Carnivores
食肉動物

lion	獅子
tiger	老虎
coyote [kaɪˋotɪ]	土狼
hawk	隼
snake	蛇
owl	貓頭鷹

Omnivores
雜食動物

bear	熊
raccoon [ræˋkun]	浣熊
mouse	老鼠 (pl. mice)
chimpanzee [ˌtʃɪmpænˋzi]	黑猩猩
human	人類

Scavengers
食腐動物

hyena [haɪˋinə]	鬣狗
crow	烏鴉
vulture [ˋvʌltʃɚ]	禿鷹
crab	蟹

Checkup

A

Write | 請依提示寫出正確的英文單字或片語。

1	食草動物	_____	
2	食肉動物	_____	
3	雜食動物	_____	
4	生產者	_____	
5	消費者	_____	
6	分解者	_____	
7	掠食性動物	_____	
8	獵物	_____	

9	食腐動物	_____	
10	寄生生物	_____	
11	追獵	h_____	
12	捕食	p_____	
13	吃完；喝光	_____	
14	（從廢棄物中）覓食	_____	
15	被分解；腐爛	_____	
16	犀牛	_____	

B

Complete the Sentences | 請在空格中填入最適當的答案，並視情況做適當的變化。

scavenger	omnivore	herbivore	prey	decomposer
predator	consumer	parasite	carnivore	producer

1 _____ can eat both plants and animals. 雜食動物吃植物也吃動物。

2 A _____ is an animal that eats only plants. 食草動物是指以植物為生的動物。

3 A _____ is an animal that only eats other animals.
食肉動物是指以其他動物為生的動物。

4 _____ are organisms that get energy by eating other organisms.
消費者是指依靠吃其他有機體獲得能量的有機體。

5 A _____ animal is one that is hunted for food by other animals.
獵物是指被其他動物捕食的動物。

6 Animals like lions that hunt others for food are _____.
像獅子這樣獵捕其他動物為生的動物，稱為掠食性動物。

7 _____ break down the bodies of dead plants and animals.
分解者分解死亡動植物的屍體。

8 _____ live on or inside the bodies of other animals.
寄生生物生活在其他動物的體內或是體表。

C

Read and Choose | 閱讀下列句子，並且選出最適當的答案。

1 Many predators (hunt | prey) on other animals at night.

2 A dead body will (decompose | scavenge) and break down.

3 Some animals (consume | scavenge) to get their food.

4 (Producers | Consumers) are organisms that get energy by eating other organisms.

Look, Read, and Write | 看圖並且依照提示，在空格中填入正確答案。

1

▶ an animal that only eats other animals

_____

4

▶ an animal that lives by hunting other animals for food

_____

2

▶ an animal that only eats plants

_____

5

▶ an animal that eats dead animals

_____

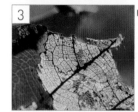
3

▶ to decay by a slow natural process

_____

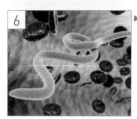
6

▶ an animal that lives on or inside the bodies of other animals

_____

E

Read and Answer | 閱讀並且回答下列問題。　● 052

Herbivores, Carnivores, and Omnivores

Every living creature needs to eat to survive. However, animals do not all eat the same things. Instead, they eat a variety of foods. Most animals can be classified into three groups. Herbivores are the first group. These are animals that only eat vegetation. So they might eat plants, fruits, or vegetables. People call them "plant eaters." Cows and horses are herbivores. So are rabbits. Huge animals can be herbivores, too. Both elephants and rhinoceroses only eat plants. Carnivores are meat eaters. They are often hunters. They are predators and must find prey to catch and eat. The members of the cat family are carnivores. This includes lions, pumas, and even house cats. Sharks are also meat eaters. Some animals eat both plants and animals. They are called omnivores. Humans are omnivores. So are pigs, wolves, and even chickens.

Answer the questions.

1　How many groups of animals are there?　_____

2　What do herbivores eat?　_____

3　What kinds of animals are sharks and lions?　_____

4　What do omnivores eat?　_____

Key Words 🔊 053

01 competition
[ˌkɑmpə`tɪʃən]

(n.) 競爭　*intense/fierce competition 激烈競爭

Animals are in **competition** with each other to survive.
動物間會彼此競爭以求生存。

02 adaptation
[ˌædæp`teʃən]

(n.) 適應；改編　*evolutionary adaptation 進化適應

Adaptation to its environment is important for an animal.
對動物來說，適應環境是很重要的。

03 survival
[sə`vaɪvl̩]

(n.) 生存；存活　*chance of survival 存活的機率　*survival instinct 生存本能

All animals are concerned about their **survival**.
所有的動物都很關切牠們的生存問題。

04 defense
[dɪ`fɛns]

(n.) 防禦；保衛　*in defense of 防禦；保衛　*line of defense 防線

A good **defense** helps animals protect themselves from predators.
好的防禦可讓動物免於落入掠食性動物之手。

05 camouflage
[`kæmə,flɑʒ]

(n.) 偽裝；掩飾　*natural camouflage 天然保護色　*camouflage jacket 迷彩夾克

Some animals use **camouflage** to hide from hunters.
有些動物利用偽裝來躲避獵人。

06 mimicry
[`mɪmɪkrɪ]

(n.) 模仿；模擬　*mimic 善於模仿的人

Looking like another organism is called **mimicry**.
看起來像另一個生物一樣稱作模仿。

07 poison
[`pɔɪzn̩]

(n.) 毒　*take poison 服毒　*food poisoning 食物中毒

Some spiders use **poison** to kill their enemies.
有些蜘蛛利用毒液來殺害牠們的敵人。

08 endangered
[ɪn`dendʒəd]

(a.) 瀕臨絕種的

Elephants, lions, and tigers are all **endangered** species.
大象、獅子以及老虎都是瀕臨絕種的物種。

09 extinct
[ɪk`stɪŋkt]

(a.) 絕種的　*become extinct 絕種　*extinct volcano 死火山

The dodo birds all died, so they are now **extinct**.
渡渡鳥全都死了，所以牠們現今已絕種。

10 destruction
[dɪ`strʌkʃən]

(n.) 破壞；毀滅　*the destruction of sth. 破壞、摧毀某物

The **destruction** of habitats is harmful to many animals.
棲息地的破壞有害於許多動物。

competition for survival

camouflage　　mimicry

destruction of habitats

adapt
[ə`dæpt]
適應
An animal that cannot adapt will die. 無法適應的動物將會死亡。

adjust
[ə`dʒʌst]
適應
An animal that cannot adjust will die. 無法適應的動物將會死亡。

defend
[dɪ`fɛnd]
保護；防禦
Many animals defend their young from predators.
許多動物保護牠們的孩子免於落入掠食性動物之手。

protect
[prə`tɛkt]
保護
Many animals protect their young from predators.
許多動物保護牠們的孩子免於落入掠食性動物之手。

defend/protect their young

perish
[`pɛrɪʃ]
死去；消滅
Old, sick, and weak animals perish very quickly.
年邁、幼小以及虛弱的動物很快就會死亡。

die out
滅絕；逐漸消失
Old, sick, and weak animals die out very quickly.
年邁、幼小以及虛弱的動物很快就會滅絕。

become extinct
滅絕
Old, sick, and weak animals become extinct very quickly.
年邁、幼小以及虛弱的動物很快就會滅絕。

Word Families 🔘 055

sharp teeth

compete
競爭；對抗
Animals compete against each other in the wild. 動物在野外彼此競爭。

share
分享；分擔
Many types of animals share the same ecosystem.
許多種類的動物同享一個生態系統。

strong claws

destroy
破壞
Humans often destroy animals' environments 人類常常破壞動物的生存環境。

harm
危害
Humans often harm animals' environments. 人類常常危害動物的生存環境。

Animal Adaptations and Defense Methods 動物的適應與防禦方法	**camouflage** 偽裝	**mimicry** 模仿
	poison 毒	**ejection** 噴出（液體）
	strong claws 利爪	**sharp teeth** 尖牙

Checkup

A

Write | 請依提示寫出正確的英文單字或片語。

1 競爭 (n.)	_____	9 絕種的	_____
2 適應；改編 (n.)	_____	10 破壞；毀滅 (n.)	_____
3 生存；存活	_____	11 適應 (v.)	_____
4 防禦；保衛 (n.)	_____	12 分享；分擔	_____
5 偽裝；掩飾	_____	13 保護	p _____
6 模仿；模擬	_____	14 死去；消滅	p _____
7 毒	_____	15 噴出（液體）	_____
8 瀕臨絕種的	_____	16 危害	_____

B

Complete the Sentences | 請在空格中填入最適當的答案，並視情況做適當的變化。

competition	mimicry	survival	camouflage	extinct
defense	endangered	destruction	adaptation	poison

1 Animals are in _____ with each other to survive.
動物間會彼此競爭以求生存。

2 All animals are concerned about their _____. 所有動物都很關切牠們的生存問題。

3 _____ to its environment is important for an animal.
對動物來說，適應環境是很重要的。

4 The dodo birds all died, so they are now _____.
渡渡鳥全都死了，所以牠們現今已絕種。

5 A good _____ helps animals protect themselves from predators.
好的防禦可讓動物免於落入掠食性動物之手。

6 Some spiders use _____ to kill their enemies.
有些蜘蛛利用毒液來殺死牠們的敵人。

7 Elephants, lions, and tigers are all _____ species.
大象、獅子以及老虎都是瀕臨絕種的物種。

8 The _____ of habitats is harmful to many animals.
棲息地的破壞有害於許多動物。

C

Read and Choose | 請選出與鋪底字意思相近的答案。

1 Many animals defend their young from predators.

   a. hide   b. care of   c. protect

2 An animal that cannot adapt will die.

   a. advise   b. adjust   c. survive

3 Old, sick, and weak animals perish very quickly.

   a. extinct   b. die out   c. destroy

Look, Read, and Write I 看圖並且依照提示，在空格中填入正確答案。

 ► the act of changing oneself to adapt for its environment

_____

 ► no longer existing

_____

 ► a way of hiding something by making them look like the natural background

_____

 ► looking like another organism

_____

E

Read and Answer I 閱讀並且回答下列問題。　○ 056

How Animals Become Extinct

There has been life on Earth for billions of years. These organisms are always changing. In fact, many organisms no longer live on Earth. They all died. So people say that they are extinct.

Many animals are extinct. The dinosaurs are extinct. The dodo bird is extinct. The woolly mammoth is also no longer alive. Why do animals become extinct? There are many reasons. Natural disasters such as fires, flood, droughts, and earthquakes can destroy habitats. People can destroy habitats, too. Pollution can also harm organisms. Some animals are hunted by people. All these things are harmful to plants and animals, and they can cause the changes to ecosystems. When a large change occurs in an ecosystem, some organisms have trouble surviving. Then they can be endangered and may become extinct. So, it is important to protect our natural environment and ecosystems. What do you think we can do for endangered animals?

What is NOT true?

1　Organisms often change.

2　The dinosaurs are extinct.

3　Only natural disasters make animals become extinct.

4　Changes in an ecosystem can make animals go extinct.

Unit 15 Earth's Rocks and Soil 地球的岩石與土壤

01 rock
[rɑk]

(n.) 岩石；石頭　*volcanic rock 火山岩　*solid as a rock = rock-solid 堅如磐石

Much of Earth's surface is made up of **rocks**. 地表大部分由岩石構成。

02 mineral
[ˈmɪnərəl]

(n.) 礦物　*metallic mineral 金屬礦　*mineral salt 礦物鹽

Rocks are usually made of many different **minerals**.
岩石通常由許多種不同的礦物組成。

03 soil
[sɔɪl]

(n.) 土壤；土　*fertile soil 沃土　*surface soil 表土

Some kinds of **soils** are silt, clay, sand, and humus.
土壤的種類有泥沙、黏土、沙和腐殖質。

04 property
[ˈprɑpətɪ]

(n.) 特性；屬性　*property 財產（personal/public property 私人／公共財產）

Each kind of soil has its own **properties**, like being powdery or sticky.
每種土壤都有不同的特性，像是粉狀或是黏稠狀。

05 igneous rock
[ˈɪgnɪəs rɑk]

(n.) 火成岩

Igneous rocks are made from melted rock. 火成岩由熔化的岩石所組成。

06 sedimentary rock
[ˌsɛdəˈmɛntərɪ rɑk]

(n.) 沈積岩

Sedimentary rock forms when layers of sand, mud, or pebbles are pressed together. 沈積岩由沙、泥或鵝卵石等地層擠壓而成。

07 metamorphic rock
[mɛtəˈmɔrfɪk rɑk]

(n.) 變質岩

Metamorphic rock is rock that has changed from one kind of rock into another. 變質岩是由某種岩石轉變而成的另一種岩石。

08 fossil
[ˈfɑsl̩]

(n.) 化石　*living fossil 活化石　*old fossil 老頑固

Fossils are the imprints or remains of plants or animals that lived long ago.
化石是指年代久遠的動植物所留下的痕跡或是遺骸。

09 fossil fuel
[ˈfɑsl̩ ˈfjʊəl]

(n.) 化石燃料

Fossil fuels like coal and gas were formed from the remains of plants or animals long ago. 煤和天然氣等化石燃料由年代久遠的動植物遺骸所形成。

10 impression
[ɪmˈprɛʃən]

(n.) 印記；壓印　*make/leave an impression in the mud 在泥地上留下痕跡

A fossil can be a footprint or an **impression** in rock.
化石可能是岩石中的一個腳印或是印記。

Fossil | imprint/remains/impression

Fossil Fuels | coal | gas

form 形成；構成
[fɔrm]
Fossils **form** when plants and animals are buried under mud or sand.
動植物被埋藏於泥沙底下便形成化石。

be formed 由……形成；由……構成
Rocks **are formed** in many different ways. 岩石由不同的方式所形成。

preserve 保存
[prɪˋzɝv]
Most fossils are **preserved** in sedimentary rocks. 大部分的化石被保存於沈積岩。

press 擠壓；推
[prɛs]
Most fossils are **pressed** on materials that later turned into rock.
大部分的化石被擠壓在後來形成岩石的物質上。

petrify 石化
[ˋpɛtrɪfaɪ]
Some animal bones **petrify** and become fossils.
有些動物的骨頭會石化，然後成為化石。

Kinds of Soils 土壤的種類

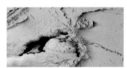

silt
泥沙

clay
黏土

sand
沙

humus [ˋhjuməs]
腐殖質

Layers of Soil 土壤的分層

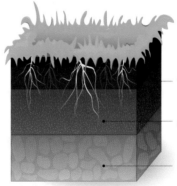

topsoil 表土

subsoil 下層土；底土

bedrock 床岩

Igneous Rocks
火成岩

granite [ˋgrænɪt]	花崗岩
pumice [ˋpʌmɪs]	輕石
basalt [bəˋsɔlt]	玄武岩

Sedimentary Rocks
沈積岩

limestone	石灰岩
sandstone	沙岩
shale [ʃel]	頁岩；泥板岩

Metamorphic Rocks
變質岩

marble	大理石
quartz [kwɔrts]	石英
slate [slet]	板岩；石板瓦

Checkup

A

Write | 請依提示寫出正確的英文單字或片語。

1	岩石；石頭	_____	9	特性；屬性	_____
2	礦物	_____	10	印記；壓印	_____
3	土壤；土	_____	11	形成；構成	_____
4	火成岩	_____	12	花崗岩	_____
5	沈積岩	_____	13	保存；保藏	_____
6	變質岩	_____	14	擠壓；推	_____
7	化石	_____	15	石化	_____
8	化石燃料	_____	16	地層	_____

B

Complete the Sentences | 請在空格中填入最適當的答案，並視情況做適當的變化。

igneous	sedimentary	rock	metamorphic	mineral
impression	property	soil	fossil fuel	fossil

1 Much of Earth's surface is made up of _____. 地表大部分由岩石所構成。

2 _____ rocks are made from melted rock. 火成岩由熔化的岩石所組成。

3 _____ rock is rock that has changed from one kind of rock into another. 變質岩是由某種岩石轉變而成的另一種岩石。

4 _____ rock forms when layers of sand, mud, or pebbles are pressed together. 沈積岩由沙、泥或鵝卵石等地層擠壓而成。

5 Each kind of soil has its own _____, like being powdery or sticky. 每種土壤都有不同的特性，像是粉狀或是黏稠狀。

6 _____ like coal and gas were formed from the remains of plants or animals long ago. 煤和天然氣等化石燃料由年代久遠的動植物遺骸所形成。

7 Some kinds of _____ are silt, clay, sand, and humus. 土壤的種類有泥沙、黏土、沙和腐殖質。

8 A fossil can be a footprint or an _____ in rock. 化石可能是岩石中的一個腳印或是印記。

C

Read and Choose | 閱讀下列句子，並且選出最適當的答案。

1 Fossils (form | change) when plants and animals are buried under mud or sand.

2 Most fossils are (impression | pressed) on materials that later turned into rock.

3 Most fossils are (preserved | remain) in sedimentary rocks.

4 Some animal bones (petrify | form) and become fossils.

Look, Read, and Write | 看圖並且依照提示，在空格中填入正確答案。

1  ▸ a natural substance in the earth, such as coal, salt, or gold

_____

4  ▸ a kind of rock that forms when layers of sand, mud, or pebbles are pressed together

_____

2  ▸ a kind of rock made from melted rock

_____

5  ▸ the imprints or remains of a plant or an animal

_____

3  ▸ a kind of rock that has changed from another type of rock

_____

6  ▸ a mark that is made when an object is pressed onto a surface

_____

E

Read and Answer | 閱讀並且回答下列問題。　🔊 060

Fossils

Sometimes people go to the museum. They see many bones of dinosaurs or other animals. There are even some plant fossils! But, what exactly are fossils? And how do fossils form? Fossils are the petrified remains of dead animals or plants. They can form in many ways. The most common way is like this: A long time ago, an animal died. Then it got buried in the ground. Over time, the skin and muscles rotted away. But the bones remained. Then, minerals entered the animal's bones. The bones then became as hard as rock. This might have taken thousands or millions of years to occur.

Scientists like to study fossils. They can learn a lot about the animals and plants that lived a long time ago. Scientists can learn how big they are. Scientists can even learn what kind of food they ate. Thanks to fossils, scientists today know a lot about dinosaurs and other animals.

Fill in the blanks.

1 Fossils are the _____ remains of animals or plants.

2 _____ enter bones to make fossils.

3 It takes thousands or millions of _____ for fossils to form.

4 _____ can learn many things from fossils.

A

Write | 請依提示寫出正確的英文單字或片語。

1	開花植物	_____	
2	針葉樹；松柏科植物	_____	
3	恆溫的；溫血的	_____	
4	變溫的；冷血的	_____	
5	食草動物	_____	
6	食肉動物	_____	
7	適應；改編 (n.)	_____	
8	防禦；保衛 (n.)	_____	
9	火成岩	_____	
10	沈積岩	_____	

11	葉綠素	_____
12	光合作用	_____
13	遺傳特質	_____
14	後天學習	_____
15	食腐動物	_____
16	寄生生物	_____
17	破壞；毀滅 (n.)	_____
18	滅絕；逐漸消失	d_____
19	變質岩	_____
20	特性；屬性	p_____

B

Choose the Correct Word | 請選出與鋪底字意思相近的答案。

1 How do animals respond to changes in the environment?

    a. reply   b. react   c. release

2 When leaves make food for a plant, they give off oxygen.

    a. take in   b. absorb   c. release

3 Many animals defend their young from predators.

    a. hide   b. care of   c. protect

4 An animal that cannot adapt will die.

    a. adjust   b. advise   c. survive

C

Complete the Sentences | 請在空格中填入最適當的答案，並視情況做適當的變化。

vertebrate	omnivore	fossil	photosynthesis

1 A _____ is an animal with a backbone.
脊椎動物是指有脊骨的動物。

2 Plants use _____ to create food for themselves.
植物利用光合作用為自己製造養分。

3 _____ can eat both plants and animals.
雜食動物吃植物也吃動物。

4 _____ are the imprints or remains of plants or animals that lived long ago.
化石是指年代久遠的動植物所留下的痕跡或是遺骸。

CHAPTER 4

Science ②

Key Words 🔊 061

01	**resource** [rɪˋsors]	*(n.)* 資源；物力 *natural resources 自然資源 *human resources 人力資源 Useful materials such as oil, coal, and water are called **resources**. 像石油、煤以及水這類有用的原料稱為資源。
02	**conservation** [ˌkɑnsəˋveʃən]	*(n.)* 保存；保護 *conservation area 保護區 *wildlife conservation 野生生物保護 The **conservation** of resources is very important these days. 保護資源是當今非常重要的事。
03	**preservation** [ˌprɛzəˋveʃən]	*(n.)* 保存；保護；維護 *the preservation of sth. 對某事物的保護 *in a good state of preservation 保存狀況良好 People need to think about the **preservation** of the environment. 人們要好好為環境的保護著想。
04	**waste** [west]	*(n.)* 廢棄物；廢料 *hazardous waste 有害廢料 *a waste of sth. 浪費、未善加利用某物 Some factories dump their **waste** in rivers or streams. 有些工廠將廢棄物傾倒於小河或溪流。
05	**spill** [spɪl]	*(n.)* 溢出；濺出 *clean up the spill 清理溢出物 *spill . . . all over sth. 把……濺滿某處 An oil **spill** can kill thousands of fish and other sea life. 海上的漏油會殺死數以千計的魚類和其他海洋生物。
06	**landfill** [ˋlændfɪl]	*(n.)* 垃圾掩埋場 (= landfill site) *dump 倒（垃圾） Putting trash in **landfills** keeps it from becoming pollution. 將垃圾倒在垃圾掩埋場可以避免造成污染。
07	**mining** [ˋmaɪnɪŋ]	*(n.)* 採礦；礦業 *mining industry 採礦業 *mine 礦；礦山 **Mining** lets people get valuable materials like coal, gold, and silver. 採礦讓人們取得像煤、黃金及銀等珍貴原料。
08	**pollution** [pəˋluʃən]	*(n.)* 污染；污染物 *noise pollution 噪音污染 *light pollution 光害 Waste that harms the air, water, or land is called **pollution**. 危害空氣、水或土地的廢棄物稱為污染。
09	**polluted** [pəˋlutɪd]	*(a.)* 受污染的 *polluted beach 被污染的海灘 The air in many big cities is **polluted**. 許多大城市的空氣都受到了污染。
10	**damaged** [ˋdæmɪdʒd]	*(a.)* 損壞的 *damaged goods 受損的貨物 The land can be **damaged** because of ground pollution. 由於土壤污染，土地可能會有所損壞。

Types of Pollution

air pollution

water pollution

ground pollution

smog

conserve 節省；保存
[kən'sɝv]
Try to **conserve** electricity whenever you can. 無論何時都要盡量省電。

preserve 保護；維護
[prɪ'zɝv]
We can help **preserve** the environment by taking care of it.
我們可以透過愛護環境來為環保盡一份力。

replace 恢復；替代；以⋯⋯代替
[rɪ'ples]
A renewable resource is a resource that can be **replaced** or used again.
所謂的再生資源是指可更新或重複使用的資源。

reduce 減少
[rɪ'djus]
Let's **reduce** the amount of energy that we use. 讓我們減少使用能源。

waste 浪費
[west]
Don't **waste** electricity by leaving lights on all the time. 不要讓燈一直開著，這樣很浪費電。

litter 亂丟廢棄物
['lɪtɚ]
Please do not **litter**. 請不要亂丟垃圾。

pollute 污染；弄髒
[pə'lut]
It is bad to **pollute** the environment. 污染環境是一件糟糕的事。

spill 溢出；濺出
[spɪl]
The tanker **spilled** its oil, so it got into the ocean. 因為油輪漏油，致使油污流入海洋。

smoke 煙霧
There is a lot of smoke coming from that factory.
很多煙霧來自於那間工廠。

fume （有害或難聞的）煙、氣
[fjum]
Smoke and fumes from factories and cars make air pollution. 工廠和汽車排出的煙和氣體造成空氣污染。

smog 煙霧
Smog is a mixture of fog and smoke.
煙霧是霧和煙的混合體。

trash 垃圾 (= garbage)
We should throw away our trash properly.
我們應該正確地丟棄垃圾。

garbage 垃圾 (= trash)
The landfill is full of garbage.
垃圾掩埋場充滿垃圾。

litter 廢棄物
If trash is not placed in a trash can, it becomes litter.
垃圾若沒有放置在垃圾桶內，就變成亂丟廢棄物。

Types of Pollutants
污染物的種類

garbage	垃圾
sewage ['sjuɪdʒ]	污水
fertilizer ['fɝtl̩ˌaɪzɚ]	肥料
oil spills	漏油
industrial waste 工業廢棄物	
smog	煙霧
smoke	煙
dust	灰塵
garbage odors	垃圾臭味
gasoline fumes	油氣

Checkup

Write | 請依提示寫出正確的英文單字或片語。

1	資源；物力	_____	9	廢棄物；廢料 _____
2	保存；保護 (n.)	_____	10	保護；維護 (v.) _____
3	溢出；濺出	_____	11	恢復；替代 _____
4	垃圾掩埋場	_____	12	減少 _____
5	採礦；礦業	_____	13	漏油 _____
6	受污染的	_____	14	亂丟廢棄物 _____
7	污染；污染物	_____	15	垃圾 g_____
8	損壞的	_____	16	（有害或難聞的）煙、氣 _____

B

Complete the Sentences | 請在空格中填入最適當的答案，並視情況做適當的變化。

pollution	recycling	preserve	waste	damaged
resource	mining	landfill	spill	conservation

1 The _____ of resources is very important these days.
保護資源是當今非常重要的事。

2 Some factories dump their _____ in rivers or streams.
有些工廠將廢棄物傾倒於小河或溪流。

3 Putting trash in _____ keeps it from becoming pollution.
將垃圾倒在垃圾掩埋場可以避免造成污染。

4 Useful materials such as oil, coal, and water are called _____.
像石油、煤以及水這類有用的原料稱為資源。

5 _____ lets people get valuable minerals like coal, gold, and silver.
採礦讓人們取得像煤、黃金及銀等珍貴礦物。

6 Waste that harms the air, water, or land is called _____.
危害空氣、水或土地的廢棄物稱為污染。

7 We can help _____ the environment by taking care of it.
我們可以透過愛護環境來為環保盡一份力。

8 The land can be _____ because of ground pollution.
由於土壤污染，土地可能會有所損壞。

C

Read and Choose | 閱讀下列句子，並且選出最適當的答案。

1 A renewable resource is a resource that can be (replaced | reduced) again.

2 Try to (conserve | waste) electricity whenever you can.

3 The air in many big cities is (pollute | polluted).

4 The tanker (preserved | spilled) its oil, so it got into the ocean.

Look, Read, and Write | 看圖並且依照提示，在空格中填入正確答案。

1 ▸ waste that harms the air, water, or land

_____

4 ▸ a release of oil into the environment

_____

2 ▸ material that is left after something has been made

_____

5 ▸ the protection of animals, plants, and natural resources

_____

3 ▸ a place where waste is buried in large amounts

_____

6 ▸ strong smelling gas or smoke that is unpleasant to breathe

_____

E

Read and Answer | 閱讀並且回答下列問題。　● 064

How to Conserve Our Resources

Earth has many natural resources. But many of them are resources that cannot be reused or replaced easily. Once nonrenewable resources are used up, they are gone forever. That means we should conserve our resources as much as possible. Everyone can help do this in many ways.

Water is a valuable resource. So we shouldn't waste it. When you're brushing your teeth, turn the water off. Don't take really long showers either. We should also be careful about using electricity. Don't turn on any lights if you aren't going to use them. Don't leave your computer on all night long. Recycling is another way to save natural resources. Try to reuse things like papers and boxes. Reducing the amount of energy you use is also a good way to conserve our resources.

Answer the questions.

1 What kind of resources cannot be replaced easily? _____

2 What should people do while brushing their teeth? _____

3 What can recycling do? _____

Key Words 🔊 065

01 **weathering**
[ˋwɛðərɪŋ]

(n.) 風化作用　*weathering effect 風化作用

Weathering is the process through which wind and water break down rocks into small pieces for many years.
風和水經多年時間將岩石瓦解為小碎塊的過程稱為風化作用。

02 **erosion**
[ɪˋroʒən]

(n.) 侵蝕；腐蝕　*soil erosion 土壤侵蝕
*the erosion of moral standards 道德淪喪（常用於比喻）

Erosion happens when weathered rocks and soil are carried away to a new place.　風化的岩石和土壤被搬運至新地點稱為侵蝕。

03 **glacier**
[ˋgleʃɚ]

(n.) 冰河　*valley glacier 山谷冰川

A **glacier** is a huge mass of moving ice that appears in cold places.
冰河是一塊會移動的巨大冰塊，出現在寒冷的地方。

04 **canyon**
[ˋkænjən]

(n.) 峽谷　*Grand Canyon 美國大峽谷　*cliff 懸崖；峭壁

Canyons are formed by water erosion over millions of years.
峽谷是由水侵蝕數百萬年而形成。

05 **mesa**
[ˋmesə]

(n.) 臺地；平頂山

A **mesa** is a large hill with a flat top and steep sides.
臺地是頂部平坦、四周陡峭的大丘陵。

06 **plateau**
[plæˋto]

(n.) 高原　*Tibetan Plateau 青藏高原

A **plateau** is a large raised area that is flat.
高原是指地勢高起而平坦的遼闊地區。

07 **sand dune**
[sænd djun]

(n.) 沙丘（= dune）

There are many **sand dunes** at beaches and in deserts.
海灘和沙漠有許多的沙丘。

08 **volcano**
[vɑlˋkeno]

(n.) 火山　*active/dormant/extinct volcano 活／休／死火山

Volcanoes sometimes spew hot ash, gas, and lava into the air.
火山有時會噴出灼熱的灰燼、氣體及熔岩。

09 **eruption**
[ɪˋrʌpʃən]

(n.) 爆發；噴出（= outburst）

A volcanic **eruption** is both powerful and dangerous.
火山爆發的威力既強大又危險。

10 **earthquake**
[ˋɝθ͵kwek]

(n.) 地震　*great/violent earthquake 大地震　*earthquake-resistant 防震的

An **earthquake** is the shaking of Earth's surface. 地表的撼動稱為地震。

glacier　　canyon　　mesa　　sand dune

tornado

weather
['wɛðɚ]
風化;損壞
Water, wind, and changing temperatures **weather** rocks.
水、風以及氣溫的變化會風化岩石。

erode
[ɪ'rod]
腐蝕;侵蝕
When the land **erodes**, it changes shape. 土地受到侵蝕會變形。

expand
[ɪk'spænd]
擴大;擴張
Glaciers often **expand** during cold weather. 冰河通常在寒冷的天氣期間擴大。

recede
[rɪ'sid]
縮減;降低
Glaciers often **recede** during hot weather. 冰河通常在炎熱的天氣期間消融。

erupt
[ɪ'rʌpt]
噴出;爆發
The volcano **erupted** and destroyed several villages. 火山爆發並摧毀許多村莊。

spew
[spju]
噴出;放出
Some volcanoes **spew** large amounts of ash into the air. 有些火山會噴出大量的灰燼。

shake
[ʃek]
搖動;震動
The ground may **shake** very much in an earthquake. 地震時地面可能會搖晃得非常厲害。

tremble
['trɛmbl̩]
搖晃;搖動
The ground may **tremble** very much in an earthquake.
地震時地面可能會搖晃得非常厲害。

Changes on Earth's Surface
地表的變化

Slow Changes 緩慢的變化	Fast Changes 劇烈的變化	
weathering 風化作用	**earthquake**	地震
erosion 侵蝕	**volcano**	火山
	hurricane	颶風
	tornado	龍捲風
	flood	洪水
	violent storm	暴風雨

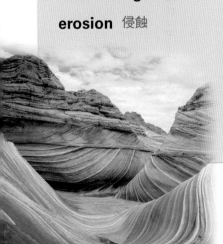

Volcano
火山

vent 火山口
lava 熔岩
crust 地殼
magma 岩漿

Checkup

A

Write | 請依提示寫出正確的英文單字或片語。

1	風化作用	_____	9	爆發；噴出 (n.)	_____
2	侵蝕；腐蝕 (n.)	_____	10	地震	_____
3	冰河	_____	11	風化；損壞 (v.)	_____
4	峽谷	_____	12	腐蝕；侵蝕 (v.)	_____
5	臺地；平頂山	_____	13	縮減；降低	_____
6	高原	_____	14	擴大；擴張	_____
7	沙丘	_____	15	噴出；放出	s_____
8	火山	_____	16	搖晃；搖動	t_____

B

Complete the Sentences | 請在空格中填入最適當的答案，並視情況做適當的變化。

weathering	erosion	earthquake	plateau	glacier
canyon	eruption	sand dune	mesa	volcano

1　_____ happens when weathered rocks and soil are carried away to a new place. 風化的岩石和土壤被搬運至新地點稱為侵蝕。

2　_____ is the process through which wind and water break down rocks into small pieces for many years. 風和水經多年時間將岩石瓦解為小碎塊的過程稱為風化作用。

3　_____ sometimes spew hot ash, gas, and lava into the air.
火山有時會噴出灼熱的灰燼、氣體及熔岩。

4　An _____ is the shaking of Earth's surface. 地表的撼動稱為地震。

5　A volcanic _____ is both powerful and dangerous.
火山爆發的威力既強大又危險。

6　A _____ is a large raised area that is flat. 高原是指地勢高起而平坦的遼闊地區。

7　There are many _____ at beaches and in deserts.
海灘和沙漠有許多的沙丘。

8　A _____ is a huge mass of moving ice that appears in cold places.
冰河是一塊會移動的巨大冰塊，出現在寒冷的地方。

C

Read and Choose | 閱讀下列句子，並且選出最適當的答案。

1　Water, wind, and changing temperatures (erode | weather) rocks.

2　When the land (erodes | weathers), it changes shape.

3　The ground may (shake | spew) very much in an earthquake.

4　Glaciers often (expand | recede) during hot weather.

Look, Read, and Write | 看圖並且依照提示，在空格中填入正確答案。

 ▶ the process in which wind and water break down rocks

_____

 ▶ a large hill with a flat top and steep sides

_____

 ▶ the bursting out of material from a volcano

_____

 ▶ the shaking of Earth's surface

_____

 ▶ a huge mass of moving ice

_____

 ▶ a large flat area of land that is higher than other areas of land that surround it

_____

E

Read and Answer | 閱讀並且回答下列問題。 ● 068

What Changes Earth's Surface?

The surface of the earth is constantly changing. Mountains and hills break down. Rocks and soil move from one place to another. Some changes are very slow. Weathering and erosion can cause these changes. Weathering occurs when wind and water break down rocks into pieces. Erosion occurs when weathered rocks or sand are carried away. There are many types of erosion. The most powerful is water. Water can break down mountains and form canyons. Water erosion made the Grand Canyon over millions of years. Water also moves dirt and soil to oceans and seas. The wind can move sand in deserts from place to place. And it can erode valuable topsoil and make deserts that way. Earthquakes, volcanoes, and violent storms can change Earth's surface quickly. Earthquakes can make huge cracks in the land. Volcanoes can cover entire cities in ash and lava. And storms can drop huge amounts of water and causes floods.

What is NOT true?

1   There are many types of erosion.
2   All changes on Earth's surface are slow.
3   The Grand Canyon was made by water erosion.
4   Volcanoes can change Earth's surface quickly.

Weather and the Water Cycle

天氣與水循環

01 atmosphere
[ˈætməsˌfɪr]

(n.) 大氣　*atmosphere 氣氛（relaxed atmosphere 放鬆的氣氛）

The air that surrounds Earth is called the atmosphere.
圍繞地球的空氣稱為大氣。

02 pattern
[ˈpætən]

(n.) 型態　*behavior pattern 行為模式　*set pattern 固定模式

A change in the weather that repeats is called a weather pattern.
重複的天氣變化稱為天氣型態。

03 temperature
[ˈtɛmprətʃə]

(n.) 溫度　*room temperature 室溫　*at a temperature of . . .°C 在攝氏⋯⋯度

The temperature tells you how hot or cold something is.
溫度告訴你冷熱的變化。

04 thermometer
[θəˈmɑmətə]

(n.) 溫度計　*the thermometer reads . . . degrees 溫度計顯示⋯⋯度

A thermometer measures the temperature. 溫度計用來測量溫度。

05 air pressure
[ɛr ˈprɛʃə]

(n.) 氣壓

You can tell if it will rain or not by checking the air pressure.
你可以經由檢測氣壓來得知是否會下雨。

06 barometer
[bəˈrɑmətə]

(n.) 氣壓計　*barometer 用於顯示或預測的事物（a barometer of sth. 某事物的指標）

A barometer measures the air pressure. 氣壓計用來測量氣壓。

07 front
[frʌnt]

(n.) 鋒　*cold/warm/occluded/stationary front 冷鋒／暖鋒／囚錮鋒／滯留鋒

When a storm front arrives, it rains. 當暴風雨鋒面來臨時，就會下雨。

08 precipitation
[prɪˌsɪpɪˈteʃən]

(n.) 降水；降水量　*a 20 percent chance of precipitation 百分之二十的降雨機率

Precipitation can fall as rain, snow, sleet, or hail.
降水可以雨、雪、霰以及冰雹的形式降下。

09 evaporation
[ɪˌvæpəˈreʃən]

(n.) 蒸發；發散

Evaporation occurs when liquid water changes into water vapor.
液態水變成水蒸氣的過程稱為蒸發。

10 condensation
[ˌkɑndɛnˈseʃən]

(n.) 凝結；凝聚；凝結物

Condensation occurs when water vapor changes into liquid water.
水蒸氣變成液態水的過程稱為凝結。

atmosphere

precipitation

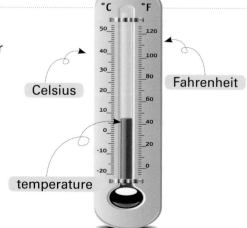
Celsius　Fahrenheit
temperature

predict
[prɪˋdɪkt]

預報；預料

Weather patterns help scientists **predict** the weather. 天氣型態有助科學家預測天氣。

fall

落下；降下

Rain **falls** very much in some areas. 某些區域雨下得很多。

come down

落下

Rain **comes down** very much in some areas. 某些區域雨下得很多。

evaporate
[ɪˋvæpə‚ret]

蒸發；揮發

Water **evaporates** in the air when the temperature is high.
當氣溫高時，水會蒸發到空氣中。

condense
[kənˋdɛns]

凝結

The water vapor **condensed** and fell as rain. 水蒸氣凝結後，會成為雨滴降下。

Word Families ▶ 071

Celsius
[ˋsɛlsɪəs]

攝氏 (0°C = 32°F)

Water freezes at 0°C. 水於攝氏零度結凍。

Fahrenheit
[ˋfærən‚haɪt]

華氏 (100°C = 212°F)

Water boils at 212°F. 水於華氏 212 度沸騰。

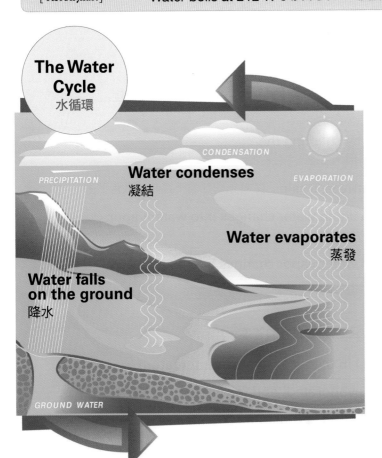

The Water Cycle
水循環

CONDENSATION

Water condenses
凝結

EVAPORATION

PRECIPITATION

Water evaporates
蒸發

Water falls on the ground
降水

GROUND WATER

Weather Equipment
氣象設備

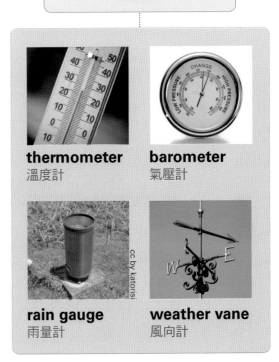

thermometer
溫度計

barometer
氣壓計

rain gauge
雨量計

cc by katorisi

weather vane
風向計

Checkup

A

Write | 請依提示寫出正確的英文單字或片語。

1	大氣	_____	9	蒸發；發散 (n.)	_____
2	型態	_____	10	凝結；凝結物	_____
3	溫度	_____	11	預報；預料	_____
4	溫度計	_____	12	落下	f_____
5	氣壓	_____	13	風向計	_____
6	氣壓計	_____	14	蒸發；揮發 (v.)	_____
7	鋒	_____	15	攝氏	_____
8	降水；降水量	_____	16	華氏	_____

B

Complete the Sentences | 請在空格中填入最適當的答案，並視情況做適當的變化。

weather pattern	temperature	precipitation	atmosphere	evaporation
air pressure	barometer	condensation	thermometer	front

1 The air that surrounds Earth is called the _____.
圍繞地球的空氣稱為大氣。

2 The _____ tells you how hot or cold something is. 溫度告訴你冷熱的變化。

3 _____ can fall as rain, snow, sleet, or hail.
降水可以雨、雪、霰以及冰雹的形式降下。

4 A change in the weather that repeats is called a _____.
重複的天氣變化稱為天氣型態。

5 You can tell if it will rain or not by checking the _____.
你可以經由檢測氣壓來得知是否會下雨。

6 When a storm _____ arrives, it rains. 當暴風雨鋒面來臨時，就會下雨。

7 _____ occurs when liquid water changes into water vapor.
液態水變成水蒸氣的過程稱為蒸發。

8 _____ occurs when water vapor changes into liquid water.
水蒸氣變成液態水的過程稱為凝結。

C

Read and Choose | 閱讀下列句子，並且選出最適當的答案。

1 Water (condenses | evaporates) in the air when the temperature is high.

2 The water vapor (condensed | evaporated) and fell as rain.

3 Weather patterns help scientists (fall | predict) the weather.

4 Rain (falls | predicts) very much in some areas.

D

Look, Read, and Write | 看圖並且依照提示，在空格中填入正確答案。

1
▸ the air that surrounds Earth

_____

4
▸ the forward edge of an advancing mass of air

_____

2
▸ It occurs when liquid water changes into water vapor.

_____

5
▸ water that falls to the ground as rain, snow, etc.

_____

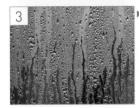
3
▸ It occurs when water vapor changes into liquid water.

_____

6
▸ equipment that measures the amount of rain

_____

E

Read and Answer | 閱讀並且回答下列問題。 ⊙ 072

Weather Equipment

Meteorologists are people who study the weather. They tell us if it will be hot or cold. They tell us if it will be sunny or rainy. They have lots of equipment to help them. The most common piece of equipment is the thermometer. A thermometer measures the temperature. By looking at it, people can tell exactly how hot or cold it is. Another common instrument is the barometer. This measures the air pressure. So people can know if it is going to rain or not. Usually, when the air pressure drops, bad weather is coming. And when it goes up, good weather is coming. There is other equipment, too. A rain gauge measures the amount of rain that has fallen in a place. And an anemometer is used to measure how fast the wind is blowing. It's really useful on windy days! And some people even have weather vanes on their homes. They show which direction the wind is blowing.

Answer the questions.

1   Who studies the weather? _____

2   What equipment measures the temperature? _____

3   What does a barometer do? _____

4   What equipment measures the speed the air is blowing? _____

Key Words 🔊 073

01	**astronomy** [əsˈtrɑnəmɪ]	*(n.)* 天文學

Astronomy is the study of the universe and everything in it.
宇宙及其中所有事物的研究稱為天文學。

02	**astronomer** [əˈstrɑnəmə]	*(n.)* 天文學家 (= stargazer)

An astronomer is someone who studies astronomy.
研究天文學的人稱為天文學家。

03	**universe** [ˈjunəˌvɝs]	*(n.)* 宇宙；全世界；天地萬物　*the universe 宇宙 *center of one's universe 某人生活的中心

The universe is the whole of space including all the stars and planets.
宇宙是指包含了星體及行星的整個空間。

04	**galaxy** [ˈgæləksɪ]	*(n.)* 星系　*the Galaxy 銀河系　*spiral galaxy 螺旋星系

A galaxy is a huge collection of stars. 星系是眾多星體的匯集。

05	**big bang theory** [bɪg bæŋ ˈθɪərɪ]	*(n.)* 大爆炸理論

The big bang theory explains how the universe first formed.
大爆炸理論解釋了宇宙形成之初的情形。

06	**inner planets** [ˈɪnə ˈplænɪts]	*(n.)* 內行星

The inner planets are the four planets closest to the sun: Mercury, Venus, Earth, and Mars. 內行星是靠太陽最近的四個行星：水星、金星、地球以及火星。

07	**outer planets** [ˈaʊtə ˈplænɪts]	*(n.)* 外行星

The outer planets are the four planets farthest from the sun: Jupiter, Saturn, Uranus, and Neptune.
外行星是離太陽最遠的四個行星：木星、土星、天王星以及海王星。

08	**asteroid belt** [ˈæstəˌrɔɪd bɛlt]	*(n.)* 小行星帶

Between Mars and Jupiter is the asteroid belt.
小行星帶介於火星和木星之間。

09	**telescope** [ˈtɛləˌskop]	*(n.)* (單筒) 望遠鏡　*through a telescope 透過望遠鏡 *radio telescope 電波望遠鏡

Astronomers observe the stars and planets with telescopes.
天文學家利用望遠鏡來觀察星體和行星。

10	**astronaut** [ˈæstrəˌnɔt]	*(n.)* 太空人 (= spaceman)

An astronaut is a person who travels in outer space in a spacecraft.
太空人是搭乘太空船航行於外太空的人。

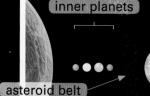

galaxy

inner planets　　outer planets

asteroid belt

asteroid belt

observe [əb`zɝv]	觀測；觀察 Astronomers have **observed** the stars for many years. 天文學家已觀測天體許多年。
look at	研究；觀察 Astronomers have **looked at** the stars for many years. 天文學家已觀察天體許多年。

wax [wæks]	漸圓；漸滿 When the moon is getting bigger, it is **waxing**. 月亮變大稱為月盈。
wane [wen]	虧；缺 When the moon is getting smaller, it is **waning**. 月亮變小稱為月虧。

blast off	發射 The rocket will **blast off** into space soon. 火箭不久後便會發射至太空。
lift off	發射；升空 The rocket will **lift off** into space soon. 火箭不久後便會發射至太空。

Milky Way Galaxy　銀河系
(= Milky Way)
The sun is located in the Milky Way Galaxy.
太陽位於銀河系。

Andromeda Galaxy　仙女座星系
[æn`drɑmədə]
The Andromeda Galaxy is a galaxy near the
Milky Way. 仙女座星系是位於銀河旁的星系。

space shuttle	太空梭 A space shuttle is a spacecraft that can travel into space and back to Earth several times. 太空梭是能往返太空與地球間好幾次的太空船。
space probe	宇宙探測器 Space probes explore many parts of outer space. 宇宙探測器探索外太空的許多部分。
spacecraft	太空船 Astronauts use spacecraft to go into outer space. 太空人利用太空船進入外太空。

space probe

cc by CamWow

Kinds of Telescopes 望遠鏡的種類	**reflecting telescope** 反射式望遠鏡	**radio telescope** 電波望遠鏡
	refracting telescope 折射式望遠鏡	**space telescope** 太空望遠鏡

Checkup

A

Write | 請依提示寫出正確的英文單字或片語。

1	天文學	_____	9	外行星	_____
2	天文學家	_____	10	小行星帶	_____
3	宇宙；全世界	_____	11	觀測；觀察	o_____
4	星系	_____	12	漸圓；漸滿	_____
5	大爆炸理論	_____	13	虧；缺	_____
6	（單筒）望遠鏡	_____	14	發射	b_____
7	太空人	_____	15	太空梭	_____
8	內行星	_____	16	宇宙探測器	_____

B

Complete the Sentences | 請在空格中填入最適當的答案，並視情況做適當的變化。

astronomy	universe	inner	galaxy	big bang
astronomer	astronaut	telescope	planet	asteroid belt

1 The _____ is the whole of space including all the stars and planets.
宇宙是指包含了星體及行星的整個空間。

2 An astronomer is someone who studies _____.
研究天文學的人稱為天文學家。

3 The _____ theory explains how the universe first formed.
大爆炸理論解釋了宇宙形成之初的情形。

4 The _____ planets are the four planets closest to the sun: Mercury, Venus, Earth, and Mars. 內行星是靠太陽最近的四個行星：水星、金星、地球以及火星。

5 Astronomers observe the stars and planets with _____.
天文學家利用望遠鏡來觀察星體和行星。

6 A _____ is a huge collection of stars. 星系是眾多星體的匯集。

7 An _____ is a person who travels in outer space in a spacecraft.
太空人是搭乘太空船航行於外太空的人。

8 Between Mars and Jupiter is the _____. 小行星帶介於火星和木星之間。

C

Read and Choose | 閱讀下列句子，並且選出最適當的答案。

1 Astronomers have (observed | formed) the stars for many years.

2 When the moon is getting bigger, it is (waning | waxing).

3 The rocket will (blast | go) off into space soon.

4 Astronauts use (space probe | spacecraft) to go into outer space.

Look, Read, and Write | 看圖並且依照提示，在空格中填入正確答案。

▶ all of space and everything in it

_____

▶ a device that you look through to see things that are far away

_____

▶ a huge collection of stars

_____

▶ the belt between Mars and Jupiter

_____

▶ These are the four planets closest to the sun.

_____

▶ a person who travels in outer space in a spacecraft

_____

E

Read and Answer | 閱讀並且回答下列問題。 ⊙ 076

The Inner and Outer Planets

The solar system has eight planets in it. These planets are divided into two groups. We call them the inner and outer planets. These two groups have their own characteristics.

The inner planets are Mercury, Venus, Earth, and Mars. They are all fairly close to the sun. Also, these planets are all small and made up of solid, rocklike materials. The earth is the largest of the inner planets. And the inner planets all have zero, one, or two moons. The outer planets are very different from the inner planets. The outer planets are much colder than the inner planets. They are farther from the sun. The outer planets are Jupiter, Saturn, Uranus, and Neptune. They are all very large. Jupiter is the largest planet in the solar system. They are mostly made up of gas. Also, the outer planets have many moons. Jupiter has at least 63 moons. The others also have many moons.

What is true? Write T(true) or F(false).

1   There are nine planets in the solar system.   _____

2   The inner planets are made up of gas.   _____

3   Saturn is one of the outer planets.   _____

4   Jupiter has at least 63 moons.   _____

The Senses 感覺官能

01 vision
[ˈvɪʒən]

(n.) 視覺；視力　　*have good/poor vision 視力好／差　　*field of vision 視野

Vision is what lets people see. 視覺讓人們能看見物體。

02 optic
[ˈɑptɪk]

(a.) 視覺的；視力的；眼的　　*optics 光學

The optic nerves help a person see things. 視神經幫助人們看見物體。

03 lens
[lɛnz]

(n.) (眼球的) 水晶體　*pl. lenses　*lens 鏡片 (contact lens 隱形眼鏡)

There is a lens in the eye that focuses light and helps you to see clearly.
眼睛裡的水晶體使光線聚焦，幫助你看得清晰。

04 eyeball
[ˈaɪˌbɔl]

(n.) 眼球；眼珠　*eyeball to eyeball 面對面地；怒目相向地

The important parts of the eye are in the eyeball. 眼睛最重要的構造都在眼球裡。

05 eyesight
[ˈaɪˌsaɪt]

(n.) 視力　*poor eyesight 視力差　*within eyesight 看得到之處

A person with good eyesight can see very well. 視力好的人可以看得很清楚。

06 reflex
[ˈriflɛks]

(a.) 反射的；反作用的 *(n.)* 反射作用　*reflex response 反射反應
*reflexes 反應能力

Reflex actions like blinking happen almost instantly.
像眨眼這樣的反射作用幾乎是立即的。

07 auditory
[ˈɔdəˌtorɪ]

(a.) 聽覺的；耳朵的　*visual 視覺的　*gustatory 味覺的

The auditory nerve carries signals to the brain, and you hear the sound.
聽覺神經將訊號傳遞到大腦，於是你能夠聽到聲音。

08 eardrum
[ˈɪrˌdrʌm]

(n.) 鼓膜

Sound waves enter the ear and make the eardrum vibrate.
聲波進入耳朵後會使鼓膜振動。

09 taste buds
[test bʌdz]

(n.) 味蕾

The tongue's taste buds let people experience various tastes.
舌頭上的味蕾讓人們體驗各種味道。

10 sensation
[sɛnˈseʃən]

(n.) 感覺；知覺；知覺能力　*a sensation of falling/hungry 墜落感／飢餓感
*a burning/stinging sensation 灼熱感／刺痛感

Sensation is the ability to feel things physically, especially through your
sense of touch. 感覺是指身體上感受事物的能力，特別是透過觸覺。

Five Human Senses

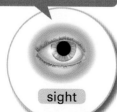
sight

smell

tasting

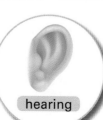
hearing

touching

refract
[rɪˈfrækt]
（使）折射
A lens refracts light. 透鏡可折射光線。

bend
[bɛnd]
（使）彎曲
A prism bends light rays. 稜鏡使光線彎曲。

reflect
[rɪˈflɛkt]
反射；照出
A mirror reflects light. 鏡子會反光。

bounce back
反射
A mirror bounces light back. 鏡子會反光。

taste buds

hear 聽見 Your ears let you hear the things around you. 耳朵能讓你聽見周遭的事物。

smell 嗅到 Your nose lets you smell things. 鼻子能讓你嗅到事物。

taste 嚐出 Your tongue helps you taste things. 舌頭能讓你嚐出事物。

sense 感覺 You can sense things through sight, smell, hearing, tasting, and touching. 你可以透過視覺、嗅覺、聽覺、味覺以及觸覺感覺事物。

transparent 可穿透的；透明的
Light can travel through something that is transparent.
光可以穿過透明的物體。

opaque
[oˈpek]
不透光的；不透明的
Light cannot travel through something that is opaque.
光無法穿過不透明的物體。

The Parts of the Eye (Seeing)
眼睛各部位（視覺）

The Parts of the Ear (Hearing)
耳朵各部位（聽覺）

optic nerve 視神經
iris 虹膜
cornea 角膜
pupil 瞳孔
retina 視網膜
lens 水晶體

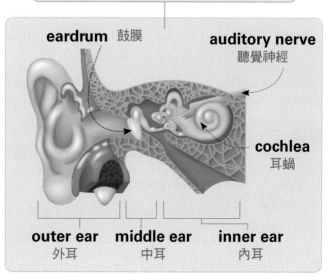

eardrum 鼓膜
auditory nerve 聽覺神經
cochlea 耳蝸
outer ear 外耳
middle ear 中耳
inner ear 內耳

Checkup

A

Write | 請依提示寫出正確的英文單字或片語。

1　視覺；視力　＿＿＿＿＿＿＿＿＿

2　視覺的；視力的；眼的　＿＿＿＿＿

3　（眼球的）水晶體　＿＿＿＿＿＿＿

4　眼球；眼珠　＿＿＿＿＿＿＿＿＿

5　視力　＿＿＿＿＿＿＿＿＿

6　反射的；反作用的　＿＿＿＿＿＿＿

7　聽覺的；耳朵的　＿＿＿＿＿＿＿

8　鼓膜　＿＿＿＿＿＿＿＿＿

9　味蕾　＿＿＿＿＿＿＿＿＿

10　感覺；知覺 (n.)　＿＿＿＿＿＿＿

11　（使）折射　＿＿＿＿＿＿＿

12　（使）彎曲　＿＿＿＿＿＿＿

13　反射；照出　r＿＿＿＿＿＿＿

14　反射　b＿＿＿＿＿＿＿

15　可穿透的；透明的　＿＿＿＿＿＿

16　不透光的；不透明的　＿＿＿＿＿

B

Complete the Sentences | 請在空格中填入最適當的答案，並視情況做適當的變化。

vision	auditory nerve	reflex action	lens	eardrum
opaque	optic nerve	taste buds	bend	eyesight

1　＿＿＿＿＿＿＿＿ is what lets people see. 視覺讓人們能看到物體。

2　There is a ＿＿＿＿＿＿＿＿ in the eye that focuses light and helps you to see clearly.
眼睛裡的水晶體使光線聚焦，幫助你看得清晰。

3　The ＿＿＿＿＿＿＿＿ help a person see things. 視神經幫助人們看見物體。

4　A person with good ＿＿＿＿＿＿＿＿ can see very well. 視力好的人可以看得很清楚。

5　The tongue's ＿＿＿＿＿＿＿＿ let people experience various tastes.
舌頭上的味蕾讓人們體驗各種味道。

6　＿＿＿＿＿＿＿＿ like blinking happen almost instantly.
像眨眼這樣的反射作用幾乎是立即的。

7　Sound waves enter the ear and make the ＿＿＿＿＿＿＿＿ vibrate.
聲波進入耳朵後會使鼓膜振動。

8　The ＿＿＿＿＿＿＿＿ carries signals to the brain, and you hear the sound.
聽覺神經將訊號傳遞到大腦，於是你能夠聽到聲音。

C

Read and Choose | 閱讀下列句子，並且選出最適當的答案。

1　A lens (reflects | refracts) light.

2　A mirror (reflects | refracts) light.

3　Your ears let you (hear | smell) the things around you.

4　Light can travel through something that is (opaque | transparent).

Look, Read, and Write | 看圖並且依照提示，在空格中填入正確答案。

 1 ▸ actions like blinking that happen almost instantly

_____

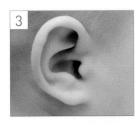 3 ▸ relating to hearing or the ears

_____

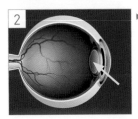 2 ▸ It focuses light and helps you to see clearly.

_____

 4 ▸ be clear or thin enough for you to see through

_____

E

Read and Answer | 閱讀並且回答下列問題。 ⊙ 080

Caring for the Five Senses

Everyone has five senses: seeing, hearing, smelling, tasting, and feeling. We need to take care of the parts of our bodies that let us use our senses.

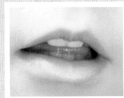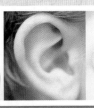

For example, you use your eyes for seeing. You should protect your eyes and have a doctor regularly check your eyesight. Don't sit too close to the TV or computer monitor, and don't read in the dark or in dim light. Never look directly at the sun or at very bright lights. Your ears let you hear the things around you. You should clean your ears all the time. Don't listen to loud music, and try to avoid places that are really loud. Your nose cleans the air you breathe and lets you smell things. Avoid things that have very strong smells. Always wash your hands after blowing your nose, playing outside, or using the restroom. Protect your skin from sunburns. Use sunscreen to protect your skin from the sun.

What is true? Write T(true) or F(false).

1 Everyone has five senses. _____

2 It is okay to sit very close to the TV. _____

3 Your ears are for smelling. _____

4 Putting sunscreen on your skin prevents sunburns. _____

Review Test 4

A

Write | 請依提示寫出正確的英文單字或片語。

1	資源；物力	_____	11	污染；弄髒	_____
2	保存；保護 (n.)	_____	12	溢出；濺出	_____
3	風化作用	_____	13	風化；損壞 (v.)	_____
4	侵蝕；腐蝕 (n.)	_____	14	腐蝕；侵蝕 (v.)	_____
5	大氣	_____	15	蒸發；揮發 (v.)	_____
6	降水；降水量	_____	16	凝結 (v.)	_____
7	星系	_____	17	內行星	_____
8	太空人	_____	18	外行星	_____
9	視力的；視覺的；眼的	_____	19	（使）折射	_____
10	聽覺的；耳朵的	_____	20	反射；照出	r_____

B

Choose the Correct Word | 請選出與鋪底字意思相近的答案。

1 Astronomers have observed the stars for many years.

   a. looked   b. served   c. looked at

2 Rain falls very much in some areas.

   a. comes down   b. comes   c. condenses

3 A lens refracts light.

   a. reflects   b. bends   c. reduces

4 A mirror reflects light.

   a. refracts   b. bounces back   c. focuses

C

Complete the Sentences | 請在空格中填入最適當的答案，並視情況做適當的變化。

pollution	air pressure	universe	weathering

1 Waste that harms the air, water, or land is called _____.
危害空氣、水或土地的廢棄物稱為污染。

2 _____ is the process through which wind and water break down rocks into small pieces for many years. 風和水經多年時間將岩石瓦解為小碎塊的過程稱為風化作用。

3 You can tell if it will rain or not by checking the _____.
你可以經由檢測氣壓來得知是否會下雨。

4 The _____ is the whole of space including all the stars and planets.
宇宙是包含了所有星體及行星的整個空間。

CHAPTER 5

Mathematics

Key Words ● 081

01	**fraction** [ˈfrækʃən]	(n.) 分數　　*fraction 片段（a fraction of sth. 某物的一小部分） When something is divided into 3 equal parts, each part is one-third, which is written as the fraction $\frac{1}{3}$. 當某物被分為三個均等的部分時，每一個部分為三分之一，分數寫作 $\frac{1}{3}$。
02	**numerator** [ˈnjumə,retɚ]	(n.) 分子　　*fraction slash 分（數）線 The numerator is the top number of a fraction. 分子是分數中位於上面的數字。
03	**denominator** [dɪˈnɑmə,netɚ]	(n.) 分母 The denominator is the bottom number of a fraction. 分母是分數中位於底下的數字。
04	**equivalent** [ɪˈkwɪvələnt]	(a.) 相等的；相同的 (n.) 相等物　　*be equivalent to 相當於 　　　　　　　　　　　　　　　　　　　*the equivalent of sth. 相當於某物的東西 Two fractions that have the same value, like $\frac{1}{2}$ and $\frac{2}{4}$, are equivalent fractions. 像 $\frac{1}{2}$ 和 $\frac{2}{4}$ 兩個數值相同的分數，稱為等值分數。
05	**whole number** [hol ˈnʌmbɚ]	(n.) 整數 A whole number is a number like 1, 2, 3, or 4 and is not a fraction. 1、2、3 或 4 這樣不是分數的數字稱為整數。
06	**mixed number** [mɪkst ˈnʌmbɚ]	(n.) 帶分數　　*proper/improper fraction 真／假分數 A number like $1\frac{2}{3}$ is called a mixed number. $1\frac{2}{3}$ 這樣的數字稱為帶分數。
07	**decimal** [ˈdɛsɪml̩]	(n.) 小數 (a.) 小數的；十進位的　　*the decimal system 十進位制 　　　　　　　　　　　　　　　　　*decimal place 小數點後面的位數 You can write the fraction $\frac{1}{10}$ as the decimal 0.1. 你可以把分數 $\frac{1}{10}$ 寫作小數 0.1。
08	**decimal point** [ˈdɛsɪml̩ pɔɪnt]	(n.) 小數點 The first place to the right of the decimal point is the tenth's place. 小數點右邊的第一位稱為十分位。（ 0.1 = $\frac{1}{10}$ ）
09	**hundredth** [ˈhʌndrədθ]	(n.) 百分之一；第一百個 The second place to the right of the decimal point is the hundredth's place. 小數點右邊的第二位稱為百分位。（ 0.01 = $\frac{1}{100}$ ）
10	**portion** [ˈporʃən]	(n.) 部分　　*a portion of 一部分 If you slice an apple in half, you have made two equal portions. 如果你將一顆蘋果切成兩半，你會得到兩個均等的部分。

whole number
0, 1, 2, 3, 4, 5, ...

fraction
$$\frac{1}{2}, \frac{2}{3}, \frac{3}{4}$$
numerator
denominator

mixed number
$$1\frac{2}{3}, 2\frac{3}{4}, 3\frac{2}{5}$$

decimal
0.1, 2.8, 4.25

represent
[ˌrɛprɪˈzɛnt]
代表
If you slice an orange into 4 parts, each portion represents $\frac{1}{4}$.
將一顆橘子切成四份，每一份代表 $\frac{1}{4}$。

be represented by
用……來表示
Fractions can be represented by decimal numbers. ($\frac{1}{10}$ =0.1)
分數可以用小數來表示。

recognize
[ˈrɛkəɡˌnaɪz]
辨別；認識
Recognize the numerator and denominator. 請辨別分子和分母。

identify
[aɪˈdɛntəˌfaɪ]
辨別；鑑定
Identify the numerator and denominator. 請辨別分子和分母。

estimate
[ˈɛstəˌmet]
估計；估量
Can you estimate the answer? 你可以估算出答案嗎？

guess
推測；猜測
Can you guess the answer? 你可以推測出答案嗎？

Word Families 🔘 083

equal parts/portions

---

equal part 等分
$\frac{1}{4}$ means 1 out of 4 equal parts. $\frac{1}{4}$ 表示從四個等分中取出一份。

equal portion 等分
$\frac{1}{4}$ means 1 out of 4 equal portions. $\frac{1}{4}$ 表示從四個等分中取出一份。

How to Read Fractions
如何讀分數

$\frac{1}{2}$	one half 2 分之 1
$\frac{3}{6}$	three sixths 6 分之 3
$\frac{5}{10}$	five tenths 10 分之 5
$\frac{2}{100}$	two hundredths 100 分之 2
$\frac{28}{100}$	twenty-eight hundredths 100 分之 28

How to Read Mixed Numbers
如何讀帶分數

$1\frac{1}{2}$	one and one half 1 又 2 分之 1
$2\frac{2}{3}$	two and two thirds 2 又 3 分之 2
$3\frac{1}{4}$	three and one fourth 3 又 4 分之 1
$5\frac{3}{100}$	five and three hundredths 5 又 100 分之 3
$6\frac{47}{100}$	six and forty-seven hundredths 6 又 100 分之 47

 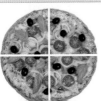 

Checkup

A Write | 請依提示寫出正確的英文單字或片語。

1	分數	_____	
2	分子	_____	
3	分母	_____	
4	相等的；相同的	_____	
5	整數	_____	
6	帶分數	_____	
7	小數	_____	
8	小數點	_____	

9	百分之一；第一百個	_____	
10	部分	_____	
11	代表	_____	
12	6 分之 3	_____	
13	辨別；認識	r	_____
14	辨別；鑑定	i	_____
15	估計；估量	_____	
16	等分	_____	

B Complete the Sentences | 請在空格中填入最適當的答案，並視情況做適當的變化。

whole number	equivalent	fraction	decimal	denominator
mixed number	numerator	hundredth's	portions	decimal point

1. When something is divided into 3 equal parts, each part is one-third, which is written as the _____ $\frac{1}{3}$.
   當某物被分為三個均等的部分時，每一個部分為三分之一，分數寫作 $\frac{1}{3}$。

2. Two fractions that have the same value, like $\frac{1}{2}$ and $\frac{2}{4}$, are _____ fractions.
   像 $\frac{1}{2}$ 和 $\frac{2}{4}$ 兩個數值相等的分數，稱為等值分數。

3. A _____ is a number like 1, 2, 3, or 4 and is not a fraction.
   1、2、3 或 4 這樣不是分數的數字稱為整數。

4. You can write the fraction $\frac{1}{10}$ as the _____ 0.1. 你可以把分數 $\frac{1}{10}$ 寫作小數 0.1。

5. A number like $1\frac{2}{3}$ is called a _____. $1\frac{2}{3}$ 這樣的數字稱為帶分數。

6. The _____ is the top number of a fraction. 分子是分數中位於上面的數。

7. The second place to the right of the decimal point is the _____ place.
   小數點右邊的第二位稱為百分位。

8. If you slice an apple in half, you have made two equal _____.
   如果你將一顆蘋果切成兩半，你會得到兩個均等的部分。

C Read and Choose | 閱讀下列句子，並且選出最適當的答案。

1. If you slice an orange into 4 parts, each portion (represented by | represents) $\frac{1}{4}$.

2. Fractions can be (represented | recognized) by decimal numbers.

3. (Divide | Identify) the numerator and denominator.

4. $\frac{1}{4}$ means 1 out of 4 (equal | decimal) parts.

Look, Read, and Write | 看圖並且依照提示，在空格中填入正確答案。

1
$$\frac{2}{5}$$
▸ a division or part of a whole number
_____

3
0, 1, 2, 3, 4, 5, ...
▸ a number like 1, 2, 3, or 4 and which is not a fraction
_____

2
$$\frac{3}{4}$$
▸ the top number of a fraction
_____

4
▸ a part of a larger amount
_____

E

Read and Answer | 閱讀並且回答下列問題。　🔘 084

Solve the Problems

1. Two oranges are the same size. Amy gets $\frac{1}{2}$ of one orange. Tom gets $\frac{1}{5}$ of the other. Who gets more of the orange?
   ⇨ $\frac{1}{2}$ is greater than $\frac{1}{5}$. So, Amy gets the larger piece.

2. Eric has one candy bar. He eats $\frac{1}{3}$ of the candy bar in the morning. Later in the day, he eats another $\frac{1}{3}$ of the candy bar. How much of the candy bar is left over?
   ⇨ He ate $\frac{2}{3}$ of the candy bar. So there is $\frac{1}{3}$ left over.

3. Mary makes a pie. She cuts it into 8 pieces. Steve takes $\frac{1}{4}$ of the pie. Then Chris takes $\frac{1}{2}$ of the pie. How much pie remains?
   ⇨ $\frac{1}{4} = \frac{2}{8}$. And $\frac{1}{2} = \frac{4}{8}$. $\frac{2}{8} + \frac{4}{8} = \frac{6}{8}$. So $\frac{6}{8}$ of the pie is gone.
   Now there are $\frac{2}{8}$ (or $\frac{1}{4}$) of the pie remaining.

4. Daniel goes shopping. He has $5\frac{1}{2}$ dollars. His brother goes shopping with him. His brother has $5\frac{2}{3}$ dollars. Who has more money?
   ⇨ $\frac{2}{3}$ is greater than $\frac{1}{2}$. So Daniel's brother has more money.

What is NOT true?

1 Amy has more of the orange than Tom.

2 Eric eats $\frac{1}{3}$ of the candy bar in the morning.

3 Steve takes more of the pie than Chris.

4 Daniel has less money than his brother.

Geometry 幾何學

Key Words ● 085

| 01 | **horizontal** | (a.) 水平的；橫的　*horizontal plane 水平面 |
| | [ˌhɑrəˈzɑntl̩] | A horizontal line goes from left to right. 由左到右的直線稱為水平線。 |

| 02 | **vertical** | (a.) 垂直的；豎的　*vertical plane 垂直平面 |
| | [ˈvɝtɪkl̩] | A vertical line goes up and down. 由上到下的直線稱為垂直線。 |

| 03 | **perpendicular** | (a.) 垂直的；成直角的 |
| | [ˌpɝpənˈdɪkjələ˞] | Two perpendicular lines intersect and form right angles.
兩條垂直線相交並構成直角。 |

| 04 | **parallel** | (a.) 平行的　*be parallel to/with sth. 與某物平行　*parallel (n.) 平行線；相似處 |
| | [ˈpærəˌlɛl] | Two parallel lines run the same direction and never intersect.
兩條平行線往同一個方向延伸，永遠不會相交。 |

| 05 | **line segment** | (n.) 線段 |
| | [laɪn ˈsɛgmənt] | A line segment is a part of a line and has two endpoints.
線段為直線的一部分，並有兩個端點。 |

| 06 | **polygon** | (n.) 多邊形 |
| | [ˈpɑlɪˌgɑn] | A polygon is a closed figure formed by line segments.
多邊形是由線段所構成的封閉圖形。 |

| 07 | **vertex** | (n.) 頂點 *pl. vertices, vertexes |
| | [ˈvɝtɛks] | The place where two line segments meet is a vertex.
兩條線段交會的地方稱為頂點。 |

| 08 | **right angle** | (n.) 直角　*acute angle 銳角　*obtuse angle 鈍角 |
| | [raɪt ˈæŋgl̩] | A right angle is an angle of ninety degrees. 直角是一個 90 度的角。 |

| 09 | **perimeter** | (n.) 周長　*diameter 直徑　*radius 半徑 |
| | [pəˈrɪmətə˞] | Perimeter is the distance around a figure. 周長是一個圖形周圍的長度。 |

| 10 | **area** | (n.) 面積　*an area of . . . square kilometer(s) 多少平方公里的面積 |
| | [ˈɛrɪə] | Multiply a figure's length and width to find its area.
將一個圖形的長乘以寬可以得到面積。 |

vertical line

horizontal line

perpendicular lines

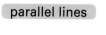

parallel lines

line segment

intersect [ˌɪntəˈsɛkt]	相交；交叉 When two lines intersect, they might form a right angle. 兩條直線相交可能會形成直角。
meet	交會 When two lines meet, they might form a right angle. 兩條直線交會可能會形成直角。

form	形成；構成 When two sides of a polygon meet, they form an angle. 多邊形的兩個邊相交會形成一個角。
create [krɪˈet]	創造；創作 It is possible to create many different polygons. 創造許多不同的多邊形是有可能的。

compute [kəmˈpjut]	計算；估算 Can you compute the area of the square? 你可以計算那個正方形的面積嗎？
find	找出；發現 Can you find the area of the square? 你可以找出那個正方形的面積嗎？
determine [dɪˈtɝmɪn]	測定；確定 Can you determine the area of the square? 你可以測定那個正方形的面積嗎？

congruent figure [ˈkɑŋgruənt]	全等圖形 Congruent figures have the same size and shape. 全等圖形有相同的大小和形狀。
symmetric figure [sɪˈmɛtrɪk]	對稱圖形 A symmetric figure can be folded in half so that both halves match. 對稱圖形對摺一半後，對半的兩邊會相合。

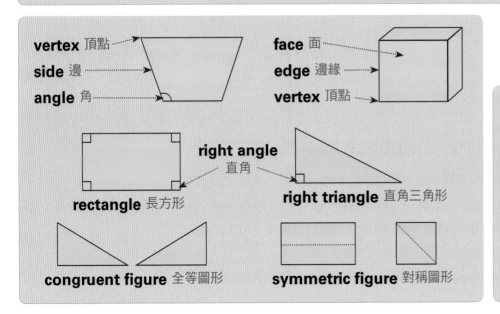

vertex 頂點
side 邊
angle 角

face 面
edge 邊緣
vertex 頂點

right angle 直角

rectangle 長方形

right triangle 直角三角形

congruent figure 全等圖形

symmetric figure 對稱圖形

Polygons
多邊形

triangle	三角形
rectangle	長方形
square	正方形
rhombus	菱形
pentagon	五邊形
hexagon	六邊形
octagon	八邊形

Checkup

A

Write | 請依提示寫出正確的英文單字或片語。

1	水平的；橫的	_____	9	垂直的；成直角的
2	垂直的；豎的	_____	10	周長
3	平行的	_____	11	相交；交叉
4	線段	_____	12	形成；構成
5	多邊形	_____	13	計算；估算
6	頂點	_____	14	測定；確定
7	直角	_____	15	全等圖形
8	面積	_____	16	對稱圖形

B

Complete the Sentences | 請在空格中填入最適當的答案，並視情況做適當的變化。

perpendicular	polygon	horizontal	parallel	line segment
right angle	area	vertex	vertical	perimeter

1　A _____ line goes up and down. 由上到下的直線稱為垂直線。

2　A _____ line goes from left to right. 由左到右的直線稱為水平線。

3　Two _____ lines intersect and form right angles.
兩條垂直線相交會形成直角。

4　A _____ is a part of a line and has two endpoints.
線段為直線的一部分，並有兩個端點。

5　Two _____ lines run the same direction and never intersect.
兩條平行線往同一個方向延伸，永遠不會相交。

6　A _____ is a closed figure formed by line segments.
多邊形是由線段所構成的封閉圖形。

7　A _____ is an angle of ninety degrees. 直角是一個 90 度的角。

8　Multiply a figure's length and width to find its _____.
將一個圖形的長乘以寬可以得到面積。

C

Read and Choose | 請選出與鋪底字意思相近的答案。

1　Can you compute the area of the square?

　　a. form　　　　　　b. find　　　　　　c. create

2　When two lines intersect, they might form a right angle.

　　a. find　　　　　　b. form　　　　　　c. meet

3　When two sides of a polygon meet, they form an angle.

　　a. create　　　　　　b. draw　　　　　　c. close

Look, Read, and Write | 看圖並且依照提示，在空格中填入正確答案。

1 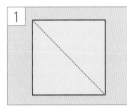 ▸ figures that have sides or halves that are the same

_____

4 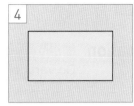 ▸ a shape with four straight sides and four right angles

_____

2 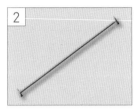 ▸ a part of a line that has two endpoints

_____

5 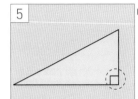 ▸ an angle that forms a square corner

_____

3 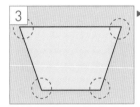 ▸ the place where two line segments meet

_____

6 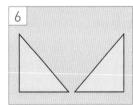 ▸ figures that have the same size and shape

_____

E

Read and Answer | 閱讀並且回答下列問題。　088

Polygons and Congruent Figures

There are many different types of polygons. There are two requirements for an object to be a polygon. It must be made of three or more line segments. And it must be a closed figure. That means that all of the lines in the polygon meet each other. A three-sided polygon is a triangle. Some four-sided polygons are squares, rectangles, or rhombuses. A five-sided one is a pentagon. An octagon has eight sides. A polygon can have any number of sides. It could have 10, 100, or even 1,000 sides! But circles are not polygons. Sometimes two polygons are congruent figures. This means they have the same shape and size. For example, two squares have sides that are three inches long. They are identical. So they are congruent figures. But if one square's sides are two inches long while the other's sides are three inches long, they are not congruent. Also, a triangle and a square can never be congruent.

Answer the questions.

1　At least how many line segments can make a polygon? _____

2　What are some four-sided polygons? _____

3　How many sides does an octagon have? _____

4　What does it mean when two figures are congruent? _____

Unit 23 Multiplication and Division

Key Words ● 089

01 vertical multiplication
[ˋvɝtɪkḷ ˌmʌltəpləˋkeʃən]

(n.) 乘法的直式計算

Do vertical multiplication like this: $\begin{smallmatrix} 5 \\ \times 2 \\ \hline 10 \end{smallmatrix}$.

作乘法的直式運算要像這樣：$\begin{smallmatrix} 5 \\ \times 2 \\ \hline 10 \end{smallmatrix}$ 。

02 square number
[skwɛr ˋnʌmbɚ]

(n.) 平方數

The square number of 3 is 9. (3×3=9) 3 的平方數為 9。

03 square root
[skwɛr rut]

(n.) 平方根

The square root of 9 is 3. (3×3=9) 9 的平方根為 3。

04 three-digit number
[θriˋdɪdʒɪt ˋnʌmbɚ]

(n.) 三位數

100, 254, and 999 are three-digit numbers.
100、254 及 999 都是三位數。

05 four-digit number
[forˋdɪdʒɪt ˋnʌmbɚ]

(n.) 四位數

1000, 4567, and 9321 are four-digit numbers.
1000、4567 及 9321 都是四位數。

06 operation
[ˌɑpəˋreʃən]

(n.) 運算

Addition, subtraction, multiplication, and division are called operations.
加、減、乘、除稱為運算。

07 inverse operation
[ɪnˋvɝs ˌɑpəˋreʃən]

(n.) 反運算

Addition and subtraction and multiplication and division are inverse operations. 加減和乘除分別為反運算。

08 equation
[ɪˋkweʃən]

(n.) 等式　*solve an equation 解方程式
　　　　　*linear/quadratic equation 一次／二次方程式

A number statement that uses an equal sign is called an equation.
使用等號的式子稱為等式。

09 inequality
[ɪnɪˋkwɑlətɪ]

(n.) 不等式

A number statement that uses the signs > or < is called an inequality.
使用 > 或 < 符號的式子稱為不等式。

10 remainder
[rɪˋmendɚ]

(n.) 餘數　*quotient 商數

The remainder is what is left over in a division problem.
除法中，除不盡而剩下來的數稱為餘數。

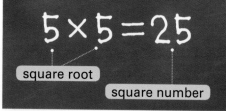

check [tʃɛk] 檢查;檢驗 Check the answer to see if it is correct. 請檢查答案是否正確。

confirm [kənˋfɝm] 確定 Confirm the answer to see if it is correct. 請確定答案是否正確。

be divided by itself 除以本身的數 Any number that **is divided by itself** equals 1. (5÷5=1)
任何數除以自己都等於 1。

be multiplied by itself 乘以本身的數 5 that **is multiplied by itself** equals 25. (5×5=25)
5 乘以自己等於 25。

positive number 正數
Positive numbers are the numbers to the right of zero on a number line.
正數是指數線上位於 0 右邊的數。

negative number 負數
Negative numbers are the numbers to the left of zero on a number line.
負數是指數線上位於 0 左邊的數。

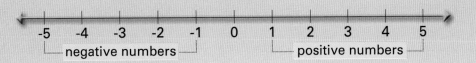

negative numbers — positive numbers

Multiplication Table for 3
3 的乘法表

$3 \times 1 = 3$ Three times one is three.
3 乘以 1 得 3

$3 \times 2 = 6$ Three times two is six.
3 乘以 2 得 6

$3 \times 3 = 9$ Three times three is nine.
3 乘以 3 得 9

$3 \times 4 = 12$ Three times four is twelve.
3 乘以 4 得 12

$3 \times 5 = 15$ Three times five is fifteen.
3 乘以 5 得 15

$3 \times 6 = 18$ Three times six is eighteen.
3 乘以 6 得 18

$3 \times 7 = 21$ Three times seven is twenty-one.
3 乘以 7 得 21

$3 \times 8 = 24$ Three times eight is twenty-four.
3 乘以 8 得 24

$3 \times 9 = 27$ Three times nine is twenty-seven.
3 乘以 9 得 27

$3 \times 10 = 30$ Three times ten is thirty.
3 乘以 10 得 30

Division Table for 3
3 的除法表

$0 \div 3 = 0$ Zero divided by three is zero.
0 除以 3 得 0

$3 \div 3 = 1$ Three divided by three is one.
3 除以 3 得 1

$6 \div 3 = 2$ Six divided by three is two.
6 除以 3 得 2

$9 \div 3 = 3$ Nine divided by three is three.
9 除以 3 得 3

$12 \div 3 = 4$ Twelve divided by three is four.
12 除以 3 得 4

$15 \div 3 = 5$ Fifteen divided by three is five.
15 除以 3 得 5

$18 \div 3 = 6$ Eighteen divided by three is six.
18 除以 3 得 6

$21 \div 3 = 7$ Twenty-one divided by three is seven.
21 除以 3 得 7

$24 \div 3 = 8$ Twenty-four divided by three is eight.
24 除以 3 得 8

$27 \div 3 = 9$ Twenty-seven divided by three is nine.
27 除以 3 得 9

Checkup

Write | 請依提示寫出正確的英文單字或片語。

1	平方數	_____	9 乘法的直式計算	_____
2	平方根	_____	10 餘數	_____
3	三位數	_____	11 檢查；檢驗	_____
4	四位數	_____	12 確定；證實	_____
5	運算	_____	13 除以本身的數	_____
6	反運算	_____	14 乘以本身的數	_____
7	等式	_____	15 正數	_____
8	不等式	_____	16 負數	_____

Complete the Sentences | 請在空格中填入最適當的答案，並視情況做適當的變化。

square number	confirm	square root	inequality	operation
inverse operation	equation	remainder	three-digit	check

1 The _____ of 3 is 9. 3 的平方數為 9。

2 The _____ of 9 is 3. 3 為 9 的平方根。

3 100, 254, and 999 are _____ numbers. 100、254 及 999 都是三位數。

4 Addition, subtraction, multiplication, and division are called _____.
加、減、乘、除稱為運算。

5 Addition and subtraction are _____. 加和減為反運算。

6 A number statement that uses an equal sign is called an _____.
使用等號的式子稱為等式。

7 A number statement that uses the signs > or < is called an _____.
使用 > 或 < 符號的式子稱為不等式。

8 The _____ is what is left over in a division problem.
除法中，除不盡剩下來的數稱為餘數。

Read and Choose | 閱讀下列句子，並且選出最適當的答案。

1 (Solve | Confirm) the answer to see if it is correct.

2 Any number (multiplied | divided) by itself equals 1.

3 Addition, subtraction, multiplication, and division are called
(inverse operations | operations).

4 The square (root | number) of 9 is 3.

Look, Read, and Write ｜ 看圖並且依照提示，在空格中填入正確答案。

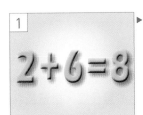 ▸ a number statement that uses an equal sign

_____

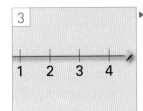 ▸ a number that produces a specified number when multiplied by itself

_____

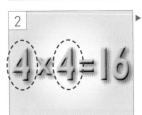 ▸ the numbers to the right of zero on a number line

_____

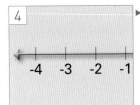 ▸ the numbers to the left of zero on a number line

_____

E

Read and Answer ｜ 閱讀並且回答下列問題。　092

Solve the Problems

1. Mrs. White is a teacher. She is giving a test to the students. Each test has 3 sheets of paper. She has 10 students in her class. How many sheets of paper does she need?
   ⇨ The answer is 30 because 3×10=30.

2. Some families are going to go on a picnic together. Each family has a mother, father, and two children. There are 8 families. How many people are going on the picnic?
   ⇨ The answer is 32 because 4×8=32.

3. Jenny has 24 pieces of candy. She wants to share all of the candy with her friends. There are 5 people plus Jenny. How many pieces of candy should each person get?
   ⇨ The answer is 4 because 24÷6=4.

4. 5 students find some coins in a jar. They want to share the coins with each other. They count the coins and see that there are 25 coins. How many coins does each student get?
   ⇨ The answer is 5 because 25÷5=5.

What is true? Write T(true) or F(false).

1　Mrs. White has thirty students in her class.　_____

2　Thirty-two people go on the picnic together.　_____

3　Jenny gives six pieces of candy to each friend.　_____

4　Six students find twenty-five coins in the jar.　_____

Key Words 🔘 093

01	**U.S. customary system** [ˈjuˌɛs ˈkʌstəmˌɛrɪ ˈsɪstəm]	*(n.)* 美國通用單位制度 The U.S. customary system is how Americans measure length, weight, and capacity. 美國通用單位制度顯示美國人如何測量長度、重量及容量。
02	**metric system** [ˈmɛtrɪk ˈsɪstəm]	*(n.)* 公制　*metric ton 公噸 The metric system measures length, weight, and capacity on a base-ten system. 公制系統以十進位基準來測量長度、重量及容量。
03	**length** [lɛŋθ]	*(n.)* 長度　*. . . in length 長度為……　*at length 經過一段長時間之後；終於 Length tells you how long something is. 長度讓你知道東西有多長。
04	**weight** [wet]	*(n.)* 重量　*gain/lose weight 增／減重　*by weight 按重量 Weight tells you how heavy something is. 重量讓你知道東西有多重。
05	**capacity** [kəˈpæsətɪ]	*(n.)* 容量　*a capacity of . . . 多少的容量　*seating capacity 座位數量 Capacity is the amount a container can hold. 容量是一個容器所能容納的量。
06	**balance scale** [ˈbæləns skel]	*(n.)* 平衡量表；天平 People use a balance scale for comparing weight. 人們使用天平來比較重量。
07	**liquid** [ˈlɪkwɪd]	*(n.)* 液體　*liquid substance 液態物質　*solid 固體 A liquid has both weight and volume. 液體有重量和體積。
08	**volume** [ˈvɑljəm]	*(n.)* 體積；容積　*a volume of . . . cubic meter(s) 多少立方公尺的體積 In the metric system, we use liters and milliliters for measuring the volume of a liquid. 在公制中，我們用公升或毫升來測量液體的體積。
09	**mass** [mæs]	*(n.)* 質量 Use grams and kilograms to measure mass. 用公克或公斤來測量質量。
10	**degree** [dɪˈgri]	*(n.)* 度數　*45 degrees Celsius/Fahrenheit 攝氏／華氏 45 度 We measure temperature in degrees. 我們以度數來測量溫度。

weight

length

capacity

weigh
[we]
秤……的重量
How much does it weigh? 這東西有多重？

hold
[hold]
容納；包含
How many cups does the container hold? 這個容器可以容納多少杯？

measure
[ˈmɛʒɚ]
測量
A gram is a unit that measures weight. 公克是測量重量的單位。

be the same as
與……相同
1 pound is the same as 16 ounces. 1 磅等於 16 盎司。

Abbreviations for Each Unit　單位的縮寫

*U.S. Customary System　美國通用單位制度

mile – **mi**	英里	yard – **yd**	碼	foot – **ft**	英尺
inch – **in**	英寸	pound – **lb**	磅	ounce – **oz**	盎司
pint – **pt**	品脫	quart – **qt**	夸脫	gallon – **gal**	加侖

*Metric System　公制

centimeter – **cm**	公分	meter – **m**	公尺	kilometer – **km**	公里
liter – **ℓ**	公升	gram – **g**	公克	kilogram – **kg**	公斤

Changing Units in the Metric System　公制單位換算

1m = 100cm　　1cm = 10mm　　1km = 1,000m　　1kg = 1,000g

Changing Units in the U.S. Customary System　美國通用單位制度單位換算

1ft = 12in　　3ft = 1yd　　2 cups = 1pt　　2pt = 1qt　　4qt = 1gal

Units for Length
長度的單位

mile	英里
yard	碼
foot	英尺
inch	英寸
centimeter	公分
meter	公尺
kilometer	公里

Units for Weight
重量的單位

ounce	盎司
pound	磅
gram	公克
kilogram	公斤

four ounces of butter

Units for Capacity
容量的單位

gallon	加侖
quart	夸脫
pint	品脫
cup	杯
liter	公升

a gallon of milk

1.5 liters of water

Checkup

A

Write | 請依提示寫出正確的英文單字或片語。

1	公制	_____	9	體積；容積	_____
2	長度	_____	10	質量	_____
3	重量	_____	11	秤……的重量	_____
4	容量	_____	12	容納；包含	_____
5	平衡量表；天平	_____	13	測量	_____
6	液體	_____	14	與……相同	_____
7	度數	_____	15	英里	_____
8	美國通用單位制度	_____	16	碼	_____

B

Complete the Sentences | 請在空格中填入最適當的答案，並視情況做適當的變化。

customary system	capacity	liquid	weight	degrees
metric system	balance scale	volume	length	mass

1　The _____ measures length, weight, and capacity on a base-ten system. 公制系統以十進位基準來測量長度、重量及容量。

2　_____ tells you how long something is. 長度讓你知道東西有多長。

3　_____ is the amount a container can hold. 容量是一個容器所能容納的量。

4　_____ tells you how heavy something is. 重量讓你知道東西有多重。

5　In the metric system, we use liters and milliliters for measuring _____ of liquid. 在公制中，我們用公升或毫升來測量液體的體積。

6　Use grams and kilograms to measure _____. 用公克或公斤來測量質量。

7　People use a _____ for comparing weight.
人們使用天平來比較重量。

8　We measure temperature in _____. 我們以度數來測量溫度。

C

Read and Choose | 閱讀下列句子，並且選出最適當的答案。

1　1 pound is the (same | scale) as 16 ounces.

2　How much does it (tall | weigh)?

3　How many cups does the container (measure | hold)?

4　A gram is a unit that measures (length | weight).

Look, Read, and Write | 看圖並且依照提示，在空格中填入正確答案。

1 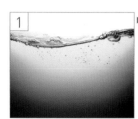 ▶ a substance that can flow, has no fixed shape, and is not a solid or a gas

_____

3  ▶ the amount a container can hold

_____

2  ▶ the heaviness of a person or thing

_____

4  ▶ a scale for comparing weight

_____

E

Read and Answer | 閱讀並且回答下列問題。　● 096

Solve the Problems

1. Mary is baking a cake. She needs to use flour to make the cake. She needs 2 pints of flour. But her measuring cup can only fill 1 cup at a time. How many cups of flour does she need?
   ⇨ She needs 4 cups. 2 cups is 1 pint. So 4 cups is 2 pints.

2. Chris likes to run. Today, he ran 2,500 meters. How many kilometers did he run?
   ⇨ He ran 2.5 kilometers. There are 1,000 meters in 1 kilometer.

3. Peter gets a ruler and measures himself. He is 60 inches tall. How many feet tall is he?
   ⇨ He is 5 feet tall. There are 12 inches in one foot. So 60÷12=5.

4. Lucy steps on a scale. She sees that she weighs 38 kilograms. How many grams does she weigh?
   ⇨ She weighs 38,000 grams. There are 1,000 grams in one kilogram. So 1,000×38=38,000.

Fill in the blanks.

1 Mary needs 4 _____ of flour to make the cake.

2 Chris ran 2.5 _____ today.

3 Peter is five feet _____.

4 Lucy weighs herself with a _____.

Review Test 5

A

Write | 請依提示寫出正確的英文單字或片語。

1	整數	_____	11 等分	_____
2	帶分數	_____	12 線段	_____
3	直角	_____	13 多邊形	_____
4	面積	_____	14 不等式	_____
5	平方數	_____	15 等式	_____
6	平方根	_____	16 正數	_____
7	餘數	_____	17 負數	_____
8	運算	_____	18 液體	_____
9	公制	_____	19 秤……的重量	_____
10	小數	_____	20 容納；包含	_____

B

Choose the Correct Word | 請選出與鋪底字意思相近的答案。

1 **Identify** the numerator and denominator.

   a. Check   b. Confirm   c. Recognize

2 Can you **compute** the area of the square?

   a. form   b. find   c. create

3 When two sides of a polygon meet, they **form** an angle.

   a. create   b. draw   c. close

4 When two lines **intersect**, they might form a right angle.

   a. find   b. form   c. meet

C

Complete the Sentences | 請在空格中填入最適當的答案，並視情況做適當的變化。

polygon	volume	portion	inverse operation

1 If you slice an apple in half, you have made two equal _____.
如果你將一顆蘋果切成兩半，你會得到兩個均等的部分。

2 A _____ is a closed figure formed by line segments.
多邊形是由線段所構成的封閉圖形。

3 Addition and subtraction are _____. 加和減為反運算。

4 In the metric system, we use liters and milliliters for measuring the _____ of a liquid. 在公制中，我們用公升或毫升來測量液體的體積。

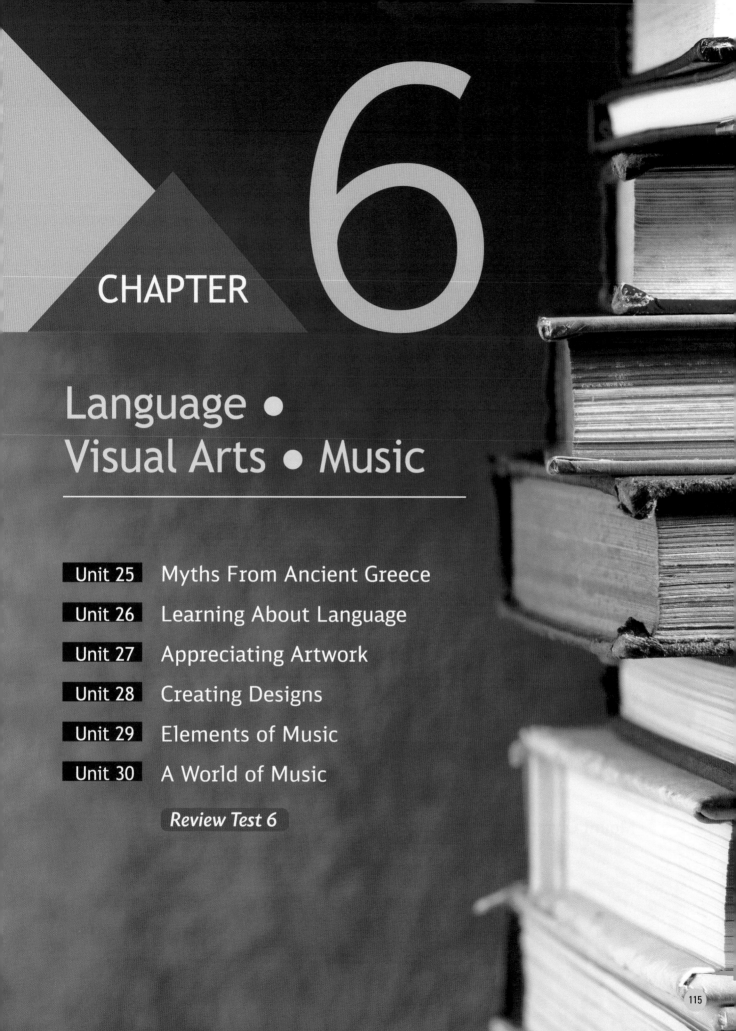

CHAPTER 6

Language • Visual Arts • Music

Myths From Ancient Greece 古希臘神話

| 01 | **myth** [mɪθ] | *(n.)* 神話（= mythology） *myth 錯誤觀念（dispel a myth 打破迷思）* |
| | | Myths tell about brave heroes, great battles, and gods and goddesses. 神話講述勇敢的英雄、偉大的戰役、神與女神。 |

| 02 | **hero** [ˋhɪro] | *(n.)* 英雄 *national hero 民族英雄 *heroine 女英雄；女傑 |
| | | Hercules and Theseus were heroes in Greek mythology. 在希臘神話中，海克力斯和特修斯都是英雄。 |

| 03 | **god** [gɑd] | *(n.)* 神；上帝 *God 上帝；造物主 *sun god/goddess 太陽神 |
| | | Zeus was the most powerful Greek god. 宙斯是最強大的希臘神。 |

| 04 | **goddess** [ˋgɑdɪs] | *(n.)* 女神 *goddess of hunting 狩獵女神 |
| | | Aphrodite was the goddess of love. 阿芙蘿黛蒂為愛之女神。 |

| 05 | **demigod** [ˋdɛməˏgɑd] | *(n.)* 半神半人 |
| | | A demigod was the child of a god or a goddess and a human. 半神半人是指神或女神和人類所生下的後代。 |

| 06 | **monster** [ˋmɑnstɚ] | *(n.)* 怪物 *sea monster 海怪 *monster 龐然大物（a monster of sth. 巨大的某物） |
| | | Greek heroes had to battle monsters like Medusa. 希臘的英雄必須和像梅杜莎這樣的怪物戰鬥。 |

| 07 | **mythical** [ˋmɪθɪkəl] | *(a.)* 神話的；虛構的 *mythical hero/monster/beast/creature 神話裡的英雄／怪物／野獸／生物 |
| | | The hydra and other monsters are mythical. 九頭蛇和其他的怪物都是神話中的事物。 |

| 08 | **Titan** [ˋtaɪtṇ] | *(n.)* 泰坦；巨人 *titan 巨人（titan of industry 工業巨擘） |
| | | Atlas and Prometheus were both powerful Titans. 亞特拉斯和普羅米修斯都是強大的泰坦。 |

| 09 | **immortal** [ɪˋmɔrtḷ] | *(a.)* 不朽的；流芳百世的 *(n.)* 不朽的人物；神 *the immortals 眾神 *mortal 會死的；凡人 |
| | | The Greek gods and goddesses were immortal and lived forever. 希臘的神和女神都是不朽之軀，永生不死。 |

| 10 | **Mount Olympus** [maʊnt oˋlɪmpəs] | *(n.)* 奧林帕斯山 |
| | | The Greek gods and goddesses lived on a mountain called Mount Olympus. 希臘的神和女神住在名為奧林帕斯山的山上。 |

Greek Gods and Goddesses

Zeus   Athena   Apollo   Poseidon   Hermes

Power Verbs 🔊 098

fight
與……戰鬥
Hercules fought the nine-headed hydra. 海克力斯與九頭蛇戰鬥。

battle
['bætl]
與……戰鬥
Hercules battled the nine-headed hydra. 海克力斯與九頭蛇戰鬥。

destroy
[dɪ'strɔɪ]
毀壞；破壞
Zeus could destroy anything with his thunderbolts.
宙斯的雷電可以摧毀任何事物。

punish
['pʌnɪʃ]
懲罰；處罰
Zeus had Prometheus tied to a rock to punish him.
宙斯將普羅米修斯綁在岩石上以懲罰他。

kill
殺死
Theseus killed the Minotaur, a monster. 特修斯殺死了米諾陶洛斯這個怪物。

slay
[sle]
殺死；殺害 (slay-slew-slain)
Theseus slew the Minotaur, a monster. 特修斯殺死了米諾陶洛斯這個怪物。

Word Families 🔊 099

Gods and Goddesses in Greek Myths 希臘神話的神與女神

Zeus	the king of the gods 宙斯，眾神之王	
Hera	the wife of Zeus and the goddess of marriage 赫拉，宙斯之妻，掌管婚姻的女神	
Poseidon	the god of the sea 波塞頓，海神	
Apollo	a son of Zeus and the god of light 阿波羅，宙斯之子，光明之神	
Artemis	the twin sister of Apollo and the goddess of the moon and hunting 阿耳忒彌斯，阿波羅的攣生姐妹，月亮及狩獵女神	
Aphrodite	the goddess of love and beauty 阿芙蘿黛蒂，愛情與美麗之女神	
Ares	the god of war 阿瑞斯，戰神	
Hermes	the messenger god 赫密士，神的信使	
Hephaestus	the god of fire and the forge 赫菲斯托斯，火神與冶煉之神	
Athena	the goddess of wisdom 雅典娜，智慧女神	
Hades	the god of the underworld 哈帝斯，冥府之神	

Titans and Heroes in Greek Myths 希臘神話的泰坦與英雄

Prometheus	the Titan who stole fire from the gods and gave it to people 普羅米修斯，從神的手中偷走火，並將其給人類的泰坦
Atlas	the Titan who held the world up on his shoulders 亞特拉斯，將世界支撐在肩膀上的泰坦
Hercules	the hero who was the strongest man on Earth 海克力斯，地球上最強壯的英雄
Theseus	the hero who killed the Minotaur 特修斯，殺死人身牛頭怪物米諾陶洛斯的英雄

Checkup

A

Write | 請依提示寫出正確的英文單字或片語。

1	神話		9	不朽的；流芳百世的
2	英雄		10	奧林帕斯山
3	神		11	與……戰鬥　f
4	女神		12	與……戰鬥　b
5	半神半人		13	毀壞；破壞
6	怪物		14	懲罰；處罰
7	神話的；虛構的		15	殺死　k
8	泰坦；巨人		16	殺死；殺害　s

B

Complete the Sentences | 請在空格中填入最適當的答案，並視情況做適當的變化。

hero	myth	mythical	goddess	Mount Olympus
monster	Titan	demigod	god	immortal

1 _____ tell about brave heroes, great battles, and gods and goddesses.
神話講述勇敢的英雄、偉大的戰役、神與女神。

2 Hercules and Theseus were _____ in Greek mythology.
在希臘神話中，海克力斯和特修斯都是英雄。

3 Aphrodite was the _____ of love. 阿芙蘿黛蒂為愛之女神。

4 A _____ was the child of a god or a goddess and a human.
半神半人是指神或女神和人類所生下的後代。

5 The Greek gods and goddesses were _____ and lived forever.
希臘的神和女神都是不朽之軀，永生不死。

6 Atlas and Prometheus were both powerful _____.
亞特拉斯和普羅米修斯都是強大的泰坦。

7 The hydra and other monsters are _____. 九頭蛇和其他的怪物都是神話中的事物。

8 Greek heroes had to battle _____ like Medusa.
希臘的英雄必須和像梅杜莎這樣的怪物戰鬥。

C

Read and Choose | 閱讀下列句子，並且選出最適當的答案。

1 Zeus could (destroy | decide) anything with his thunderbolts.

2 Zeus had Prometheus tied to a rock to (battle | punish) him.

3 Theseus (slew | slow) the Minotaur, a monster.

4 Hercules (found | fought) the nine-headed hydra.

Look, Read, and Write | 看圖並且依照提示，在空格中填入正確答案。

 ▸ stories about brave heroes, battles, and gods and goddesses

_____

 ▸ an imaginary creature that is large and frightening

_____

 ▸ a female god

_____

 ▸ one of a family of giants in Greek mythology

_____

E

Read and Answer | 閱讀並且回答下列問題。 ⊙ 100

The Greek Gods and Goddesses

Myths are stories that have been around for thousands of years or more. Myths tell about brave heroes, great battles, monsters, and gods and goddesses. Some wonderful myths come to us from ancient Greece. These tales are a part of Greek mythology. Now, let's meet some of the main Greek gods and goddesses.

The Greeks believed that the gods lived on Mount Olympus, a mountain in Greece. At Mount Olympus, Zeus was the most powerful god. He was the king of the gods. He controlled the heavens and decided arguments among the gods. Poseidon was the god of the sea, and Hades was the god of the underworld. They were the three strongest gods. Hera was Zeus's wife. She was the goddess of marriage. Athena was Zeus's daughter. She was the goddess of wisdom. Apollo and Artemis were twins. Apollo was the god of light, and Artemis was the goddess of the hunt. Ares was the god of war. And Aphrodite was the goddess of love. There were some other gods. But they were the most powerful of all.

Fill in the blanks.

1 _____ tell about heroes, battles, monsters, gods, and goddesses.

2 The Greek gods lived on Mount _____.

3 _____ was Zeus's wife.

4 The god of war was _____.

Key Words 🔘 101

01	**declarative** [dɪˋklærətɪv]	*(a.)* 陳述的；敘述的　　*(in) the declarative（以）敘述形式 A declarative sentence makes a statement about something. 陳述句是對某事進行陳述。
02	**interrogative** [ˌɪntəˋrɑgətɪv]	*(a.)* 疑問的；詢問的　　*interrogative pronoun 疑問代名詞 　　　　　　　　　　　*(in) the interrogative（以）疑問形式 An interrogative sentence asks a person something. 疑問句是詢問他人某件事。
03	**exclamatory** [ɪkˋsklæməˌtorɪ]	*(a.)* 感嘆的；尖叫的　　*exclamatory point/mark 驚嘆號 An exclamatory sentence shows surprise or excitement. 感嘆句用來表示驚訝或是興奮。
04	**imperative** [ɪmˋpɛrətɪv]	*(a.)* 祈使法的；命令式的　　*imperative verb 使役動詞 　　　　　　　　　　　　*it is imperative to do sth. 做某事是迫切的 An imperative sentence gives a person an order. 祈使句是給他人一個命令。
05	**prefix** [ˋpriˌfɪks]	*(n.)* 字首 *Un-*, *dis-*, and *im-* are prefixes that mean "not." 字首 un-、dis- 以及 im- 表示否定的意思。
06	**suffix** [ˋsʌfɪks]	*(n.)* 字尾 A suffix goes at the end of a word. 字尾出現在一個單字的結尾。
07	**synonym** [ˋsɪnəˌnɪm]	*(n.)* 同義字　　*synonym of/for 某字的同義字 "Pretty" and "beautiful" are synonyms.　pretty 和 beautiful 為同義字。
08	**antonym** [ˋæntəˌnɪm]	*(n.)* 反義字　　*antonym of/for 某字的反義字 The antonym of "cold" is "hot."　cold 的反義字為 hot。
09	**homophone** [ˋhɑməˌfon]	*(n.)* 異義同音字 Two words that sound alike but are spelled differently—like hear and here—are homophones. 像 hear 和 here 這兩個發音相同但拼寫不同的單字，稱為異義同音字。
10	**paragraph** [ˋpærəˌgræf]	*(n.)* 文章的（段或節） A paragraph is a group of sentences that share the same idea. 一起表達同一個概念的一組句子稱為段落。

prefix

unhappy
dislike
impossible

wonder**ful**
play**er**
quick**ly**　suffix

synonym
big - large
sea - ocean

antonym
alive - dead
present - absent

state 陳述；聲明
State a fact with a declarative sentence. 使用陳述句來陳述一個事實。

question 詢問
Question someone with an interrogative sentence. 用疑問句來詢問他人。

ask 問；詢問
Ask someone a question with an interrogative sentence. 用疑問句來問他人問題。

exclaim 大聲說；喊著說出
[ɪksˋklem]
Exclaim something with an exclamatory sentence. 用感嘆句來大聲說出某事。

order 命令；指揮
Order a person to do something with an imperative sentence. 用祈使句來命令某人做事。

indent 縮排；縮格
[ɪnˋdɛnt]
Always indent the first line of a paragraph. 每段的首句一定要縮排。

Word Families 🔊 103

dictionary 字典
A dictionary gives the definitions of words. 字典提供每個單字的意義。

thesaurus 分類辭典；同類詞辭典
[θɪˋsɔrəs]
A thesaurus gives synonyms and antonyms of words.
分類辭典提供單字的同義字與反義字。

encyclopedia 百科全書
[ɪnˌsaɪkləˋpidɪə]
An encyclopedia gives information about many different subjects.
百科全書提供許多不同主題的資訊。

Four Kinds of Sentences
四種句型

declarative sentence
(= statement) 陳述句

interrogative sentence
(= question) 疑問句

exclamatory sentence
(= exclamation) 感嘆句

imperative sentence
(= command) 祈使句

Punctuation Marks
標點符號

period 句號　　　**question mark** 問號

comma 逗號　　　**exclamation point** 驚嘆號

colon 冒號　　　**semicolon** 分號

dash 破折號　　　**hyphen** 連字號

slash 斜線　　　**quotes** 引號

apostrophe 撇號

Checkup

A

Write l 請依提示寫出正確的英文單字或片語。

1	陳述的；敘述的	_____
2	疑問的；詢問的	_____
3	感嘆的；尖叫的	_____
4	祈使法的；命令式的	_____
5	字首	_____
6	字尾	_____
7	同義字	_____
8	反義字	_____
9	異義同音字	_____
10	文章的（段或節）	_____
11	陳述；聲明	_____
12	大聲說出	_____
13	命令；指揮	_____
14	縮排；縮格	_____
15	分類辭典；同類詞辭典	_____
16	百科全書	_____

B

Complete the Sentences l 請在空格中填入最適當的答案，並視情況做適當的變化。

exclamatory	prefix	paragraph	indent	homophone
interrogative	synonym	imperative	suffix	declarative

1 An _____ sentence gives a person an order. 祈使句是給他人一個命令。

2 An _____ sentence asks a person something.
疑問句是詢問他人某件事。

3 A _____ sentence makes a statement about something.
陳述句是對某事進行陳述。

4 Un-, dis-, and im- are _____ that mean "not."
字首 un-、dis- 以及 im- 表示否定的意思。

5 A _____ goes at the end of a word. 字尾出現在一個單字的結尾。

6 "Pretty" and "beautiful" are _____. pretty 和 beautiful 為同義字。

7 A _____ is a group of sentences that share the same idea.
一起表達同一個概念的一組句子稱為段落。

8 Two words that sound alike but are spelled differently – like hear and here – are
_____. 像 hear 和 here 這兩個發音相同但拼寫不同的單字，稱為異義同音字。

C

Read and Choose l 閱讀下列句子，並且選出最適當的答案。

1 (Ask | State) a fact with a declarative sentence.

2 A (dictionary | thesaurus) gives synonyms and antonyms of words.

3 (Exclaim | Order) a person to do something with an imperative sentence.

4 Always (question | indent) the first line of a paragraph.

Look, Read, and Write | 看圖並且依照提示，在空格中填入正確答案。

 ▸ a group of sentences that share the same idea

_____

 ▸ a sentence type that asks a person something

_____

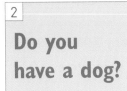 ▸ a sentence type that shows surprise or excitement

_____

 ▸ a letter or group of letters added to the beginning of a word to change its meaning

_____

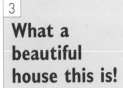 ▸ two words that sound alike but are spelled differently

_____

 ▸ a word that means the opposite of another word

_____

E

Read and Answer | 閱讀並且回答下列問題。 🔘 104

Different Types of Sentences

There are four types of sentences in English. They are declarative, interrogative, exclamatory, and imperative sentences. Declarative sentences are the most common. They are just statements. Use them to state facts. You always end these sentences with a period. All of the sentences in this paragraph are declarative ones. An interrogative is a question. Use this kind of sentence to ask other people about something. They always end with a question mark. You know what that is, don't you? Sometimes, you might be really excited about something. Or perhaps you are happy. Or maybe you have a strong emotion. Then you use an exclamatory sentence. You end these with an exclamation point! Finally, you might want to give a person an order. Use an imperative sentence to do this. In these sentences, the subject is "you." But don't say that word. Instead, just give the order.

Answer the questions.

1 What is the most common kind of sentence? _____

2 What is an interrogative? _____

3 How do you end an exclamatory sentence? _____

4 What is an imperative sentence? _____

Key Words ⊙ 105

| 01 | **artwork** | (n.) 藝術品；美術品　　*contemporary artwork 當代藝術品 |
| | [ˋɑrtˌwɝk] | A museum has a lot of **artwork** on display.　博物館展示了許多藝術品。 |

| 02 | **masterpiece** | (n.) 名作；傑作　　*literary masterpiece 文學傑作 |
| | [ˋmæstɚˌpis] | A **masterpiece** is an outstanding work of art. 名作是指出色的藝術作品。 |

03	**master**	(n.) 大師；主人　　*a master of 某方面的能手
	[ˋmæstɚ]	*be (the) master of one's destiny 掌握自己的命運
		Michelangelo, Rembrandt, and Picasso were all **masters**.
		米開朗基羅、林布蘭特以及畢卡索都是大師。

04	**contemporary**	(a.) 當代的；同時代的　　*contemporary poetry 現代詩
	[kənˋtɛmpəˌrɛrɪ]	*be contemporary with . . . 與……同期、同時代
		Contemporary art is another name for modern art.
		現代藝術又稱當代藝術。

05	**element**	(n.) 元素　　*chemical element 化學元素　　*element 因素（key element 關鍵因素）
	[ˋɛləmənt]	Lines, shapes, and colors are all **elements** of a painting.
		線條、形狀以及色彩都是繪畫的元素。

06	**contrast**	(n.) 對比；對照　　*a contrast to sth./sb. 與某事物／某人的對照
	[ˋkɑnˌtræst]	*by contrast 相較之下
		Many works of art have a **contrast** between bright and dark colors.
		許多藝術作品會以亮色和暗色作對比。

07	**reflection**	(n.) 反射；反映　　*a reflection of 反映出　　*on reflection 深思熟慮之後
	[rɪˋflɛkʃən]	The artist captured the **reflection** from the light very well.
		那位藝術家巧妙地捕捉了光線的反射。

08	**dimension**	(n.)【數】維；方面　　*the room's dimensions 房間的長寬高
	[dɪˋmɛnʃən]	*give sth. a new dimension 為……增添新的風貌
		Artists may paint in either two or three **dimensions**.
		畫家會從二維空間或三維空間來繪畫。

09	**foreground**	(n.) 前景　　*in the foreground 在前景中
	[ˋforˌɡraʊnd]	The **foreground** shows what is happening at the front of the painting.
		前景顯現了畫作前部的景象。

10	**background**	(n.) 背景　　*in the background 在背景中　　*background information 背景資料
	[ˋbækˌɡraʊnd]	The **background** shows what is happening at the back of the painting.
		背景顯現了畫作後部的景象。

Master and Masterpiece

Leonardo da Vinci

Mona Lisa

Michelangelo

Pietà

appreciate 欣賞
[ə`priʃɪˌet]
Many people visit a gallery to **appreciate** the art. 許多人到畫廊欣賞藝術品。

observe 觀看；觀察
[əb`zɝv]
Many people visit a gallery to **observe** the art. 許多人到畫廊觀看藝術品。

exhibit 展示
[ɪg`zɪbɪt]
The gallery is **exhibiting** some works of Picasso's. 畫廊正在展示一些畢卡索的作品。

display 展示；展出
[dɪ`sple]
The gallery is **displaying** some works of Picasso's. 畫廊正在展示一些畢卡索的作品。

contrast 對照；比較
[kən`træst]
The bright and dark colors **contrast** each other. 亮色和暗色互相對比。

affect 影響
[ə`fɛkt]
Light **affects** people's facial expressions. 光線會影響人的面部表情。

capture 留存；紀錄；拍攝
[`kæptʃɚ]
The artist has **captured** the image perfectly. 藝術家完美地捕捉了影像。

brighten 使明亮
[`braɪtn̩]
It is necessary to **brighten** paintings so that they are not too dark.
使畫作明亮是必要的，如此才不致太暗。

darken 使變暗
[`dɑrkn̩]
It is necessary to **darken** paintings so that they are not too bright.
使畫作變暗是必要的，如此才不致太亮。

Elements of Painting 繪畫的元素

light and shadow 光影

bright colors and dark colors 亮色與暗色

shapes and lines 形狀與線條

a sense of space 空間感

contrast 對比

reflections from the light 光線的反射

Landscape Topics 風景主題

forest	森林
field	野外
farm	農場
river	河川
lake	湖泊
sky	天空
flower	花朵
weather	天氣

Sculpture Materials 雕刻素材

marble	大理石
clay	黏土
bronze	青銅
concrete	混凝土
wax	蠟

Checkup

A

Write | 請依提示寫出正確的英文單字或片語。

1	藝術品；美術品	_____	9	【數】維；方面	_____
2	名作；傑作	_____	10	前景	_____
3	大師；主人	_____	11	欣賞；賞識	_____
4	當代的；同時代的	_____	12	觀看；觀察	_____
5	元素	_____	13	展示	e_____
6	對比；對照	_____	14	展示；陳列	d_____
7	反射；反映	_____	15	使明亮	_____
8	背景	_____	16	影響	_____

B

Complete the Sentences | 請在空格中填入最適當的答案，並視情況做適當的變化。

element	masterpiece	background	artwork	dimension
reflection	contemporary	foreground	master	contrast

1 A _____ is an outstanding work of art. 名作是指出色的藝術作品。

2 A museum has a lot of _____ on display. 博物館展示了許多藝術品。

3 Lines, shapes, and colors are all _____ of a painting.
線條、形狀以及色彩都是繪畫的元素。

4 The artist captured the _____ from the light very well.
那位藝術家巧妙地捕捉了光線的反射。

5 Artists may paint in either two or three _____.
畫家會從二維空間或三維空間來繪畫。

6 The _____ shows what is happening at the back of the painting.
背景顯現了畫作後部的景象。

7 Many works of art have a _____ between bright and dark colors.
許多藝術作品會以亮色和暗色作對比。

8 The _____ shows what is happening at the front of the painting.
前景顯現了畫作前部的景象。

C

Read and Choose | 閱讀下列句子，並且選出最適當的答案。

1 Many people visit a gallery to (appreciate | exhibit) the art.

2 The gallery is (appreciating | exhibiting) some works of Picasso's.

3 The bright and dark colors (display | contrast) each other.

4 It is necessary to (darken | brighten) paintings so that they are not too dark.

Look, Read, and Write | 看圖並且依照提示，在空格中填入正確答案。

 ▸ paintings and other pieces of art

_____

 ▸ the front part of a scene or picture

_____

 ▸ an outstanding work of art

_____

 ▸ difference in color or brightness between parts

_____

E

Read and Answer | 閱讀並且回答下列問題。 ⊙ 108

Elements of Painting

People often visit art galleries and museums to look at paintings. There are many famous paintings in places around the world. People call the greatest paintings "masterworks." What makes a painting great? There are many different elements.

First, the lines and shapes that an artist uses are important. Realistic artists make their lines and shapes imitate reality. Abstract artists do not. The way of using lines and shapes is the main difference between realistic and abstract art. Also, the colors in the painting are important. The colors should go well with each other. Light and shadows are important elements of paintings, too. Light can affect the way you feel. The way that artists use light in their paintings can affect your emotions as well. So some artists may use a sharp contrast between dark and light. An artist should also have a good sense of space. This means that the painting should not be too crowded or too empty. The painter should always try to find balance in a painting. That makes great art.

What is NOT true?

1 Great paintings are called masterworks.

2 Realistic artists and abstract artists make different kinds of art.

3 Light and shadows are not important in art.

4 A painting should not be too crowded.

Creating Designs 創造設計

Key Words 🔊 109

01	**symmetrical**	*(a.)* 對稱的；勻稱的　*symmetrical pattern 對稱圖案
	[sɪ`mɛtrɪkl̩]	Symmetrical lines are important when making art. 對稱的線條對創作藝術來說非常重要。
02	**balance**	*(n.)* 均衡；平衡　*keep/lose one's balance 保持／失去平衡 *sense of balance 平衡感
	[`bæləns]	Balance will make something a better work of art. 平衡會使藝術品更出色。
03	**pattern**	*(n.)* 圖案；型態　*geometric pattern 幾何圖案　*floral pattern 花紋
	[`pætən]	Many quilt artworks have patterns that repeat. 許多拼布藝術品運用了不斷重複的圖案。
04	**primary**	*(a.)* 原始的；主要的　*primary concern 主要考量　*primary source 原始資料
	[`praɪ,mɛrɪ]	Red, yellow, and blue are three primary colors. 紅色、黃色以及藍色為三原色。
05	**complementary**	*(n.)* 互補的；補充的　*be complementary to . . . 與……相輔相成
	[ˌkɑmplə`mɛntərɪ]	Red and green are complementary colors that go together. 紅色和綠色是相配的互補色。
06	**vivid**	*(n.)* (色彩) 鮮豔的，鮮明的；生動的；活潑的　*vivid red 鮮紅 *vivid imagination 生動的想像
	[`vɪvɪd]	When complementary colors are placed side by side, they appear more vivid. 把互補色擺在一起會顯得更加生動。
07	**quilt**	*(n.)* 拼布
	[kwɪlt]	Some people enjoy making quilts in their free time. 有些人喜歡在閒暇時從事拼布創作。
08	**collage**	*(n.)* 拼貼畫
	[kə`lɑʒ]	You can assemble a collage by using many different things. 你可以用許多不同的東西來組合拼貼畫。
09	**mosaic**	*(n.)* 馬賽克　*mosaic tile 馬賽克磚　*in mosaic 以鑲嵌方式
	[mə`zeɪk]	Mosaics can be made of stone, glass, or other objects. 馬賽克可由石頭、玻璃或其他東西來組成。
10	**folk art**	*(n.)* 民俗藝術
	[fok ɑrt]	Every culture in the world has its own folk art. 世界上的每個文化都有自己的民俗藝術。

quilt

collage

mosaic

mix	使混合
	Artists **mix** paints to get different colors. 畫家混合顏料來得到不同的顏色。
combine [kəm`baɪn]	使結合;使組合;使混合
	Artists **combine** paints to get different colors. 畫家結合顏料來得到不同的顏色。

cut	裁剪
	Cut the cloth with the scissors. 用剪刀裁剪布料。
snip [snɪp]	剪去;喀擦剪斷
	Snip a small part of the cloth with the scissors. 用剪刀剪下一小塊布料。

paste [pest]	用漿糊黏貼
	He is **pasting** something on to the collage. 他正用漿糊把一些材料黏到拼貼畫上。
glue [glu]	用膠水黏合;黏牢
	He is **gluing** something on to the collage. 他正用膠水把一些材料黏到拼貼畫上。

weave [wiv]	編製;編織
	She likes to **weave** quilts. 她喜歡編製拼布。

Painting Materials
繪畫材料

canvas	油畫布
paper	紙張
fabric	布料
wool	絨;羊毛
thread	線
wall	牆
glass	玻璃

Primary Colors
原色

	red	紅色
	yellow	黃色
	blue	藍色

Secondary Colors
二次色

	orange	橘色
	green	綠色
	purple	紫色

Complementary Colors
互補色

	red and green	紅色與綠色
	**blue and orange**	藍色與橘色
	yellow and purple	黃色與紫色

Checkup

A

Write | 請依提示寫出正確的英文單字或片語。

1	對稱的；勻稱的	_____	9	馬賽克	_____
2	均衡；平衡	_____	10	民俗藝術	_____
3	圖案；型態	_____	11	使混合	_____
4	原始的；主要的	_____	12	使結合；使組合	_____
5	互補的；補充的	_____	13	剪去；喀擦剪斷	_____
6	生動的；活潑的	_____	14	用漿糊黏貼	_____
7	拼布	_____	15	用膠水黏合；黏牢	_____
8	拼貼畫	_____	16	編製；編織	_____

B

Complete the Sentences | 請在空格中填入最適當的答案，並視情況做適當的變化。

pattern	symmetrical	vivid	collage	balance
quilt	complementary	primary	folk art	mosaic

1 _____ will make something a better work of art. 平衡會讓藝術品更出色。

2 _____ lines are important when making art. 對稱的線條對創作藝術來說很重要。

3 Red, yellow, and blue are three _____ colors. 紅色、黃色以及藍色為三原色。

4 Red and green are _____ colors that go together.
   紅色和綠色是相配的互補色。

5 When complementary colors are placed side by side, they appear more
   _____. 把互補色擺在一起會顯得更加生動。

6 _____ can be made of stone, glass, or other objects.
   馬賽克可由石頭、玻璃或是其他東西來組成。

7 You can assemble a _____ by using many different things.
   你可以用許多不同的東西來組合拼貼畫。

8 Every culture in the world has its own _____.
   世界上的每個文化都有自己的民俗藝術。

C

Read and Choose | 請選出與鋪底字意思相近的答案。

1 Snip a small part of the cloth with the scissors.

   a. Paint   b. Weave   c. Cut

2 He is pasting something on to the collage.

   a. cutting   b. gluing   c. weaving

3 Artists combine paints to get different colors.

   a. mix   b. snip   c. draw

D

Look, Read, and Write | 看圖並且依照提示，在空格中填入正確答案。

 ▶ a picture or method made by sticking various materials onto paper

_____

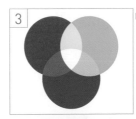 ▶ a pattern or picture made of many small colored pieces of stone, glass, etc.

_____

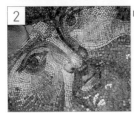 ▶ colors like red, yellow, and blue

_____

 ▶ to make something (such as cloth) by crossing threads

_____

E

Read and Answer | 閱讀並且回答下列問題。　🔊 112

Unique Art

Most people think that art is just painting or drawing. But there are many other kinds of unique art.

For example, some artists love cold weather. The reason they like the cold is that they make ice sculptures. They take huge blocks of ice and use saws, hammers, and chisels to create sculptures. Of course, when the weather gets warmer, their artwork disappears.

Most people don't think of bed covers as art, but others do. Many people make quilts. These are bed covers. But the quilt makers put many designs on their quilts. The designs can be simple, or they can be very complicated. But no two quilts are ever alike. Quilt making is a popular form of folk art in some places.

In America, Native Americans have many unique forms of art. Some of them paint rocks. Others make tiny sculptures from rocks, wood, or bone. And some Native Americans even use sand to make art! This is called sand painting. It can produce many beautiful pieces of art.

Answer the questions.

1　What do artists use to make ice sculptures?　_____

2　What is another name for a bed cover?　_____

3　What kinds of designs do quilts have?　_____

4　Who does sand painting?　_____

Elements of Music 音樂的元素

Key Words 🎧 113

01	**musical scale**	*(n.)* 音階
	[ˋmjuzɪkḷ skel]	The notes on a musical scale all have a different pitch. 音階上的音符具有不同的音高。

02	**note**	*(n.)* 音符　*whole note 全音符　*note 單音（wrong note 錯音）
	[not]	A musical note includes the pitch and length of a musical sound. 音符包含了樂音的音高及長短。

03	**staff**	*(n.)* 五線譜 *pl. staves
	[stæf]	Notes are written on a staff. 音符被書寫在五線譜上。

04	**clef**	*(n.)* 譜號　*bass clef 低音譜號
	[klɛf]	A clef is a symbol on the left side of each staff that shows the pitch of the notes. 譜號是位於五線譜左方的符號，用來顯示音符的音高。

05	**treble clef**	*(n.)* 高音譜號　*treble 最高聲部的
	[ˋtrɛbḷ klɛf]	The treble clef is the swirling symbol on the left side of each staff. 高音譜號是位於五線譜左方的旋轉符號。

06	**G clef**	*(n.)* G 譜號；高音譜號　*F clef 低音譜號
	[dʒi klɛf]	Sometimes, the treble clef is called the G clef. 有時候高音譜號又被稱作 G 譜號。

07	**measure**	*(n.)* (音樂) 小節　*a few measures/bars 幾個小節
	[ˋmɛʒɚ]	Musicians divide music into measures to make it easier to read so many notes. 為了方便閱讀眾多的音符，音樂家將音樂分為許多小節。

08	**bar line**	*(n.)* 小節線
	[bɑr laɪn]	The line that shows each measure is called a bar line. 分割每個小節的線條稱為小節線。

09	**time signature**	*(n.)* 拍子記號
	[taɪm ˋsɪgnətʃɚ]	The time signature indicates the meter of the music. 拍子記號顯示音樂的節拍。

10	**rest**	*(n.)* 休止符　*whole/half/quarter 全／二分／四分休止符
	[rɛst]	A musician does not play when there is a rest. 休止符出現時，音樂家便停止演奏。

sit

位於；座落於
On a musical staff, each note sits either on a line or on a space between lines.
在五線譜上，每個音符位於線上或是線與線之間。

keep

保持
The performers keep time so that they can play together.
表演者要合拍子，如此才能讓他們的演奏和諧。

beat
[bit]

（隨著音樂）打拍子
The musicians beat the time to keep up with the others.
音樂家隨著音樂打拍子來跟上其他人。

rest
[rɛst]

停止；靜止
The rest sign tells the musician to keep quiet and to rest during that beat.
休止符是告訴音樂家，這一拍要靜音、停止演奏。

last
[læst]

持續；繼續
A quarter rest lasts the same amount of time as a quarter note.
四分休止符持續的時間和四分音符相同。

represent
[ˌrɛprɪˈzɛnt]

表示；象徵
Each sound in a piece of music is represented by a musical note.
一首音樂裡的每一個音符都代表著一個音。

Word Families 🔊 115

Musical Scales 音階	**Time Signatures** 拍子記號	**Rests** 休止符

Musical Scales		
major scale	大音階
minor scale	小音階
C major	C 大調
D major	D 大調
E major	E 大調
F major	F 大調
G major	G 大調
A minor	A 小調
C minor	C 小調
D minor	D 小調

Time Signatures		
$\frac{4}{4}$ (four-four time)	四四拍
$\frac{3}{4}$ (three-four time)	三四拍
$\frac{2}{4}$ (two-four time)	二四拍

Rests		
whole rest	全休止符
half rest	二分休止符
quarter rest	四分休止符
eighth rest	八分休止符

Checkup

A Write | 請依提示寫出正確的英文單字或片語。

1	音階	_____	9	G 譜號	_____
2	音符	_____	10	F 譜號	_____
3	五線譜	_____	11	拍子記號	_____
4	譜號	_____	12	位於；座落於	_____
5	高音譜號	t_____	13	保持	_____
6	（音樂）小節	_____	14	（隨著音樂）打拍子	_____
7	小節線	_____	15	持續；繼續	_____
8	休止符	_____	16	表示；象徵	_____

B Complete the Sentences | 請在空格中填入最適當的答案，並視情況做適當的變化。

staff	bar line	clef	musical scale	musical note
rest	measure	G clef	time signature	treble clef

1 The notes on a _____ all have a different pitch.
音階上的音符具有不同的音高。

2 Notes are written on a _____. 音符被書寫在五線譜上。

3 A _____ includes the pitch and length of a musical sound.
音符包含了樂音的音高及長短。

4 A _____ is a symbol on the left side of each staff that shows the pitch of the notes. 譜號是位於五線譜左方的符號，顯示音符的音高。

5 The _____ is the swirling symbol on the left side of each staff.
高音譜號是位於五線譜左方的旋轉符號。

6 Musicians divide music into _____ to make it easier to read so many notes.
為了方便閱讀眾多的音符，音樂家將音樂分為許多小節。

7 A musician does not play when there is a _____.
休止符出現時，音樂家便停止演奏。

8 The _____ indicates the meter of the music. 拍子記號顯示音樂的節拍。

C Read and Choose | 閱讀下列句子，並且選出最適當的答案。

1 The performers (last | keep) time so that they can play together.

2 A quarter rest (lasts | beats) the same amount of time as a quarter note.

3 On a musical staff, each note (keeps | sits) either on a line or on a space between lines.

4 Each sound in a piece of music is (represent | represented) by a musical note.

Look, Read, and Write | 看圖並且依照提示，在空格中填入正確答案。

1 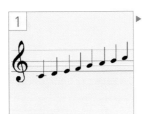 ▸ a series of musical notes going up or down in pitch in a fixed order

_____

4  ▸ It indicates the meter of the music.

_____

2  ▸ a symbol on the left side of each staff that shows the pitch of the notes

_____

5  ▸ the line that shows each measure

_____

3  ▸ any of the sections that a line of printed music is divided into

_____

6  ▸ the five horizontal lines on which music is written

_____

Read and Answer | 閱讀並且回答下列問題。 ◉ 116

Composers and Their Music

There have been many great classical music composers. Three of the greatest were Johann Sebastian Bach, Wolfgang Amadeus Mozart, and Ludwig van Beethoven. Bach came first. He composed music during the Baroque Period. Much of his music was for the church. He wrote tunes for orchestras, choirs, and solo instruments. *The Brandenburg Concertos* are some of his most famous works. Mozart was one of the most brilliant musicians of all time. He was a child genius. He started writing music at a very young age. He wrote all kinds of music. His opera *The Marriage of Figaro* is still famous. So is his *Great Mass in C Minor*. Beethoven was a great pianist and composer. His *Moonlight Sonata* was very famous. He went deaf later in his life. But he still conducted orchestras. His *9th Symphony* is one of the greatest of all pieces of classical music.

Bach

Mozart

Beethoven

What is true? Write T(true) or F(false).

1 Bach lived during the Baroque Period. _____

2 Bach wrote *The Marriage of Figaro*. _____

3 Mozart went deaf later in life. _____

4 Beethoven composed *Moonlight Sonata*. _____

A World of Music 音樂的世界

Key Words 🔊 117

01 reed
[rid]
(n.) 簧舌；簧片
Without a reed, you cannot play the clarinet. 沒有簧片就無法演奏單簧管。

02 mouthpiece
[ˋmaʊθ͵pis]
(n.) (樂器的) 吹嘴
The trumpet needs a mouthpiece to make music. 小號利用吹嘴來演奏音樂。

03 slide
[slaɪd]
(n.) 滑管；拉管
A trombone has a slide that moves back and forth.
長號有一根可以前後滑動的滑管。

04 ballet
[ˋbæle]
(n.) 芭蕾　　*go to a ballet 觀賞芭蕾舞表演　　*ballerina 芭蕾女伶
A ballet involves a combination of music and dancing.
芭蕾是音樂與舞蹈的結合。

05 theme
[θim]
(n.) 主旋律　　*theme song (to/from a movie, show, etc.) (電影、表演等的) 主題曲
The theme of the music helps to set the mood.
這首音樂的主旋律有助於營造氣氛。

06 movement
[ˋmuvmənt]
(n.) 樂章
The first movement of Beethoven's 5th Symphony is very famous.
貝多芬《第五號交響曲》的首樂章非常受歡迎。

07 suite
[swit]
(n.) 組曲　　*Nutcracker Suite 胡桃鉗組曲
A suite is a set of instrumental or orchestral pieces normally performed in a concert. 組曲是指在音樂會上演奏套曲形式的器樂曲或管弦樂曲。

08 overture
[ˋovət͡ʃʊr]
(n.) 序曲；前奏曲
An overture is the introductory piece to an opera or a longer musical piece. 序曲是指歌劇或長篇樂曲的開場音樂。

09 march
[mɑrt͡ʃ]
(n.) 進行曲　　*Turkish March 土耳其進行曲
A march is music that is often appropriate for marching.
進行曲是指適合用於行軍的音樂。

10 live performance
[laɪv pəˋfɔrməns]
(n.) 現場表演
The band will give a live performance this evening.
樂團將在今晚進行現場表演。

reed

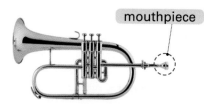
mouthpiece

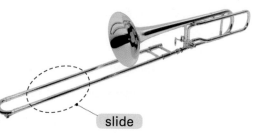
slide

slide
[slaɪd]
滑動；滑行
The trombone has a tube that **slides** in and out to change the sound.
長號有一根滑管，前後滑動可以改變音高。

toot
[tut]
吹奏出
The musicians are **tooting** on their horns. 音樂家正在吹奏他們的管樂器。

blow
[blo]
吹響；吹奏
You play the French horn by **blowing** into the mouthpiece.
對著吹嘴吹氣來演奏法國號。

bang
[bæŋ]
砰地敲
The drummer **bangs** on a drum and helps keep the beat.
鼓手砰地敲著鼓來幫助保持節拍。

tap
[tæp]
輕拍；輕敲
Tap on the cymbals to make music. 輕拍鐃鈸來奏出音樂。

shake
[ʃek]
搖動；震動
The musician is **shaking** the tambourine. 那位音樂家正搖動著鈴鼓。

The Nutcracker

Word Families 🔊 119

Famous Ballets
著名芭蕾舞曲

The Nutcracker	胡桃鉗
Swan Lake	天鵝湖
The Sleeping Beauty	睡美人
Giselle	吉賽兒

Famous Ballet Composers
著名芭蕾作曲家

Peter Tchaikovsky	彼得・柴可夫斯基
Igor Stravinsky	伊果・史特拉汶斯基
Aaron Copland	艾朗・柯普蘭
Sergei Prokofiev	謝爾蓋・普羅高菲夫

Famous Operas
著名歌劇

The Marriage of Figaro	費加洛婚禮
Aida	阿依達
La Boheme	波西米亞人
Carmen	卡門
The Barber of Seville	塞維里亞的理髮師

Famous Opera Composers
著名歌劇作曲家

Wolfgang Amadeus Mozart 沃夫岡・阿瑪迪斯・莫札特	
Giuseppe Verdi	朱瑟貝・威爾第
Giacomo Puccini	賈科莫・普契尼
Georges Bizet	喬治・比才
Giovanni Paisiello	喬瓦尼・帕伊謝洛

Checkup

A

Write I 請依提示寫出正確的英文單字或片語。

1	簧舌；簧片	_____	9	進行曲	_____
2	（音樂的）吹嘴	_____	10	現場表演	_____
3	滑管；拉管	_____	11	滑動；滑行	_____
4	芭蕾	_____	12	吹奏出	t_____
5	主旋律	_____	13	吹響；吹奏	b_____
6	樂章	_____	14	砰地敲	_____
7	組曲	_____	15	輕拍；輕敲	_____
8	序曲；前奏曲	_____	16	搖動；震動	_____

B

Complete the Sentences I 請在空格中填入最適當的答案，並視情況做適當的變化。

march	reed	mouthpiece	ballet	overture
theme	suite	movement	slide	live performance

1 Without a _____, you cannot play the clarinet. 沒有簧片就無法演奏單簧管。

2 A trombone has a _____ that moves back and forth.
長號有一根可以前後滑動的滑管。

3 The trumpet needs a _____ to make music. 小號利用吹嘴來演奏音樂。

4 An _____ is the introductory piece to an opera or a longer musical piece.
序曲是指歌劇或長篇樂曲的開場音樂。

5 The _____ of the music helps to set the mood.
這首音樂的主旋律有助於營造氣氛。

6 The first _____ of Beethoven's 5th Symphony is very famous.
貝多芬《第五號交響曲》的首樂章非常受歡迎。

7 The band will give a _____ this evening.
樂團將在今晚進行現場表演。

8 A _____ is a set of instrumental or orchestral pieces normally performed in a concert. 組曲是指在音樂會上演奏套曲形式的器樂曲或管弦樂曲。

C

Read and Choose I 閱讀下列句子，並且選出最適當的答案。

1 The drummer (slides | bangs) on a drum and helps keep the beat.

2 The trombone has a tube that (slides | bangs) in and out to change the sound.

3 (Tap | Blow) on the cymbals to make music.

4 The musicians are (tooting | ringing) on their horns.

Look, Read, and Write | 看圖並且依照提示，在空格中填入正確答案。

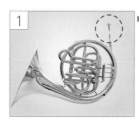 ► the part that you put into your mouth to play a brass instrument

_____

 ► a tube in a trombone that moves back and forth to change the sound

_____

 ► a combination of music and dancing

_____

 ► to make a soft knocking sound

_____

 ► a performance which is given before an audience

_____

 ► music that is often appropriate for marching

_____

E

Read and Answer | 閱讀並且回答下列問題。 🔘 120

The Nutcracker

Every Christmas season, people all around the world go to the ballet. And many of them see _The Nutcracker_. It is one of the most famous and popular ballets in the world. It was composed by Peter Tchaikovsky. In the story, it is Christmas Eve. Clara receives a nutcracker as a present. She falls asleep in a room with the nutcracker. Suddenly, the nutcracker and the toys grow big, and they come to life. Then, they battle an army of mice and defeat them. The nutcracker becomes a prince, and he and Clara go to his castle. They watch many dances there. Then, Clara wakes up and learns it was only a dream. The music and dances in _The Nutcracker_ are very famous. The music is beautiful, and the dances require great skill. Along with the story, they have made _The Nutcracker_ an important part of Christmas for many people.

Fill in the blanks.

1   _The Nutcracker_ was composed by Peter _____.

2   The events in _The Nutcracker_ take place on _____ Eve.

3   The nutcracker turns into a _____.

4   The music and _____ in _The Nutcracker_ are very famous.

A

Write | 請依提示寫出正確的英文單字或片語。

1	神話	_____	11	毀壞；破壞 (v.) _____
2	陳述的；敘述的	_____	12	懲罰；處罰 (v.) _____
3	疑問的；詢問的	_____	13	不朽的；流芳百世的 _____
4	對稱的；勻稱的	_____	14	異義同音字 _____
5	拼貼畫	_____	15	文章的（段或節） _____
6	藝術品；美術品	_____	16	欣賞；賞識 (v.) _____
7	休止符	_____	17	展示 (v.)　e_____
8	音階	_____	18	對照；比較 _____
9	組曲	_____	19	吹奏出　t_____
10	序曲；前奏曲	_____	20	拍子記號 _____

B

Choose the Correct Word | 請選出與鋪底字意思相近的答案。

1　Theseus **slew** the Minotaur, a monster.

　　a. punished　　　　　b. killed　　　　　　c. destroyed

2　The gallery is **exhibiting** some works of Picasso's.

　　a. observing　　　　　b. constructing　　　c. displaying

3　**Snip** a small part of the cloth with the scissors.

　　a. Paint　　　　　　　b. Weave　　　　　　c. Cut

4　He is **pasting** something on to the collage.

　　a. cutting　　　　　　b. gluing　　　　　　c. weaving

C

Complete the Sentences | 請在空格中填入最適當的答案，並視情況做適當的變化。

Mount Olympus	treble clef	element	suffix

1　The _____ is the swirling symbol on the left side of each staff.
高音譜號是位於五線譜左方的旋轉符號。

2　Lines, shapes, and colors are all _____ of a painting.
線條、形狀以及色彩都是繪畫的元素。

3　A _____ goes at the end of a word. 字尾出現在一個單字的結尾。

4　The Greek gods and goddesses lived on a mountain called
_____. 希臘眾神住在名為奧林帕斯山的山上。

Index

Index

ANSWERS AND TRANSLATIONS

01 Unit ● Laws and Rules (p.12)

A

1 court 2 judge 3 jury 4 lawyer 5 defendant
6 legal 7 illegal 8 punishment 9 guilty
10 innocent 11 break the law 12 fine 13 accuse
14 prosecutor 15 commit 16 sentence

B

1 Judges 2 court 3 jury 4 punishment
5 guilty 6 innocent 7 legal 8 prosecution

C

1 break 2 prosecute 3 defense 4 accuse

D

1 jury 2 judge 3 defendant 4 fine
5 prosecutor 6 court

E 陪審團制度

　　美國大部分的刑事案件都需經過陪審團的審判，陪審團審理是司法制度上很重要的一個部分。陪審團由普通公民組成，可分為大陪審團和小陪審團兩種。大陪審團由 12 到 23 人組成，他們根據檢察官提供的證據來決定罪證是否足夠進行審判。若陪審團認為罪證足夠，則會進行接下來的審判；若罪證不足，則否。小陪審團也可稱作 trial jury，通常由 12 名陪審員組成。陪審員會在場旁聽案件的審理並聽取所有的證據，接著，在審判結束前，他們會決定被告的有罪與否。

* **case** 案件；訴訟 **trial** 審判；審問 **justice** 司法；審判
  grand jury 大陪審團 **petit jury** 小陪審團

回答下列問題。
1 陪審團可分為幾種？(two)
2 大陪審團由多少人擔任？(12 to 23)
3 小陪審團的另一個名稱是什麼？(petit jury)
4 小陪審團的職責為何？
　(It decides if the defendant is innocent or guilty.)

02 Unit ● Earning, Spending, and Saving (p.16)

A

1 income 2 spending 3 savings 4 budget
5 profit 6 demand 7 supply 8 goods
9 service 10 product 11 balance 12 manage
13 make a budget 14 make a profit 15 deposit
16 invest

B

1 Income 2 savings 3 spending 4 budget
5 demand 6 supply 7 Goods 8 products

C

1 balance 2 budget 3 profit 4 deposit

D

1 budget 2 goods 3 deposit 4 income
5 needs 6 invest

E 金錢管理

　　人們工作所得到的報酬稱為收入。有了收入，人們就可以進行消費和儲蓄這兩件事。大部分的人會將兩者互相搭配。首先，他們必須將錢花費在許多事情上，像是房子、食物、衣服、保險、交通費甚至是娛樂開銷等方面。通常在這些花費外，還會有一些錢剩下來。人們通常會把這些錢存在銀行或是投資股票市場。遺憾的是，有些人開銷太大，他們入不敷出，因而開始欠債。債務對許多人來說是個很大的問題。其實，人們可以透過計畫性的購物來妥善安排他們的收入、開銷以及儲蓄。預算幫助人們管理金錢並進行儲蓄。

* **debt** 負債

以下何者為非？（1）
1 人們工作所賺來的錢就是他們的儲蓄。
2 人們通常會花費或是儲蓄他們的收入。
3 有些人把錢存在銀行。
4 預算幫助人們管理金錢。

03 Unit ● Goods and Resources (p.20)

A

1 renewable 2 nonrenewable 3 human resource
4 producer 5 assembly line 6 international trade
7 free trade 8 interdependence 9 tariff
10 scarcity 11 mass-produce 12 consumer
13 specialize in 14 take advantage of 15 export
16 collect

B

1 producer 2 Renewable 3 Nonrenewable
4 assembly lines 5 scarcity 6 Consumers
7 human 8 interdependence

C

1 mass-produce 2 specialize 3 imports 4 tariff

D

1 export 2 renewable resource
3 human resource 4 assembly line

E 資源的所有種類

　　地球上有許多種不同的資源，其中有四種非常重要，它們是可再生資源、不可再生資源、人力資源以及資本資源。可再生資源可以重複利用，並且可以在短時間之內更新。有些能源資源屬於可再生資源，像是太陽能、潮汐能、水力以及風力。此外，植物與動物也屬於可再生資源。然而，人們依舊要加以小心愛護，不可隨意浪費。不可再生資源的供應有限，一旦使用了，它們便會永久消失。它們無法更新。許多能源資源都屬此類，像是煤、天然氣以及石油。人力資源是指人以及他們所具備的技能，這當中也包含了人所擁有的知識與資訊。人們使用可再生與不可再生資源來製造產品，機器亦被用來生產商品。用來生產商品的機器與工具稱作資本資源。

回答下列問題。
1 四種重要的資源是什麼？
　(renewable, nonrenewable, human, and capital resources)
2 可再生資源有哪些？
　(energy from the sun, tides, water, and wind)
3 煤、天然氣以及石油屬於哪種資源？
　(nonrenewable resources)
4 什麼是資本資源？
　(machines and tools used to produce goods)

A

1 communication   2 postal service   3 telegraph
4 invention   5 wireless   6 transportation
7 railroad   8 automobile   9 technology
10 vaccination   11 transport   12 broadcast
13 send out   14 advance   15 prevent   16 vaccinate

B

1 technology   2 invention   3 communication
4 wireless   5 Railroads   6 automobile
7 advancing   8 vaccine

C

1 transmit   2 vaccine   3 inventors   4 broadcast

D

1 telegraph   2 wireless   3 vaccination
4 broadcast

E 科技如何幫助人類

　　現今，我們活在一個先進的世界，我們使用了許多過去的人從未想像過的新發明。從前人們無法經常與彼此溝通，寄送一封信要耗時幾天、幾週甚至是幾個月。由於當時沒有電話，人們必須要面對面才能溝通。現在，用手機就能聯絡到世界上任何角落的任何人，我們還能利用網路立即傳送電子郵件給他人。在過去，短程旅行也相當耗時，人們只能走路或是騎馬。而今，大部分的人擁有自己的車，他們可以在短時間內開車到達路途遙遠之地，人們甚至能搭乘飛機前往世界各地。過去人們經常死於醫療的貧乏，甚至連牙痛亦能致人於死！如今，疫苗讓人們免於疾病之苦，而且，醫生每天都有越來越多的醫療新發現。

* **thanks to** 由於　**medical treatment** 醫療

填空
1 我們活在一個先進的世界。(advanced)
2 現今人們可以用手機聯絡他人。(cell)
3 人們可以搭乘飛機前往世界各地。(fly)
4 疫苗讓人們免於疾病之苦。(Vaccines)

A

1 tropical   2 temperate   3 Mediterranean
4 arctic   5 rain forest   6 woodland   7 tundra
8 drought   9 flood   10 tropical storm   11 affect
12 be affected by   13 vary   14 depend on
15 be found in   16 extreme

B

1 Mediterranean   2 tropical   3 Temperate
4 rain forest   5 drought   6 Tropical storms
7 hazardous   8 extreme

C

1 affected   2 vary   3 depends   4 found

D

1 typhoon   2 arctic   3 tundra   4 drought
5 woodland   6 broadleaf forest

E 極端天氣狀況

　　很多人住在有四季變化的地區，通常夏天炎熱，冬天寒冷，春天和秋天的天氣非暖即涼。這些都是非常正常的天氣狀況，但有時候也會有極端的天氣狀況發生，這通常會帶給人們許多麻煩。有時候，某個地方可能有好長一段時間沒降雨，湖泊、河川以及溪流的水量減少，草木枯死，人們和動物感到口渴難耐，這就是所謂的乾旱。有時候，雨可能會持續下很多天，水位也會高出正常值。此時水常常會流至平地，甚至淹到市區街道，這就是所謂的水災。許多溫暖近海的地區會有熱帶風暴，這些暴風雨會挾帶豪雨狂風。熱帶風暴能在幾小時內降下數英寸高的雨量。有些地方每年都可能會有兩到三個的熱帶風暴。

* **weather conditions** 天氣狀況

回答下列問題。
1 許多人居住在有幾個季節變化的地區？(four)
2 旱災出現時會發生什麼事？
　(It doesn't rain for a long time.)
3 水位太高時稱作什麼？(flood)
4 熱帶風暴的影響為何？
　(They drop several inches of rain in a few hours.)

Review Test 1

A

1 court   2 judge   3 income   4 spending
5 renewable   6 nonrenewable   7 invention
8 wireless   9 temperate   10 Mediterranean
11 jury   12 break the law   13 balance
14 make a budget   15 mass-produce   16 scarcity
17 technology   18 vaccination   19 tropical storm
20 affect

B

1 (b)   2 (a)   3 (c)

C

1 illegal   2 budget   3 assembly lines
4 communication   5 Needs

A

1 globe   2 map scale   3 feature   4 grid
5 border   6 equator   7 hemisphere   8 latitude
9 longitude   10 prime meridian   11 be divided into
12 be connected to   13 run   14 intersect
15 cardinal directions   16 intermediate directions

B

1 globe   2 features   3 grid   4 map scale
5 Hemisphere   6 equator   7 longitude   8 latitude

C

1 divided   2 border   3 intersect   4 North

D

1 intersect   2 equator   3 hemisphere
4 lines of latitude   5 lines of longitude
6 prime meridian

地球是一個大行星，但我們可以將它分成較小的區塊，這些區塊稱為半球。每一個半球都是地球的二分之一，有一條假想線環繞於地球的東西之間，它位於地球的中心，我們稱之為赤道。赤道將地球分為北半球以及南半球，北半球包含了亞洲、歐洲以及北美洲；赤道以下的區塊稱為南半球，它包含了澳洲、南極洲以及大部分的南美洲和非洲。我們也可以將地球分為東西半球，區分東西兩半球的稱為本初子午線，這條線由北向南延伸，剛好通過英國的格林威治。東半球包含歐洲、非洲以及亞洲；西半球包含北美洲和南美洲。

以下何者為非？（2）
1 赤道由西向東延伸。
2 澳洲位於北半球。
3 地球可分為東半球和西半球。
4 北美洲和南美洲位於西半球。

07 ● The Government (p.38)

A
1 executive branch　2 legislative branch
3 judicial branch　4 candidate　5 consent　6 bill
7 veto　8 enforcement　9 taxation
10 community service　11 determine　12 carry out
13 apply　14 approve　15 vote for　16 reject/refuse

B
1 legislative　2 executive　3 judicial　4 bills
5 consent　6 enforcement　7 Taxation
8 determines

C
1 (b)　2 (a)　3 (b)

D
1 community service　2 judicial branch
3 legislative branch　4 candidate　5 veto
6 consent

E 政府三部門

政府分為三個部門：行政部門、立法部門以及司法部門。這三個部門負責法律的制訂及執行，它們有各自的權責。

立法部門為國會，負責提議、討論並表決法案，法案一旦通過並經總統簽署，就正式成為法律，法律通過後會被執行。行政部門負責執行法律，行政部門是指總統以及其屬下。司法部門為法院系統，負責裁決違法與否，當人們違反法律，司法部門就會處理他們的案件。

填空
1 政府的三個部門負責法律的制訂和執行。(laws)
2 國會為立法部門。(legislative)
3 總統簽署法案使其成為法律。(signs)
4 法院系統為司法部門。(court)

08 ● Ancient Egypt (p.42)

A
1 pharaoh　2 pyramid　3 Sphinx　4 mummy
5 tomb　6 Nile River　7 Egyptian　8 god-king
9 hieroglyphics　10 cuneiform　11 ziggurat
12 erect　13 flood　14 overflow　15 regard
16 enormous

B
1 god-kings　2 pyramids　3 tombs　4 Nile River
5 hieroglyphics　6 Cuneiform　7 Egyptian
8 mummy

C
1 (c)　2 (b)　3 (b)

D
1 cuneiform　2 pyramid　3 Sphinx　4 mummy
5 hieroglyphics　6 tomb

E 古埃及文明

埃及文明起源於五千年前，以尼羅河為中心。尼羅河每年都會氾濫，氾濫的河水為尼羅河兩岸帶來肥沃的土地，同時也利於農業，這也開啟了埃及文明的大門。

埃及人的生活以法老為中心，法老是統治整個國家的神王。大部分的埃及人都是奴隸，他們為服侍法老而活。法老非常富有，他們建造了巨大的紀念碑、金字塔以及獅身人面像。埃及到處遍佈著許多金字塔。埃及有屬於自己的書寫方式，稱作象形文字，它是一種圖畫書寫的形式。象形文字並非使用字母，而是運用圖畫來表達意義。這些圖畫各自代表著不同的聲音與詞彙。

以下何者為「是」？請在空格中填入「T」或「F」。
1 埃及文明源於 500 年前。(F)
2 埃及的法老是奴隸。(F)
3 埃及人建造了金字塔和獅身人面像。(T)
4 象形文字是一種圖畫書寫的形式。(T)

09 ● Ancient Greece (p.46)

A
1 democracy　2 Olympics　3 city-state　4 Athens
5 Sparta　6 birthplace　7 tyrant　8 philosophy
9 philosopher　10 civilization　11 take part in
12 take charge of　13 compete　14 cooperate
15 tough　16 rough

B
1 Olympics　2 City-states　3 birthplace　4 Sparta
5 Democracy　6 Tyrants　7 philosophy
8 civilization

C
1 competed　2 Athenians　3 trained　4 took part

D
1 Olympics　2 cruel　3 city-state　4 cooperate

E 雅典與斯巴達

古希臘有許多城邦，這些城邦控制了它們四周的土地。其中兩個最有名的就是雅典和斯巴達，這兩個城邦彼此大相逕庭。

首先，雅典是民主的發源地，它讓平民投票並協助城邦的運作。雅典是一個非常開放的社會，它有奴隸的存在，但許多人仍是自由的。斯巴達與雅典差異甚大，它是一個非常好戰的城邦，男人自幼便被訓練成為戰士，斯巴達人也擁有許多自己的奴隸，有時候斯巴達和雅典之間會互相征戰。

雅典以許多成就而著名，它有許多大思想家，像蘇格拉底和柏拉圖就是世界上最偉大的兩位哲學家。柏拉圖記錄了許多自己和蘇格拉底的思想，人們今天仍舊閱讀著他的著作。

填空

1 雅典和斯巴達是最有名的城邦。(Sparta)
2 雅典首先實行民主制度。(Democracy)
3 斯巴達人擁有許多奴隸。(slaves)
4 蘇格拉底和柏拉圖是兩位偉大的雅典哲學家。
　(philosophers)

10 ● Ancient Rome (p.50)

A

1 republic　2 Senate　3 citizen　4 patrician
5 plebeian　6 emperor　7 Latin　8 chariot
9 forum　10 barbarian　11 take over　12 enslave
13 invade　14 fall　15 senator　16 consul

B

1 republic　2 Senate　3 Patricians　4 Latin
5 Chariots　6 enslaved　7 forum　8 barbarians

C

1 expanded　2 took over　3 senators　4 invaded

D

1 Senate　2 plebeians　3 patricians　4 emperor
5 chariot　6 gladiator

E 條條大路通羅馬

　羅馬帝國版圖擴張最大時，幅員非常遼闊。它佔領了已知世界的眾多土地，往北延伸至英國，往西控制了西班牙和西非的土地，往南佔領了非洲大部分的土地，往東延伸至中東。然而，整個帝國的中心始終是羅馬。有句重要的諺語說道：「條條大路通羅馬。」在當時，羅馬皇帝想將各偏遠省分連結到首都，因此建築了許多條道路。這些道路都通向首都。羅馬強盛時，帝國隨之強盛；羅馬衰敗時，帝國亦隨之衰敗。多年後，羅馬被來自日耳曼的入侵者擊敗。這些入侵者是如何抵達羅馬呢？他們靠的就是羅馬的其中一條道路！

以下何者為非？（3）

1 羅馬帝國非常龐大。
2 羅馬人建造了許多道路。
3 羅馬曾統治過美國本土。
4 征服羅馬的入侵者是沿著羅馬帝國的道路行進。

Review Test 2

1 globe　2 equator　3 executive branch
4 legislative branch　5 pharaoh　6 pyramid
7 democracy　8 city-state　9 republic　10 Senate

11 hemisphere　12 latitude　13 judicial branch
14 veto　15 hieroglyphics　16 cuneiform
17 philosophy　18 civilization　19 senator　20 consul

B

1 (b)　2 (a)　3 (c)　4 (b)

C

1 prime meridian　2 enforcement　3 Egyptian
4 birthplace

11 ● A World of Plants (p.56)

A

1 embryo　2 seedling　3 flowering plant
4 conifer　5 chlorophyll　6 photosynthesis
7 carbon dioxide　8 heredity　9 deciduous
10 coniferous　11 germinate　12 biennial
13 release　14 birch　15 absorb　16 pass on

B

1 embryo　2 Chlorophyll　3 photosynthesis
4 Coniferous　5 Heredity　6 Flowering
7 seedling　8 germinate

C

1 give off　2 take in　3 on　4 annual

D

1 embryo　2 seedling　3 carbon dioxide
4 photosynthesis　5 chlorophyll　6 deciduous trees

E 光合作用

　每一個生物體都需要水和食物來生存，缺乏水和食物，生物就會死亡。植物也是生物體，因此也需要這些東西。植物可以自行製造食物，而這個製造的過程稱作光合作用。植物需要陽光來產生能量。首先，當太陽照射時，植物體中的葉綠素會汲取陽光，陽光就是能量，也就是說葉綠素是在吸收能量。接著，在光合作用發生時，植物還需要另外兩種東西：水以及二氧化碳。光合作用中，植物會經歷一種化學反應，由於有葉綠素，光合作用產生了糖分，植物也從中得到滋養。這個反應也會產生氧氣，植物釋放氧氣到空氣中，人們才得以吸收。所以，沒有光合作用，人們也無法存活。

* **creature** 生物　**capture** 汲取　**feed off** 從……得到滋養

以下何者為「是」？請在空格中填入「T」或「F」。

1 植物可自行製造水分。（F）
2 植物需要陽光來存活。（T）
3 葉綠素幫助植物進行光合作用。（T）
4 植物吸收氧氣。（F）

12 ● A World of Animals (p.60)

A

1 warm-blooded　2 cold-blooded　3 vertebrate
4 invertebrate　5 instinct　6 migration
7 hibernation　8 organism　9 trait　10 reproduction
11 respond to/react to　12 mammal　13 sponge
14 exhibit　15 inherited trait　16 learned trait

B

1 organism   2 Cold-blooded   3 Warm-blooded
4 traits   5 invertebrate   6 vertebrate   7 instinct
8 Reproduction

C

1 respond   2 inherited   3 migrate   4 exhibit

D

1 warm-blooded animals   2 cold-blooded animals
3 invertebrate   4 vertebrate   5 organism
6 inherited trait

E　恆溫動物與變溫動物

　　所有的動物不是恆溫動物就是變溫動物，主要視他們如何維持體溫而定。恆溫動物可以控制自己的體溫，所以就算室外很冷，他們仍能保持溫暖，但恆溫動物需要大量進食，他們利用食物產生的能量來維持體溫，哺乳類和鳥類都屬於恆溫動物。變溫動物則靠陽光來獲取熱能，因此他們的體溫一直隨著時間而變化，這些動物通常會在太陽底下休息好幾個小時，讓身體吸收熱能、變得溫暖。大部分的變溫動物不會居住在寒冷的地方，反之，它們會選擇溫暖的地方。爬蟲類、兩棲類以及魚類都屬於變溫動物。

* **regulate** 控制　**soak up** 吸收

填空

1 恆溫動物可以控制自己的體溫。(Warm-blooded)
2 哺乳類和鳥類都屬於恆溫動物。(birds)
3 變溫動物靠陽光來獲取熱能。(sun)
4 爬蟲類、兩棲類以及魚類都屬於變溫動物。(fish)

Unit 13 ● Food Chains (p.64)

A

1 herbivore   2 carnivore   3 omnivore
4 producer   5 consumer   6 decomposer
7 predator   8 prey   9 scavenger   10 parasite
11 hunt   12 prey on   13 consume   14 scavenge
15 decompose   16 rhinoceros

B

1 Omnivores   2 herbivore   3 carnivore
4 Consumers   5 prey   6 predators
7 Decomposers   8 Parasites

C

1 prey   2 decompose   3 scavenge   4 Consumers

D

1 carnivore   2 herbivore   3 decompose
4 predator   5 scavenger   6 parasite

E　食草動物、食肉動物與雜食動物

　　每一個生物體都需要靠吃來維生，然而，動物並不是都吃同一種東西，反之，他們吃各式各樣的食物。大部分的動物可分為三類，食草動物屬於第一類，他們只吃植物，也就是說，他們可能會吃植物、水果和蔬菜，人們稱他們為「食草者」，母牛、馬以及兔子就屬此類。大型動物也可以是食草動物，像是大象和犀牛都只吃草。食肉動物為食肉者，他們常是狩獵者，食肉動物為掠食性動物，他們必須尋找獵物並且捕捉食用。貓科動物的成員都是食肉動物，其中包含了獅子、美洲獅，甚至家貓，鯊魚也是食肉者。有些動物吃植物亦吃動物，他們稱作雜食動物，人類是雜食動物，豬、狼以及雞都是。

* **vegetation** 植物

回答下列問題。

1 動物可分為幾類？(three)
2 食草動物吃什麼？(vegetation, plants)
3 鯊魚和獅子屬於哪一類動物？(carnivores)
4 雜食動物吃什麼？(meat and vegetation)

Unit 14 ● Ecosystems (p.68)

A

1 competition   2 adaptation   3 survival
4 defense   5 camouflage   6 mimicry   7 poison
8 endangered   9 extinct   10 destruction
11 adapt/adjust   12 share   13 protect   14 perish
15 ejection   16 harm

B

1 competition   2 survival   3 Adaptation   4 extinct
5 defense   6 poison   7 endangered   8 destruction

C

1 (c)   2 (b)   3 (b)

D

1 adaptation   2 extinct   3 camouflage   4 mimicry

E　動物如何絕種

　　生命自數十億年前便已存在於地球上，這些有機體一直在改變。事實上，許多有機體已經從地球上消失，它們全都死了，所以人們稱這些動物絕種了。

　　許多動物都已絕種，恐龍、渡渡鳥以及長毛象都絕種了。為什麼動物會滅絕呢？這其中有很多的原因，火災、洪水、旱災以及地震這樣的天災會摧毀棲息地，人類也會摧毀棲息地。污染會危害到有機體，有些動物被人類獵殺，這些都會傷害動植物，造成生態系統的改變。一旦生態系統發生巨大的變化，有些動物便面臨了生存問題，接著他們會瀕臨絕種，並可能繼而滅絕。因此，保護我們的自然環境和生態系統是很重要的。你認為我們能為瀕臨絕種的動物做些什麼事呢？

以下何者為非？（3）

1 有機體常常在改變。
2 恐龍絕種了。
3 只有天災會導致動物滅絕。
4 生態系統的改變會導致動物絕種。

Unit 15 ● Earth's Rocks and Soil (p.72)

A

1 rock   2 mineral   3 soil   4 igneous rock
5 sedimentary rock   6 metamorphic rock
7 fossil   8 fossil fuel   9 property   10 impression
11 form   12 granite   13 preserve   14 press
15 petrify   16 layer

B

1 rocks   2 Igneous   3 Metamorphic   4 Sedimentary
5 properties   6 Fossil fuels   7 soils   8 impression

C

1 form 2 pressed 3 preserved 4 petrify

D

1 mineral 2 igneous rock 3 metamorphic rock
4 sedimentary rock 5 fossil 6 impression

E 化石

　　有時候人們到博物館參觀，可以看到許多恐龍和其他動物的骨頭，甚至還有一些植物的化石！但是，化石到底是什麼呢？化石是如何形成的呢？所謂的化石是動植物死後石化的殘骸，其成因有很多種，最常見的方式如下：很久以前，某隻動物死後被埋入土壤中。牠的皮膚和肌肉隨著時間逐漸腐爛，不過骨頭依舊存在，接著礦物質進入動物的骨頭中，骨頭隨之變得像岩石一樣硬，這過程通常要耗時數千年或數百萬年才會發生。

　　科學家喜歡研究化石，他們可以從中瞭解很久以前的動植物。從化石中，科學家可以得知動植物的大小、甚至是牠們吃的食物。由於化石的存在，現今的科學家才能對恐龍和其他動物有深入的了解。

填空

1 化石是動植物死後石化的殘骸。(petrified)
2 無機物進入骨頭中進而形成化石。(Minerals)
3 化石的形成耗時數千年或數百萬年。(years)
4 科學家可以從化石中得知許多事情。(Scientists)

Review Test 3

A

1 flowering plant 2 conifer 3 warm-blooded
4 cold-blooded 5 herbivore 6 carnivore
7 adaptation 8 defense 9 igneous rock
10 sedimentary rock 11 chlorophyll
12 photosynthesis 13 inherited trait
14 learned trait 15 scavenger 16 parasite
17 destruction 18 die out 19 metamorphic rock
20 property

B

1 (b) 2 (c) 3 (c) 4 (a)

C

1 vertebrate 2 photosynthesis 3 Omnivores
4 Fossils

Unit 16 • Conserving Our Resources (p.78)

A

1 resource 2 conservation/preservation 3 spill
4 landfill 5 mining 6 polluted 7 pollution
8 damaged 9 waste 10 preserve/conserve
11 replace 12 reduce 13 oil spill 14 litter
15 garbage 16 fume

B

1 conservation 2 waste 3 landfills 4 resources
5 Mining 6 pollution 7 preserve 8 damaged

C

1 replaced 2 conserve 3 polluted 4 spilled

D

1 pollution 2 waste 3 landfill 4 oil spill
5 conservation 6 fume

E 如何保存我們的資源

　　地球有許多自然資源，但其中有很多資源都不易重複使用或是恢復。不可更新資源一旦被用盡，就是永遠消失，因此我們要盡量保存我們的資源，每個人都可以在許多方面盡自己的一份力。

　　水是珍貴的資源，所以我們不可以浪費，刷牙時請把水關上，洗澡也不要洗太久。我們也要盡量節約用電，電燈不使用時不要一直開著，電腦也不要整夜都開著。回收是維護自然資源的另一個方法，盡量重複使用紙和盒子這樣的物品。節能也是維護自然資源的另一個好方法。

回答下列問題。

1 哪一種資源不易恢復？(nonrenewable resources)
2 刷牙時應該要做什麼？(turn the water off)
3 回收的好處為何？(It can save natural resources.)

Unit 17 • Earth's Changing Surface (p.82)

A

1 weathering 2 erosion 3 glacier 4 canyon
5 mesa 6 plateau 7 sand dune 8 volcano
9 eruption 10 earthquake 11 weather 12 erode
13 recede 14 expand 15 spew 16 tremble

B

1 Erosion 2 Weathering 3 Volcanoes
4 earthquake 5 eruption 6 plateau
7 sand dunes 8 glacier

C

1 weather 2 erodes 3 shake 4 recede

D

1 weathering 2 eruption 3 glacier 4 mesa
5 earthquake 6 plateau

E 地表的變化

　　地表一直在改變，高山和丘陵會崩落，岩石和土壤會搬移。有些改變非常緩慢，像是風化和侵蝕。風和水將岩石瓦解為小碎塊的過程稱為風化，風化的岩石或沙粒被搬至新地稱為侵蝕。侵蝕可分為很多種，其中水是作用最大的一種，水可以侵蝕高山使其形成峽谷，美國大峽谷即是數百萬年的水侵蝕所造就的產物，河水亦可將塵土運至海洋。風能將沙漠中的沙四處搬移，亦能以此方式侵蝕珍貴的表土使之成為沙漠。地震、火山以及劇烈的暴風雨都能迅速改變地表，地震會在陸地上造成許多巨大的裂縫，火山用灰燼和熔岩覆蓋整座城市，暴風雨挾帶豪雨造成水患。

以下何者為非？（2）

1 侵蝕可分為很多種。
2 地表的所有改變都很緩慢。
3 大峽谷是由河水侵蝕而成。
4 火山能迅速改變地表。

18 ● Weather and the Water Cycle (p.86)

A
1 atmosphere 2 pattern 3 temperature
4 thermometer 5 air pressure 6 barometer
7 front 8 precipitation 9 evaporation
10 condensation 11 predict 12 fall
13 weather vane 14 evaporate 15 Celsius
16 Fahrenheit

B
1 atmosphere 2 temperature 3 Precipitation
4 weather pattern 5 air pressure 6 front
7 Evaporation 8 Condensation

C
1 evaporates 2 condensed 3 predict 4 falls

D
1 atmosphere 2 evaporation 3 condensation
4 front 5 precipitation 6 rain gauge

E 氣象設備
　　氣象學家是指研究天氣的人,他們告訴我們天氣的冷熱和晴雨。氣象學家有很多的輔助設備,其中最常見的就是溫度計。溫度計用來測量溫度,經由觀測溫度計,人們可以得知確切的冷熱。另一個常見的儀器是氣壓計,用來測量氣壓,人們藉此可以得知未來下雨的可能性。通常氣壓下降代表即將變天,氣壓上升則會有好天氣。還有另一種設備稱作雨量計,用來測量一地的降雨量。風速計則用來測量風速,遇到颱風天特別實用!有些人甚至在家中裝設自己的風向計,可以觀測風向。

* **meteorologist** 氣象學者

回答下列問題。
1 誰研究天氣?(meteorologists)
2 什麼儀器用來測量溫度?(a thermometer)
3 氣壓計的功能為何?(It measures air pressure.)
4 什麼儀器用來測量風速?(an anemometer)

19 ● The Universe (p.90)

A
1 astronomy 2 astronomer 3 universe 4 galaxy
5 big bang theory 6 telescope 7 astronaut
8 inner planets 9 outer planets 10 asteroid belt
11 observe 12 wax 13 wane 14 blast off
15 space shuttle 16 space probe

B
1 universe 2 astronomy 3 big bang 4 inner
5 telescopes 6 galaxy 7 astronaut 8 asteroid belt

C
1 observed 2 waxing 3 blast 4 spacecraft

D
1 universe 2 galaxy 3 inner planets 4 telescope
5 asteroid belt 6 astronaut

E 內行星與外行星
　　太陽系共有八顆行星。這些行星可分為內行星和外行星兩類,各自有其特色。

　　內行星包含水星、金星、地球以及火星,它們非常靠近太陽。再者,這幾個行星的體積都很小,全都由堅硬如岩石般的物質組成,地球是內行星中體積最大的,這幾個內行星各擁有零到兩顆的衛星。外行星與內行星差異甚大,外行星比內行星寒冷許多,因為它們離太陽較遠。外行星包含木星、土星、天王星以及海王星,它們的體積都非常大,木星是太陽系中最大的一顆行星。外行星大部分由氣體組成,並擁有許多衛星,木星就有至少 63 顆衛星,其他的外行星也有很多顆衛星。

以下何者為「是」?請在空格中填入「T」或「F」。
1 太陽系共有九顆行星。(F)
2 內行星由氣體組成。(F)
3 土星是外行星。(T)
4 木星擁有至少 63 顆衛星。(T)

20 ● The Senses (p.94)

A
1 vision 2 optic 3 lens 4 eyeball 5 eyesight
6 reflex 7 auditory 8 eardrum 9 taste buds
10 sensation 11 refract 12 bend 13 reflect
14 bounce back 15 transparent 16 opaque

B
1 Vision 2 lens 3 optic nerves 4 eyesight
5 taste buds 6 Reflex actions 7 eardrum
8 auditory nerve

C
1 refracts 2 reflects 3 hear 4 transparent

D
1 reflex actions 2 lens 3 auditory 4 transparent

E 關心我們的五種感官
　　每個人都有五種感官:視覺、聽覺、嗅覺、味覺以及觸覺,我們必須照顧好這些能讓我們運用感官的身體部位。
　　舉例來說,你用眼睛來看東西,因此要好好保護眼睛並定期就醫、檢查視力,不要離電視或電腦螢幕太近,不可在昏暗或是微弱的燈光下閱讀,不可直視太陽或強光。你的耳朵讓你能聽見周遭的聲音,應該要時常清潔耳朵,聽音樂時音量不要調太大聲,避免待在過於喧鬧的地方。你的鼻子幫助你清理吸入的空氣,並使你能聞到氣味,應避免過於刺鼻的氣味,在擤鼻子、室外玩耍以及上完廁所後,記得要洗手。小心不要讓皮膚曬傷,要擦防曬油以避免皮膚受到日照的傷害。

以下何者為「是」?請在空格中填入「T」或「F」。
1 人有五種感官。(T)
2 近距離看電視是沒有大礙的。(F)
3 你的耳朵是用來聞東西的。(F)
4 擦防曬油能避免曬傷。(T)

Review Test 4

A
1 resource 2 conservation, preservation
3 weathering 4 erosion 5 atmosphere
6 precipitation 7 galaxy 8 astronaut 9 optic

10 auditory 11 pollute 12 spill 13 weather
14 erode 15 evaporate 16 condense
17 inner planets 18 outer planets 19 refract
20 reflect

B
1 (c) 2 (a) 3 (b) 4 (b)

C
1 pollution 2 Weathering 3 air pressure
4 universe

Unit 21 ● Fractions (p.100)

A
1 fraction 2 numerator 3 denominator
4 equivalent 5 whole number 6 mixed number
7 decimal 8 decimal point 9 hundredth
10 portion 11 represent 12 three sixths
13 recognize 14 identify 15 estimate
16 equal part/portion

B
1 fraction 2 equivalent 3 whole number
4 decimal 5 mixed number 6 numerator
7 hundredth's 8 portions

C
1 represents 2 represented 3 Identify 4 equal

D
1 fraction 2 numerator 3 whole number
4 portion

E 解題

1. 兩顆同樣大小的橘子。艾美拿到其中一顆的 $\frac{1}{2}$，湯姆
   拿到另一顆的 $\frac{1}{5}$。請問誰拿到比較多的橘子？
   ⇨ $\frac{1}{2}$ 大於 $\frac{1}{5}$，所以艾美拿到比較大塊。

2. 艾瑞克有一塊巧克力棒。他早上吃了 $\frac{1}{3}$ 的巧克力棒。
   當天不久後他又吃了另外的 $\frac{1}{3}$。請問巧克力棒還剩下
   多少？
   ⇨ 他吃了 $\frac{2}{3}$ 的巧克力棒，所以最後還剩下 $\frac{1}{3}$ 的巧克
   力棒。

3. 瑪麗做了一個派，她把派切成八份。史帝夫拿走派的
   $\frac{1}{4}$，然後克里斯又拿走派的 $\frac{1}{2}$。請問派最後還剩下多
   少？
   ⇨ $\frac{1}{4} = \frac{2}{8}$，而且 $\frac{1}{2} = \frac{4}{8}$。$\frac{2}{8} + \frac{4}{8} = \frac{6}{8}$。所以 $\frac{6}{8}$ 的派被
   拿走了，最後還剩下 $\frac{2}{8}$（$\frac{1}{4}$）個派。

4. 丹尼爾去購物，他有 $5\frac{1}{2}$ 塊錢，他的弟弟和他一起去購
   物，他有 $5\frac{2}{3}$ 塊錢。請問誰的錢比較多？
   ⇨ $\frac{2}{3}$ 大於 $\frac{1}{2}$，所以丹尼爾弟弟的錢比較多。

以下何者為非？（3）
1 艾美的橘子比湯姆多。
2 艾瑞克早上吃了 $\frac{1}{3}$ 的巧克力棒。

3 史帝夫拿走的派比克里斯多。
4 丹尼爾的錢比他弟弟少。

Unit 22 ● Geometry (p.104)

A
1 horizontal 2 vertical 3 parallel 4 line segment
5 polygon 6 vertex 7 right angle 8 area
9 perpendicular 10 perimeter 11 intersect
12 form 13 compute 14 determine
15 congruent figure 16 symmetric figure

B
1 vertical 2 horizontal 3 perpendicular
4 line segment 5 parallel 6 polygon
7 right angle 8 area

C
1 (b) 2 (c) 3 (a)

D
1 symmetric figures 2 line segment 3 vertex
4 rectangle 5 right angle 6 congruent figures

E 多邊形與全等圖形

　　多邊形有許多種，構成多邊形有兩個必要條件：必須
由三條以上的線段組成，而且要是一個封閉圖形。也就是
說，多邊形的所有線段都會交會。三個邊的多邊形稱為三
角形，四個邊的多邊形有可能是正方形、長方形或是菱
形，五個邊的多邊形稱為五角形，八邊形有八個邊。多邊
形可以有任何數量的邊，例如 10 個、100 個，甚至 1,000
個邊！然而圓形則不屬於多邊形。有時候兩個多邊形會是
全等圖形，亦即它們的形狀相同、大小相等。舉例來說，
兩個邊長皆為三英寸的正方形，它們完全相同，因此是全
等圖形。但如果一個正方形的邊長為二英寸，另一個正方
形的邊長為三英寸，那它們就不是全等圖形。同樣地，三
角形和正方形也不是全等圖形。

回答下列問題。
1 一個多邊形至少要有幾個邊？(three)
2 四個邊的多邊形有哪些？
  (squares, rectangles, and rhombuses)
3 八邊形有幾個邊？(eight)
4 兩個圖形全等是什麼意思？(They are identical.)

Unit 23 ● Multiplication and Division (p.108)

A
1 square number 2 square root
3 three-digit number 4 four-digit number
5 operation 6 inverse operation 7 equation
8 inequality 9 vertical multiplication
10 remainder 11 check 12 confirm
13 be divided by itself 14 be multiplied by itself
15 positive number 16 negative number

B
1 square number 2 square root 3 three-digit
4 operations 5 inverse operations 6 equation
7 inequality 8 remainder

C
1 Confirm　2 divided　3 operations　4 root
D
1 equation　2 square root　3 positive numbers
4 negative numbers

E 解題
1. 懷特太太是一位老師，她出了一份考卷給學生，每份考卷有三張。她的班上有 10 個學生，請問她需要多少張紙？
　⇨ 答案是 30，因為 3 乘以 10 等於 30。
2. 有幾個家庭要一起去野餐，每個家庭都有媽媽、爸爸以及兩個小孩。一共有八個家庭要參加，請問會有多少人去野餐？
　⇨ 答案是 32，因為 4 乘以 8 等於 32。
3. 珍妮有 24 顆糖果，她想把糖果分給她的朋友。一共有五個朋友再加上珍妮，請問每個人可以分到幾顆糖果？
　⇨ 答案是 4，因為 24 除以 6 等於 4。
4. 5 個學生發現一罐硬幣，他們想把硬幣分一分。他們數了一共有 25 個硬幣，請問每個人可以分到幾個硬幣？
　⇨ 答案是 5，因為 25 除以 5 等於 5。

以下何者為「是」？請在空格中填入「T」或「F」。
1 懷特太太的班上有 30 個學生。(F)
2 32 個人要一起去野餐。(T)
3 珍妮給了每個朋友 6 顆糖。(F)
4 6 個學生在罐子裡發現了 25 個硬幣。(F)

24 ● Measurement (p.112)

A
1 metric system　2 length　3 weight　4 capacity
5 balance scale　6 liquid　7 degree
8 U.S. customary system　9 volume　10 mass
11 weigh　12 hold　13 measure　14 be the same as
15 mile　16 yard
B
1 metric system　2 Length　3 Capacity　4 Weight
5 volume　6 mass　7 balance scale　8 degrees
C
1 same　2 weigh　3 hold　4 weight
D
1 liquid　2 weight　3 capacity　4 balance scale

E 解題
1. 瑪麗正在烘焙蛋糕，她需要一些麵粉來製作。瑪麗需要兩品脫的麵粉，但她的量杯一次只能量一杯，請問她一共需要幾杯麵粉？
　⇨ 她需要四杯。因為兩杯是一品脫，所以四杯是兩品脫。
2. 克里斯喜歡跑步。今天他跑了 2,500 公尺，請問他跑了幾公里？
　⇨ 他跑了 2.5 公里，因為 1,000 公尺為一公里。
3. 彼德拿了一把尺測量自己，他的高度為 60 英寸，請問他高幾英尺？
　⇨ 他高五英尺。因為 12 英寸為一英尺，所以 60 除以 12 等於 5。

4. 露西站在體重計上，她看見她的體重為 38 公斤。請問她重幾克？
　⇨ 她重 38,000 克。因為 1,000 克為一公斤，所以 1,000 乘以 38 等於 38,000。

填空
1 瑪麗需要四杯麵粉來做蛋糕。(four)
2 克里斯今天跑了 2.5 公里。(kilometers)
3 彼德高五英尺。(tall)
4 露西用體重計測量自己的體重。(scale)

Review Test 5
A
1 whole number　2 mixed number　3 right angle
4 area　5 square number　6 square root
7 remainder　8 operation　9 metric system
10 decimal　11 equal part/portion　12 line segment
13 polygon　14 inequality　15 equation
16 positive number　17 negative number　18 liquid
19 weigh　20 hold
B
1 (c)　2 (b)　3 (a)　4 (c)
C
1 portions　2 polygon　3 inverse operations
4 volume

25 ● Myths from Ancient Greece (p.118)

A
1 myth　2 hero　3 god　4 goddess　5 demigod
6 monster　7 mythical　8 Titan　9 immortal
10 Mount Olympus　11 fight　12 battle　13 destroy
14 punish　15 kill　16 slay
B
1 Myths　2 heroes　3 goddess　4 demigod
5 immortal　6 Titans　7 mythical　8 monsters
C
1 destroy　2 punish　3 slew　4 fought
D
1 myths　2 goddess　3 monster　4 Titan

E 希臘眾神
　神話是指流傳數千年以上的故事，它述說著勇敢的英雄、偉大的戰役、怪物以及眾神們的事蹟。有些我們熟知的美麗神話來自古希臘，這些故事都是希臘神話的一部分。現在就讓我們與希臘眾主神相遇吧。
　希臘人相信眾神們住在希臘的奧林帕斯山。在奧林帕斯山上，宙斯是權力最大的神，也是眾神之王。宙斯掌管天國並裁決眾神的紛爭。波塞頓為海神，哈帝斯為冥府之神，他們三個共為希臘最強大的神。赫拉是宙斯之妻，也是掌管婚姻的女神。雅典娜是宙斯之女，也是智慧之神。阿波羅和阿耳忒彌斯為雙胞胎，阿波羅是光明之神，阿耳忒彌斯則是狩獵之神。阿瑞斯為戰神，阿芙蘿黛蒂為愛之女神。還有其他希臘神，而上述的權力則凌駕於其他之上。

填空
1 神話述說著英雄、戰役、怪物以及眾神的事蹟。(Myths)
2 眾神們住在奧林帕斯山。(Olympus)
3 赫拉是宙斯之妻。(Hera)
4 戰神是阿瑞斯。(Ares)

Unit 26 ● Learning about Language (p.122)

A
1 declarative　2 interrogative　3 exclamatory
4 imperative　5 prefix　6 suffix　7 synonym
8 antonym　9 homophone　10 paragraph
11 state　12 exclaim　13 order　14 indent
15 thesaurus　16 encyclopedia

B
1 imperative　2 interrogative　3 declarative
4 prefixes　5 suffix　6 synonyms　7 paragraph
8 homophones

C
1 State　2 thesaurus　3 Order　4 indent

D
1 paragraph　2 interrogative sentence
3 exclamatory sentence　4 prefix　5 homophones
6 antonym

E 句子的種類
　　英文句子分為四種：陳述句、疑問句、感嘆句以及祈使句。陳述句是最常見的一種，屬於說明性的句子，用來陳述事實，在陳述句的句末要使用句號。本段文章的每個句子都是陳述句。疑問句是一個問題，用來向他人提問，在疑問句的句末要使用問號，你知道那是什麼吧？有時候，你會對某事感到興奮，你可能很開心或是情感豐沛，此時你就可以使用感嘆句。在感嘆句的句末要使用驚嘆號！最後，你也許會想下一道指令給他人，此時你可以使用祈使句。祈使句的主詞就是「你」，但是不需要講出這個字，只要表達命令就好。

回答下列問題。
1 哪一種句子最常見？(a declarative sentence)
2 什麼是疑問句？(a question)
3 如何結束感嘆句？(with an exclamation point)
4 什麼是祈使句？(an order)

Unit 27 ● Appreciating Artwork (p.126)

A
1 artwork　2 masterpiece　3 master
4 contemporary　5 element　6 contrast
7 reflection　8 background　9 dimension
10 foreground　11 appreciate　12 observe
13 exhibit　14 display　15 brighten　16 affect

B
1 masterpiece　2 artwork　3 elements
4 reflection　5 dimensions　6 background
7 contrast　8 foreground

C
1 appreciate　2 exhibiting　3 contrast　4 brighten

D
1 artwork　2 masterpiece　3 foreground
4 contrast

E 繪畫的元素
　　人們常常會到畫廊和博物館欣賞畫作。世界各地都有許多著名的畫作，人們稱之為「名作」，是什麼讓這些畫作如此出色呢？這其中包含許多因素。
　　首先，畫家所使用的線條和形狀是很重要的，寫實派畫家運用線條和形狀模擬真實世界，抽象派畫家則否，運用線條和形狀的手法正是寫實派與抽象派藝術之間的差異。其次，色彩對於畫作也是很重要的，顏色必須要彼此搭配。光影也是畫作的重要元素之一，光線和畫家運用光線的方式亦能影響你的感受，所以有些畫家會在畫作上使用強烈的明暗對比。畫家也要有好的空間概念，意即一幅畫作不能顯得太過擁擠或太過空曠。畫家必須隨時掌握畫作的和諧，如此方能造就偉大的藝術。

以下何者為非？（3）
1 偉大的畫作稱為名作。
2 寫實派畫家與抽象派畫家創作不同類型的藝術。
3 光影的變化對藝術並不重要。
4 一幅畫作不能太過擁擠。

Unit 28 ● Creating Designs (p.130)

A
1 symmetrical　2 balance　3 pattern　4 primary
5 complementary　6 vivid　7 quilt　8 collage
9 mosaic　10 folk art　11 mix　12 combine　13 snip
14 paste　15 glue　16 weave

B
1 Balance　2 Symmetrical　3 primary
4 complementary　5 vivid　6 Mosaics　7 collage
8 folk art

C
1 (c)　2 (b)　3 (a)

D
1 collage　2 mosaic　3 primary colors　4 weave

E 獨特的藝術
　　大多數人都認為藝術就是指繪畫或是圖畫，然而，其實還有許多其他類型的獨特藝術。
　　舉例來說，有些藝術家喜愛寒冷的天氣，如此便能創作冰雕。他們取用大型的冰塊，並利用鋸子、鐵鎚與鑿子來創造冰雕。當然，一旦天氣轉暖，他們的藝術品也隨之消失。
　　多數人不會認為被單是什麼藝術，但對某些人卻不然。許多人從事拼布創作，也就是被單。這些創作者將許多圖案運用在拼布上，這些圖案可簡可繁，但幾乎不會重複，在某些地方拼布創作是一種普遍的民俗藝術。
　　美國的印第安人擁有許多獨特的藝術，有些人彩繪岩石，有些人利用岩石、木材或是骨頭來製作小型雕刻。有的印第安人甚至會利用沙子來創作藝術！稱之為沙畫，可以創作出許多美麗的作品。

回答下列問題。
1 藝術家利用什麼來創作冰雕？
　(blocks of ice, saws, hammers, and chisels)
2 被單的另一個名稱為何？(a quilt)
3 拼布有什麼樣的設計？
　(simple or complicated ones)
4 誰製作沙畫？(Native Americans)

Unit 29 ● Elements of Music (p.134)

A
1 musical scale　2 note　3 staff　4 clef
5 treble clef　6 measure　7 bar line　8 rest
9 G clef　10 F clef　11 time signature　12 sit
13 keep　14 beat　15 last　16 represent

B
1 musical scale　2 staff　3 musical note　4 clef
5 treble clef　6 measures　7 rest　8 time signature

C
1 keep　2 lasts　3 sits　4 represented

D
1 musical scale　2 clef　3 measure
4 time signature　5 bar line　6 staff

E 作曲家與其音樂
　　從古至今有許多偉大的古典音樂作曲家，其中有三位分別是巴哈、莫札特以及貝多芬。巴哈為其先驅，他於巴洛克時期創作音樂。巴哈大部分的音樂是為教堂而作，曾為管弦樂團、唱詩班以及獨奏樂器譜曲，《布蘭登堡協奏曲》是他最著名的作品之一。莫札特是史上最天才的音樂家之一，他自幼便是個音樂神童，很年輕就開始從事音樂創作。莫札特寫過的音樂涵蓋各種類型，其歌劇作品《費加洛婚禮》至今仍為人所稱道，《C 小調大彌撒》亦是。貝多芬是傑出的鋼琴家兼作曲家，他的《月光奏鳴曲》非常受到歡迎。儘管貝多芬晚年失聰，他仍繼續指揮管弦樂隊，他的《第九號交響曲》是古典音樂史上最偉大的作品之一。

以下何者為「是」？請在空格中填入「T」或「F」。
1 巴哈生活在巴洛克時期。(T)
2 巴哈創作了《費加洛婚禮》。(F)
3 莫札特晚年失聰。(F)
4 貝多芬創作了《月光奏鳴曲》。(T)

Unit 30 ● A World of Music (p.138)

A
1 reed　2 mouthpiece　3 slide　4 ballet　5 theme
6 movement　7 suite　8 overture　9 march
10 live performance　11 slide　12 toot　13 blow
14 bang　15 tap　16 shake

B
1 reed　2 slide　3 mouthpiece　4 overture
5 theme　6 movement　7 live performance　8 suite

C
1 bangs　2 slides　3 Tap　4 tooting

D
1 mouthpiece　2 slide　3 ballet　4 tap
5 live performance　6 march

E 胡桃鉗
　　每年到了聖誕時節，世界各地有許多人會去欣賞芭蕾舞，其中很多人觀看《胡桃鉗》，它是全世界最出名且最受歡迎的芭蕾舞之一。《胡桃鉗》是由彼得‧柴可夫斯基所創作，故事的背景為聖誕夜，克萊拉收到了一個胡桃鉗禮物，她拿著胡桃鉗在房間裡睡著了。突然間，胡桃鉗和其他玩具突然變大，而且有了生命，他們和一群老鼠軍團交戰並將之擊敗。胡桃鉗化身為王子，並和克萊拉前往他的城堡，在那裡欣賞了許多舞蹈表演。接著，克萊拉突然醒了，並發現一切只是一場夢。《胡桃鉗》中的音樂和舞蹈都非常有名。它的音樂極為優美，舞蹈技巧也非常高超，加上動人的故事內容，使《胡桃鉗》成為許多人在聖誕節的重要一部分。

填空
1《胡桃鉗》由彼得‧柴可夫斯基創作。(Tchaikovsky)
2《胡桃鉗》的故事背景為聖誕夜。(Christmas)
3 胡桃鉗化身為王子。(prince)
4《胡桃鉗》中的音樂和舞蹈都非常受歡迎。(dances)

Review Test 6

A
1 myth　2 declarative　3 interrogative
4 symmetrical　5 collage　6 artwork　7 rest
8 musical scale　9 suite　10 overture　11 destroy
12 punish　13 immortal　14 homophone
15 paragraph　16 appreciate　17 exhibit
18 contrast　19 toot　20 time signature

B
1 (b)　2 (c)　3 (c)　4 (b)

C
1 treble clef　2 elements　3 suffix
4 Mount Olympus

AMERICAN SCHOOL TEXTBOOK
VOCABULARY KEY

Workbook

GRADE **3**

Michael A. Putlack

FÜN學美國英語課本
各學科關鍵英單 二版

A Listen to the passage and fill in the blanks.

🎧 121 **The Jury System**

Most criminal cases in the United States are done in a trial by 1._____.
Jury trials are an important part of the 2._____ system. A jury is made
up of regular 3._____. There are two kinds of juries: a 4._____ jury
and a 5._____ jury. A grand jury has between 12 and 23 members. The
6._____ presents his or her 7._____ to the grand jury. Then, the
grand jury decides if there is enough evidence to have a 8._____. If the
jury says yes, then there will be a trial. If the jury says no, there will be no trial.
A petit jury is also called a trial jury. This jury has usually 12 members. The
members listen to actual 9._____ cases. They hear all of the evidence.
Then, at the end of the trial, they must make a decision. They decide if the
10._____ is 11._____ or 12._____.

B Read the passage above and answer the following questions.

_____ 13. What is a trial?
   a A meeting to decide if someone committed a crime.
   b A group of people who decides if someone committed a crime.
   c The person who decides what evidence is allowed.
   d A place where criminals are held.

_____ 14. In the United States, who decides if a criminal is guilty or innocent?
   a A prosecutor.
   b A police officer.
   c A jury.
   d A lawyer.

_____ 15. "A jury is made up of **regular** citizens." Another word for "regular" is _____.
   a rich
   b normal
   c smart
   d professional

🎧 122 **Money Management**

When people work, they get paid. This money is called 1._____. With their earnings, they can do two things: spend or 2._____ their money. Most people do a combination of these two. First, they have to 3._____ their money on many things. They have to pay for their home. They have to pay for food and clothes. And they have to pay for 4._____, 5._____, and even 6._____ costs. Usually, there is some money left over. People often save this money. They might put it in the bank. Or they might 7._____ in the stock market. Unfortunately, some people spend too much money. They spend more than they earn. So they go into 8._____. Debt is a big problem for many people. People can plan to buy something if they 9._____ their 10._____, 11._____, and 12._____. A budget helps people to 13._____ money and to save it.

_____ 14. Which statement is closest to the main idea of the article?
  a People go into debt when they spend too much money.
  b People need to manage their money.
  c People aren't careful with their money.
  d People prefer saving over spending.

_____ 15. Which of the following statements is NOT true?
  a People have to spend their money on investments.
  b People have to spend money on food.
  c People have to spend money on insurance.
  d People have to spend money on transportation.

_____ 16. "People can plan to buy something if they **budget** their income, spending, and savings." In this sentence, "budget" means _____.
  a invest   b increase
  c plan   d save

Unit 03

Listen to the passage and fill in the blanks.

🎧 123 **All Kinds of Resources**

There are many kinds of 1._____ on the earth. Four of them are very important. They are 2._____, 3._____, 4._____, and capital resources. Renewable resources can be used again and again. They can be replaced within a short time. Some 5._____ resources are renewable. The energy from the sun, tides, water, and wind is renewable. Also, trees and animals are renewable. But humans still need to take good care of them. We should not 6._____ them at all. Nonrenewable resources are limited 7._____. Once we use them, they disappear forever. They can't be replaced. Many energy resources are like this. Coal, 8._____, and oil are all nonrenewable. Human resources are people and the 9._____ they have. This also includes the 10._____ and and information that humans have. People make products using renewable and nonrenewable resources. Machines are often used to 11._____ goods. The machines and tools that are used to produce goods are called 12._____ resources.

B Read the passage above and answer the following questions.

_____ 13. Which statement is closest to the main idea of the passage?
　a There are only four types of resources in the world.
　b Human resources are the most important type of resource.
　c There are four kinds of very important resources.
　d People must protect nonrenewable resources.

_____ 14. "**Renewable** resources can be used again and again." "Renewable" has a similar meaning to the word _____.
　a basic 　　b replaceable 　　c careful 　　d different

_____ 15. Which of the following statements is NOT true?
　a Renewable resources disappear once we use them.
　b Humans are considered important resources.
　c Machines and tools are examples of capital resources.
　d People need to take care of renewable resources.

Unit 04

🎧 124

How Technology Helps People

Nowadays, we live in an 1._____ world. We use many new 2._____ that people long ago never imagined. In the past, people could not regularly 3._____ with others. It took days, weeks, or even months just to send a letter. There were no telephones. So people had to talk face to face. Nowadays, we use 4._____ to call anyone anywhere in the world. And we send email to people instantly thanks to 5._____. In the past, traveling short 6._____ took a long time. People either walked or rode on a horse. Now, most people own cars. They can drive long distances in short periods of time. And people can even fly around the world on 7._____ now. In the past, people often died because of poor 8._____. Even a toothache could sometimes kill a person! Now, 9._____ protect people from diseases. And doctors are making more and more 10._____ every day.

B Read the passage above and answer the following questions.

_____ 11. This article is mostly about _____.
   a useful inventions
   b the Internet
   c cell phones
   d famous people

_____ 12. What is the main idea of this article?
   a New things are not being discovered anymore.
   b The Internet is the most important invention ever.
   c Life is a lot easier now than it was in the past.
   d A toothache is a dangerous medical problem.

_____ 13. According to the article, we are protected from many diseases now thanks to _____.
   a the Internet   b email
   c cars   d vaccines

Unit 05

🎧 125 **Extreme Weather Conditions**

Many people live in areas with four 1._____. It's hot in summer and cold in winter. The weather in spring and fall is either warm or cool. These are very normal weather 2._____. But sometimes there are 3._____ weather conditions. These can cause many problems for people. Sometimes, it might not rain somewhere for a long time. Lakes, rivers, and 4._____ have less water in them. Trees and grasses die. People and animals become very thirsty. This is called a 5._____. Other times, it rains constantly for many days. Water 6._____ become much higher than normal. Water often goes on the ground and even onto city streets. These are called 7._____. In many warm places near the water, there are 8._____. These storms drop heavy rains and have very strong winds. Tropical storms can drop several inches of rain in a few hours. Some places might get two or three tropical storms every year.

B Read the passage above and answer the following questions.

_____ 9. Which of the following statements is TRUE?
  a Most places have two or three tropical storms per year.
  b Drought happens when water goes into cities.
  c Tropical storms usually happen in cold places.
  d Floods can happen when it rains a lot.

_____ 10. "These storms **drop heavy rains** and have very strong winds."
  The phrase "drop heavy rains" means to _____.
  a cause a lot of rain to fall
  b stop rain from falling
  c create a lot of small drops of rain
  d make few drops of heavy rain

_____ 11. Which statement is closest to the main idea of the passage?
  a Warm climates have the most extreme weather.
  b It is dangerous to live close to the water in warm places.
  c Extreme weather can affect people in negative ways.
  d We need to try to stop extreme weather from happening.

Unit 06

A Listen to the passage and fill in the blanks.

🎧126 **Understanding Hemispheres**

Earth is a big planet. But we can make it smaller by 1._____ it into sections. We call these sections 2._____. One hemisphere is half of the earth. There is an 3._____ line that 4._____ from east to west all around the earth. It is in the center of the earth. We call it the 5._____. The equator divides the 6._____ Hemisphere from the 7._____ Hemisphere. The Northern Hemisphere includes Asia and Europe. North America is also in it. Below the equator is the Southern Hemisphere. Australia and 8._____ are in it. So are most of South America and Africa. We can also divide Earth into the 9._____ and 10._____ hemispheres. The line that does this is the 11._____. It runs from north to south. It goes directly through 12._____, England. The Eastern Hemisphere includes Europe, Africa, and Asia. The Western Hemisphere includes North and South America.

B Read the passage above and answer the following questions.

_____ 13. Which of the following statements is closest to the main idea of the passage?
    ⓐ The earth is made up of four different hemispheres.
    ⓑ Earth is a big planet.
    ⓒ The equator divides the earth into four hemispheres.
    ⓓ Most of Earth's land is found in the Western Hemisphere.

_____ 14. The earth can be divided by a line that runs from north to south called _____.
    ⓐ the equator   ⓑ the prime meridian
    ⓒ the Southern Hemisphere   ⓓ the Northern Hemisphere

_____ 15. "There is an **imaginary** line that runs from east to west all around the earth." The word "imaginary" is similar in meaning to the word _____.
    ⓐ unreal   ⓑ faint   ⓒ dotted   ⓓ dreamy

Unit 07

127 **The Three Branches of Government**

The government is made up of three 1._____ . They are the 2._____ ,
3._____ , and 4._____ branches. These three branches of the
government make and 5._____ laws. All three of them have their own
duties and responsibilities.

The legislative branch is 6._____ . Congress proposes 7._____ and
discusses them. Then Congress 8._____ on the bills. If the bills pass and
the president 9._____ them, then they become laws. After a law has been
passed, it must be 10._____ , or enforced. The executive branch
enforces laws. The executive branch is the president and everyone who works
for him. The judicial branch is the 11._____ . The judicial branch
determines if laws have been broken. When people 12._____ , the
judicial branch takes care of their cases.

B Read the passage above and answer the following questions.

_____ 13. Which sentence is closest to the main idea of the passage?
  a The judicial branch is the most important branch of the government.
  b The president is the highest authority in the government.
  c Once important laws are made, they should not be broken by citizens.
  d The three branches of government have different duties and
     responsibilities.

_____ 14. Who enforces bills that have been made into laws?
  a All citizens of the United States.
  b Only the president of the United States.
  c The president and everyone who works for him.
  d The judicial branch of the government.

_____ 15. "After a law has been **passed**, it must be carried out, or enforced."
     In this sentence, the word "passed" is closest in meaning to _____ .
  a changed   b rejected   c approved   d handed over

Unit 08

128

Ancient Egyptian Civilization

Over 5,000 years ago, 1._____ civilization began. It was centered on the 2._____. Every year, the Nile 3._____. The water from the floods made the land around the Nile very 4._____. So it was good for farming. This let a civilization start in Egypt.

Egyptian life was centered on the 5._____. They were 6._____ who ruled the entire land. Most Egyptians were 7._____. They lived their lives to serve the pharaohs. The pharaohs were very wealthy. They built 8._____ monuments. They also 9._____ the 10._____ and the 11._____. There are many pyramids all through Egypt. Egypt also had its own form of writing. It was called 12._____. It was a kind of picture writing. It didn't use letters. Instead, it used pictures. They represented different sounds and words.

B Read the passage above and answer the following questions.

_____ 13. This article is mostly about _____.
- a buildings
- b a very old culture
- c the Nile
- d hieroglyphics

_____ 14. Which of the following is NOT true of the pharaohs of ancient Egypt?
- a They were very wealthy.
- b They had many slaves.
- c They dressed up like animals.
- d They built the Sphinx.

_____ 15. "They also **constructed** the pyramids and the Sphinx." Another word for "constructed" is _____.
- a built
- b found
- c drew
- d saw

Unit 09

Listen to the passage and fill in the blanks.

🎧 129 **Athens and Sparta**

There were many 1._____ in ancient Greece. They controlled the land around them. Two of the most famous were 2._____ and 3._____. These two city-states were very different from each other.

First, Athens was the 4._____ of 5._____. It let regular people vote and help run the city. Athens had a very open society. There were slaves in Athens, but many people were still 6._____. Sparta was a lot different. It was a very 7._____ city-state. The men there 8._____ to be soldiers from a young age. And the Spartans owned many slaves, too. Sparta and Athens sometimes 9._____ wars against each other.

Athens is also known for its many accomplishments. There were many great 10._____ in Athens. Socrates and Plato were two of the world's greatest 11._____. Plato recorded many of his and Socrates's 12._____. People still read his works today.

B **Read the passage above and answer the following questions.**

_____ 13. Which sentence below best expresses the main idea?
a Athens and Sparta were two very different city-states.
b Athens was known for its many accomplishments.
c Socrates and Plato were born in Athens.
d Sparta was a city-state that fought many wars.

_____ 14. Which of the following is TRUE of ancient Athens?
a It was a very warlike city-state.
b Citizens did not control their government.
c There were no slaves.
d It had some great philosophers.

_____ 15. "Athens is also known for its many **accomplishments**." The word with the same meaning as "accomplishments" is _____.
a thoughts   b successes   c prisoners   d pleasures

Unit 10

🎧130 **All Roads Lead to Rome**

When it ruled the most land, the Roman Empire was 1._____ . It 2._____ much of the known world. To the north, it 3._____ as far as England. To the west, it 4._____ land in Spain and western Africa. To the south, it covered much land in Africa. And to the east, it stretched far into the 5._____ . However, the most important city in the empire was always Rome. There was an important saying: All roads 6._____ to Rome. At that time, the 7._____ were trying to be connected to their provinces far from the 8._____ . So they built many roads. And all of them led back to the capital. When Rome was 9._____ , the empire was powerful, too. When Rome was 10._____ , the empire was weak. In later years, Rome was 11._____ by 12._____ from Germany. How did the invaders get to Rome? They went there on one of the Roman roads!

B Read the passage above and answer the following questions.

_____ 13. What is closest to the main point the author wants to make?
   [a] The Roman Empire ruled over the Middle East.
   [b] Rome was defeated by the same roads that made it great.
   [c] The size of the Roman Empire will never be matched again.
   [d] England was the hardest country for Rome to defeat.

_____ 14. Which of the following places was NOT in the Roman Empire?
   [a] North America.
   [b] Northern Africa.
   [c] The Middle East.
   [d] Europe.

_____ 15. "All roads **lead** to Rome." The word with the same meaning as "lead" is _____.
   [a] cover   [b] hunt
   [c] return   [d] point

Listen to the passage and fill in the blanks.

🎧 131 | **Photosynthesis**

Every living creature needs food and water to 1._____. Without food and water, a creature would die. Plants are also living creatures. So they need to have these things, too. Plants can create their own food. They do this in a process called 2._____. Plants need 3._____ in order to make energy. First, when the sun shines, 4._____ in the plants 5._____ the sunlight. Sunlight is just energy. So the chlorophyll is capturing energy. Then a plant needs two more things: water and 6._____. That is when photosynthesis can 7._____. In photosynthesis, a plant undergoes a 8._____ reaction. Thanks to the chlorophyll, it creates sugar. The plant 9._____ of the sugar. The reaction also 10._____ oxygen. The plant 11._____ oxygen into the air, and people 12._____ it. So, without photosynthesis, people could not survive either.

B **Read the passage above and answer the following questions.**

_____ 13. This article focuses on _____.
     ⓐ a chemical reaction
     ⓑ an animal
     ⓒ a plant used for food
     ⓓ sunlight

_____ 14. In order to make energy, plants need _____.
     ⓐ animals
     ⓑ nutrients
     ⓒ sunlight
     ⓓ people

_____ 15. "The **reaction** also produces oxygen." The word "reaction" means _____.
     ⓐ an action that goes very slowly
     ⓑ an action in response to something else
     ⓒ an action that is very dangerous
     ⓓ an action that cannot be stopped

Unit 12

🎧 132 **Warm-Blooded vs. Cold-Blooded Animals**

All animals are either 1._____ or 2._____. This refers to how the animals maintain their 3._____. Warm-blooded animals can 4._____ their body temperature. So, even if it is very cold outside, their bodies will stay warm. But warm-blooded animals have to eat a lot of food. They use the food to 5._____ energy. That helps keep their bodies warm. Mammals are warm-blooded, and so are birds. Cold-blooded animals 6._____ the sun for heat. So their 7._____ temperatures can change all the time. These animals often rest in the sun for hours. This lets their bodies 8._____ heat and become warm. Most cold-blooded animals don't live in cold places. They prefer hot places instead. Reptiles, 9._____, and fish are all cold-blooded.

B Read the passage above and answer the following questions.

_____ 10. What is closest to the main point the author wants to make in this article?
　　[a] The temperature of an animal's blood affects its behavior.
　　[b] Birds are the only known warm-blooded animal.
　　[c] All animals are either warm-blooded or cold-blooded.
　　[d] Cold-blooded animals rely on the sun for heat.

_____ 11. Which of the following is TRUE about warm-blooded animals?
　　[a] They rely on the sun for heat.
　　[b] They can't live in cold places.
　　[c] They include reptiles and amphibians.
　　[d] They include mammals.

_____ 12. "This refers to how the animals **maintain** their body temperature." Which of the following is closest in meaning to "maintain"?
　　[a] Keep.
　　[b] Reduce.
　　[c] Stop.
　　[d] Increase.

A **Listen to the passage and fill in the blanks.**

🎧 133   **Herbivores, Carnivores, and Omnivores**

Every living creature needs to eat to survive. However, animals do not all eat the same things. Instead, they eat 1._____ foods. Most animals can be classified into three groups. Herbivores are the first group. These are animals that only eat 2._____. So they might eat plants, fruits, or vegetables. People call them "3._____." Cows and horses are 4._____. So are rabbits. Huge animals can be herbivores, too. Both elephants and 5._____ only eat plants. Carnivores are 6._____. They are often 7._____. They are 8._____ and must find 9._____ to catch and eat. The members of the cat family are 10._____. This includes lions, pumas, and even house cats. Sharks are also meat eaters. Some animals eat both plants and animals. They are called 11._____. Humans are omnivores. So are pigs, wolves, and even 12._____.

B **Read the passage above and answer the following questions.**

_____ 13. According to the article, animals can be classified into three groups, which are _____.
  ⓐ mammals, reptiles, and amphibians
  ⓑ herbivores, carnivores, and omnivores
  ⓒ preditors, prey, and scavengers
  ⓓ bird family, cat family, and humans

_____ 14. Which of the following statements is TRUE?
  ⓐ Herbivores are all small animals, like rabbits.
  ⓑ Omnivores eat both plants and other animals.
  ⓒ Not all of the living creature need to eat to survive.
  ⓓ Predators are hunted by prey for their meat.

_____ 15. "Instead, they eat **a variety of** foods." Which of the following has the same meaning as "a variety of"?
  ⓐ a wide range of   ⓑ plenty of
  ⓒ a matter of   ⓓ a portion of

Unit 14

🎧 134   **How Animals Become Extinct**

There has been life on Earth for billions of years. These 1._____ are always changing. In fact, many organisms no longer live on Earth. They all died. So people say that they are 2._____.

Many animals are extinct. The dinosaurs are extinct. The dodo bird is extinct. The woolly mammoth is also no longer 3._____. Why do animals 4._____? There are many reasons. Natural 5._____ such as fires, flood, droughts, and earthquakes can destroy 6._____. People can destroy habitats, too. Pollution can also harm organisms. Some animals are 7._____ by people. All these things are 8._____ to plants and animals, and they can cause the changes to 9._____. When a large change occurs in an ecosystem, some organisms have trouble 10._____. Then they can be 11._____ and may become extinct. So, it is important to 12._____ our natural environment and ecosystems. What do you think we can do for endangered animals?

B Read the passage above and answer the following questions.

_____ 13. Which sentence best expresses the main idea of this article?
- ⓐ The planet is currently experiencing a crisis.
- ⓑ The dinosaurs were the last animals to go extinct.
- ⓒ There are many things that will cause animals to die out.
- ⓓ Pollution is the number one cause of extinction.

_____ 14. Which of the following is NOT mentioned as something that can lead to an animal's extinction?
- ⓐ Natural disasters.
- ⓑ Pollution.
- ⓒ Diet changes.
- ⓓ Hunting.

_____ 15. "Then they can be **endangered** and may become extinct." Another word for "endangered" is _____.
- ⓐ discovered
- ⓑ abandoned
- ⓒ threatened
- ⓓ hunted

15

Listen to the passage and fill in the blanks.

🎧 135　Fossils

Sometimes people go to the museum. They see many 1._____ of dinosaurs or other animals. There are even some plant 2._____! But, what exactly are fossils? And how do fossils 3._____? Fossils are the 4._____ remains of dead animals or plants. They can form in many ways. The most common way is like this: A long time ago, an animal died. Then it got 5._____ in the ground. Over time, the skin and muscles rotted away. But the bones 6._____. Then, 7._____ entered the animal's bones. The bones then became as hard as 8._____. This might have taken thousands or millions of years to occur.

Scientists like to 9._____ fossils. They can learn a lot about the animals and plants that lived a long time ago. Scientists can learn how big they are. Scientists can even learn what kind of food they ate. Thanks to fossils, scientists today know a lot about dinosaurs and other animals.

Read the passage above and answer the following questions.

_____ 10. Another good title for this article is _____.
- a Five Things You Must Know About Fossils
- b How to Dig Up Your Own Fossils
- c Remains That Are Millions of Years in the Making
- d The Biggest Fossils Known to Man

_____ 11. "Over time, the skin and muscles **rotted** away." The word "rot" means _____.

a to become stronger	b to break down and disappear
c to get sick	d to become attached

_____ 12. According to the article, fossils are made when minerals enter bones and _____.

a make them hollow	b produce nutrients
c make them hard	d leave clues

A Listen to the passage and fill in the blanks.

🎧 136 **How to Conserve Our Resources**

Earth has many natural 1._____. But many of them are resources that cannot be reused or 2._____ easily. Once nonrenewable resources are 3._____, they are gone forever. That means we should 4._____ our resources as much as possible. Everyone can help do this in many ways.

Water is a valuable resource. So we shouldn't 5._____ it. When you're brushing your teeth, turn the water 6._____. Don't take really long showers either. We should also be careful about using 7._____. Don't 8._____ any lights if you aren't going to use them. Don't leave your computer on all night long. Recycling is another way to 9._____ natural resources. Try to reuse things like papers and boxes. Reducing the amount of 10._____ you use is also a good way to conserve our resources.

B Read the passage above and answer the following questions.

_____ 11. Which statement best expresses the main idea of this article?
  a We must find new resources in space.
  b Earth's resources will never be used up.
  c We must be more careful with Earth's resources.
  d We must find new ways to use Earth's resources.

_____ 12. According to the article, which of the following is a good way to save water?
  a Take more baths.
  b Take shorter showers.
  c Reuse water bottles.
  d Drink bottled water.

_____ 13. "That means we should **conserve** our resources as much as possible."
  The word "conserve" means _____.
  a to discover more of something
  b to research something
  c to find new ways of using something
  d to use less of something

Listen to the passage and fill in the blanks.

🎧 137 **What Changes Earth's Surface?**

The surface of the earth is 1._____ changing. Mountains and 2._____ break down. Rocks and soil move from one place to another. Some changes are very slow. Weathering and 3._____ can cause these changes. Weathering occurs when wind and water 4._____ rocks into pieces. Erosion occurs when 5._____ rocks or sand are carried away. There are many types of erosion. The most powerful is water. Water can break down mountains and form 6._____. Water erosion made the Grand Canyon over millions of years. Water also moves dirt and soil to oceans and seas. The wind can move 7._____ in deserts from place to place. And it can 8._____ valuable 9._____ and make deserts that way. Earthquakes, 10._____, and 11._____ can change Earth's surface quickly. Earthquakes can make huge cracks in the land. Volcanoes can cover entire cities in ash and 12._____. And storms can drop huge amounts of water and causes floods.

B Read the passage above and answer the following questions.

_____ 13. This article focuses on a(n) _____.
- [a] part of the earth
- [b] natural disaster
- [c] type of weather
- [d] volcano

_____ 14. According to the article, which of the following is NOT something that can change the earth's surface?
- [a] Skyscrapers.
- [b] Volcanoes.
- [c] Erosion.
- [d] Earthquakes.

_____ 15. "The surface of the earth is **constantly** changing." The word with the same meaning as "constantly" is _____.
- [a] entirely
- [b] formerly
- [c] always
- [d] partially

A Listen to the passage and fill in the blanks.

138 **Weather Equipment**

Meteorologists are people who study the 1._____. They tell us if it will be hot or cold. They tell us if it will be sunny or 2._____. They have lots of equipment to help them. The most common piece of equipment is the 3._____. A thermometer measures the 4._____. By looking at it, people can tell exactly how hot or cold it is. Another common instrument is the 5._____. This measures the 6._____. So people can know if it is going to rain or not. Usually, when the air pressure 7._____, bad weather is coming. And when it goes up, good weather is coming. There is other equipment, too. A 8._____ measures the amount of rain that has fallen in a place. And an 9._____ is used to measure how fast the wind is 10._____. It's really useful on windy days! And some people even have 11._____ on their homes. They show which 12._____ the wind is blowing.

B Read the passage above and answer the following questions.

_____ 13. What is the main idea of the article?
   a Meteorologists are people who study the weather.
   b A thermometer is the most important piece of weather equipment.
   c There are many pieces of equipment that help meteorologists.
   d Meteorologists don't need weather equipment to predict the weather.

_____ 14. "Usually, when the air pressure **drops**, bad weather is coming." A word that has the opposite meaning of "drops" as it is used in this sentence is

_____.
   a rises   b floats
   c steadies   d hangs

_____ 15. According to the article, a rain gauge measures the _____ of rain.
   a equipment   b temperature
   c pressure   d amount

Unit 19

139 **The Inner and Outer Planets**

The solar system has eight 1._____ in it. These planets are divided into two groups. We call them the 2._____ and 3._____ planets. These two groups have their own characteristics.

The inner planets are 4._____, Venus, Earth, and 5._____. They are all fairly close to the sun. Also, these planets are all small and made up of 6._____, rocklike materials. The earth is the largest of the inner planets. And the inner planets all have zero, one, or two 7._____. The outer planets are very different from the inner planets. The outer planets are much colder than the inner planets. They are 8._____ from the sun. The outer planets are Jupiter, 9._____, Uranus, and 10._____. They are all very large. Jupiter is the largest planet in the solar system. They are mostly 11._____ gas. Also, the outer planets have many moons. Jupiter has 12._____ 63 moons. The others also have many moons.

B Read the passage above and answer the following questions.

_____ 13. Which of the following statements is NOT true?
  [a] The solar system is divided into two groups.
  [b] Earth is the largest of the inner planets.
  [c] The outer planets are closer to the sun.
  [d] The inner planets are smaller than the outer planets.

_____ 14. Which planet is the largest in the solar system?
  [a] Earth.   [b] Saturn.
  [c] Uranus.   [d] Jupiter.

_____ 15. "They are mostly **made up** of gas." In this sentence, "made up" is closest in meaning to _____.
  [a] thought   [b] created
  [c] pretended   [d] faked

20

Unit 20

🎧 140 **Caring for the Five Senses**

Everyone has five senses: seeing, 1._____, smelling, 2._____, and 3._____. We need to take care of the parts of our bodies that let us use our senses.

For example, you use your eyes for 4._____. You should protect your eyes and have a doctor regularly check your 5._____. Don't sit too close to the TV or computer monitor, and don't read in the dark or in 6._____ light. Never look 7._____ at the sun or at very bright lights. Your ears let you hear the things around you. You should 8._____ your ears all the time. Don't listen to loud music, and try to avoid places that are really loud. Your 9._____ cleans the air you breathe and lets you 10._____ things. Avoid things that have very strong smells. Always wash your hands after 11._____ your nose, playing outside, or using the restroom. Protect your skin from 12._____. Use sunscreen to protect your skin from the sun.

B Read the passage above and answer the following questions.

_____ 13. Which statement best expresses the main idea of this article?
- a People should practice using their senses.
- b People should protect their senses.
- c People should learn more about their senses.
- d People should stop using their senses.

_____ 14. According to the article, what's a good way to maintain your sense of smell?
- a Only smell foods that you like to eat.
- b Close your nose and try not to smell anything.
- c Practice smelling for five minutes every day.
- d Avoid anything that has a very strong smell.

_____ 15. ". . . don't read in the dark or in **dim** light." The opposite of "dim" is _____.
- a bright
- b colored
- c weak
- d low

A Listen to the passage and fill in the blanks.

141 Solve the Problems

1. Two oranges are the same size. Amy gets $\frac{1}{2}$ of one orange. Tom gets
    1._____ of the other. Who gets more of the orange?

    ⇨ $\frac{1}{2}$ is greater than $\frac{1}{5}$. So, Amy gets the larger piece.

2. Eric has one candy bar. He eats 2._____ of the candy bar in the morning.

    Later in the day, he eats another $\frac{1}{3}$ of the candy bar. How much of the

    candy bar is left over?

    ⇨ He ate 3._____ of the candy bar. So there is $\frac{1}{3}$ left over.

3. Mary makes a pie. She cuts it into 8 pieces. Steve takes 4._____ of the

    pie. Then Chris takes 5._____ of the pie. How much pie remains?

    ⇨ $\frac{1}{4} = \frac{2}{8}$. And $\frac{1}{2} = \frac{4}{8}$. $\frac{2}{8} + \frac{4}{8} = \frac{6}{8}$. So $\frac{6}{8}$ of the pie is gone. Now there are

    6._____ (or $\frac{1}{4}$) of the pie remaining.

4. Daniel goes shopping. He has 7._____ dollars. His brother goes shopping

    with him. His brother has 8._____ dollars. Who has more money?

    ⇨ $\frac{2}{3}$ is greater than 9._____. So Daniel's brother has more money.

B Read the passage above and answer the following questions.

_____ 10. Another good title for this article would be _____.
- a How to Cut Food into Equal Parts
- b The Fractions of Food
- c Adding, Subtracting, and Comparing Fractions
- d The Easiest Way to Multiply and Divide Fractions

_____ 11. "Now there are 2/8 (or 1/4) of the pie **remaining**." Another way to say
   "remaining" is _____.
- a equaling
- b left over
- c adding up
- d subtracted

_____ 12. "Mary makes a pie. She cuts it into 8 **pieces**." For a word with a similar
   meaning to "pieces" as it is used in this sentence is _____.
- a slices
- b dozens
- c loaves
- d cups

Unit 22

🎧 142

Polygons and Congruent Figures

There are many different types of 1._____. There are two requirements for an object to be a polygon. It must be made of three or more 2._____. And it must be a 3._____ figure. That means that all of the lines in the polygon 4._____ each other. A three-sided polygon is a 5._____. Some four-sided polygons are squares, 6._____, or 7._____. A five-sided one is a 8._____. An 9._____ has eight sides. A polygon can have any number of sides. It could have 10, 100, or even 1,000 sides! But circles are not polygons. Sometimes two polygons are 10._____. This means they have the same shape and size. For example, two 11._____ have sides that are three inches long. They are 12._____. So they are congruent figures. But if one square's sides are two inches long while the other's sides are three inches long, they are not congruent. Also, a triangle and a square can never be congruent.

B Read the passage above and answer the following questions.

_____ 13. What is closest to the main point the author wants to make?
- [a] A rhombus is considered to be a polygon.
- [b] A triangle and a square can never be congruent, but two rectangles can be.
- [c] There are many different kinds of congruent and noncongruent polygons.
- [d] An octagon has more sides than a pentagon.

_____ 14. Which of the following statements is NOT true?
- [a] Two identical squares are congruent.
- [b] A polygon must have fewer than 10 sides.
- [c] All the lines of a polygon must meet.
- [d] A triangle is an example of a polygon.

_____ 15. "It must be made of three or more line **segments**." A word with the same meaning as "segments" is _____.
- [a] pieces
- [b] situations
- [c] resources
- [d] operators

Listen to the passage and fill in the blanks.

🎧 143   Solve the Problems

1. Mrs. White is a teacher. She is 1._____ to the students. Each test has 3 2._____ of paper. She has 10 students in her class. How many sheets of paper does she need?

    ⇨ The answer is 30 because 3 3._____ 10 = 30.

2. Some families are going to 4._____ together. Each family has a mother, father, and two children. There are 8 families. How many people are going on the picnic?

    ⇨ The answer is 32 because 4 × 8 = 32.

3. Jenny has 24 5._____ of candy. She wants to 6._____ all of the candy with her friends. There are 5 people 7._____ Jenny. How many pieces of candy should each person get?

    ⇨ The answer is 4 because 24 8._____ 6 = 4.

4. 5 students find some 9._____ in a jar. They want to share the coins with each other. They 10._____ the coins and see that there are 25 coins. How many coins does each student get?

    ⇨ The answer is 5 because 25 ÷ 5 = 5.

B Read the passage above and answer the following questions.

_____ 11. According to the article, how many families went on a picnic?
    a 2   b 3   c 5   d 8

_____ 12. This article focuses on _____.
    a word puzzles   b picnics
    c math problems   d a girl named Jenny

_____ 13. How many sheets of paper does the test that Mrs. White gives to her class have?
    a One.   b Two.
    c Three.   d Four.

Unit 24

🎧 144

Solve the Problems

1. Mary is baking a cake. She needs to use flour to make the cake. She needs 2 1._____ of flour. But her 2._____ can only fill 1 3._____ at a time. How many cups of flour does she need?

   ⇨ She needs 4 cups. 2 cups is 1 pint. So 4 cups is 2 pints.

2. Chris likes to run. Today, he ran 2,500 4._____. How many 5._____ did he run?

   ⇨ He ran 2.5 kilometers. There are 1,000 meters in 1 kilometer.

3. Peter gets a ruler and 6._____ himself. He is 60 7._____ tall. How many 8._____ tall is he?

   ⇨ He is 5 feet tall. There are 12 inches in one foot. So 60 ÷ 12 = 5.

4. Lucy steps on a 9._____. She sees that she 10._____ 38 11._____. How many 12._____ does she weigh?

   ⇨ She weighs 38,000 grams. There are 1,000 grams in one kilogram. So 1,000 × 38 = 38,000.

_____ 13. According to the article, how much does Lucy weigh?
   a She weighs 38 grams.
   b She weighs 38 kilograms.
   c She weighs 38 feet.
   d She weighs 38 meters.

_____ 14. "But her measuring cup can only **fill** 1 cup at a time." The word with the opposite meaning to "fill" is _____.
   a empty   b break   c drink   d store

_____ 15. "Lucy steps on a scale." A scale is something used to _____.
   a cook food   b wash feet
   c weigh things   d make things smell good

Unit 25

A **Listen to the passage and fill in the blanks.**

🎧 145 **The Greek Gods and Goddesses**

Myths are stories that have been around for thousands of years or more. Myths tell about brave 1._____, great battles, 2._____, and 3._____. Some wonderful myths come to us from ancient Greece. These tales are a part of Greek 4._____. Now, let's meet some of the main Greek gods and goddesses.

The Greeks believed that the gods lived on 5._____, a mountain in Greece. At Mount Olympus, 6._____ was the most powerful god. He was the king of the gods. He controlled the heavens and decided arguments among the gods. Poseidon was the god of the sea, and Hades was the god of the 7._____. They were the three strongest gods. Hera was Zeus's wife. She was the goddess of 8._____. Athena was Zeus's daughter. She was the goddess of 9._____. Apollo and Artemis were twins. Apollo was the god of 10._____, and Artemis was the goddess of the 11._____. Ares was the god of 12._____. And Aphrodite was the goddess of love. There were some other gods. But they were the most powerful of all.

B **Read the passage above and answer the following questions.**

_____ 13. Which sentence below best expresses the main idea of this article?
- a Greek myths are the oldest myths known to man.
- b In Greek mythology, Zeus is the king of the gods, and Hera is his wife.
- c Zeus's wife is the goddess of marriage.
- d Some interesting myths about gods come from ancient Greece.

_____ 14. In Greek mythology, who was the god or goddess of the hunt?
- a Apollo.　　b Hera.　　c Zeus.　　d Artemis.

_____ 15. "Myths tell about brave heroes, great battles, **monsters**, and gods and goddesses." The word "monster" means _____.
- a a helper for heroes　　b a scary creature
- c a brave warrior　　d a type of weapon

Unit 26

🎧 146 Different Types of Sentences

There are four types of sentences in English. They are 1._____, 2._____, 3._____, and 4._____ sentences. Declarative sentences are the most common. They are just statements. Use them to state 5._____. You always end these sentences with a 6._____. All of the sentences in this 7._____ are declarative ones. An interrogative is a 8._____. Use this kind of sentence to ask other people about something. They always end with a 9._____. You know what that is, don't you? Sometimes, you might be really excited about something. Or perhaps you are happy. Or maybe you have a strong 10._____. Then you use an exclamatory sentence. You end these with an 11._____! Finally, you might want to give a person an 12._____. Use an imperative sentence to do this. In these sentences, the subject is "you." But don't say that word. Instead, just give the order.

B Read the passage above and answer the following questions.

_____ 13. What is another good title for this article?
- [a] How to Write a Good Sentence
- [b] Making Sentences Easier to Read
- [c] What Kind of Sentence Is It?
- [d] Two Steps to Perfect Imperative Sentences

_____ 14. An exclamatory sentence will always end with a(n) _____.
- [a] period
- [b] exclamation point
- [c] question mark
- [d] comma

_____ 15. The article mentions that declarative sentences are "statements."
A "statement" is _____.
- [a] something said clearly and strongly
- [b] a question that is asked
- [c] something said with excitement
- [d] something whispered

Unit 27

Listen to the passage and fill in the blanks.

🎧147 **Elements of Painting**

People often visit art galleries and museums to look at paintings. There are many famous paintings in places around the world. People call the greatest paintings "1._____." What makes a painting great? There are many different 2._____.

First, the 3._____ that an artist uses are important. Realistic artists make their lines and shapes 4._____ reality. Abstract artists do not. The way of using lines and shapes is the main difference between realistic and 5._____ art. Also, the colors in the painting are important. The colors should 6._____ each other. Light and 7._____ are important elements of paintings, too. Light can affect the way you feel. The way that artists use light in their paintings can affect your emotions as well. So some artists may use a sharp 8._____ between 9._____. An artist should also have a good sense of 10._____. This means that the painting should not be too 11._____ or too empty. The painter should always try to find 12._____ in a painting. That makes great art.

B Read the passage above and answer the following questions.

_____ 13. What is closest to the main point the author wants to make?
　　　 ⓐ A sense of space makes a good painting.
　　　 ⓑ Only certain people can become artists.
　　　 ⓒ Great paintings require several elements.
　　　 ⓓ People often visit galleries to view paintings.

_____ 14. "Realistic artists make their lines and shapes **imitate** reality." The word "imitate" means _____.
　　　 ⓐ to study　　　 ⓑ to reject
　　　 ⓒ to copy　　　 ⓓ to discuss

_____ 15. "So some artists may use a sharp **contrast** between dark and light." A word with the opposite meaning of "contrast" is _____.
　　　 ⓐ sum　　　 ⓑ distance　　　 ⓒ likeness　　　 ⓓ conclusion

148 Unique Art

Most people think that art is just painting or 1._____. But there are many other kinds of unique art.

For example, some artists love cold weather. The reason they like the cold is that they make 2._____. They take huge 3._____ of ice and use saws, hammers, and chisels to create sculptures. Of course, when the weather gets warmer, their 4._____ disappears.

Most people don't think of 5._____ as art, but others do. Many people make 6._____. These are bed covers. But the quilt makers put many designs on their quilts. The designs can be 7._____, or they can be very complicated. But no two quilts are ever alike. Quilt making is a popular form of 8._____ in some places.

In America, Native Americans have many unique forms of art. Some of them paint 9._____. Others make tiny sculptures from rocks, 10._____, or bone. And some Native Americans even use 11._____ to make art! This is called sand painting. It can produce many beautiful 12._____ of art.

_____ 13. Another good title for this article is _____.
   a The Wide World of Art   b The World's Most Expensive Art
   c The Importance of Art   d The Growing Popularity of Art

_____ 14. Which of the following is NOT a unique kind of art mentioned in the article?
   a Rock painting.   b Sculpture.   c Tattooing.   d Sand painting.

_____ 15. "Quilt making is a popular form of **folk** art in some places." In this sentence, the word "folk" means _____.
   a something that is very expensive
   b something that is in a museum
   c something that is done by common people
   d something that is beautiful but strange

Unit 29

A Listen to the passage and fill in the blanks.

🎧 149 **Composers and Their Music**

There have been many great classical music 1._____. Three of the greatest were Johann Sebastian Bach, Wolfgang Amadeus Mozart, and Ludwig van Beethoven. Bach came first. He 2._____ music during the Baroque Period. Much of his music was for the church. He wrote 3._____ for orchestras, 4._____, and 5._____ instruments. *The Brandenburg Concertos* are some of his most famous works. Mozart was one of the most brilliant 6._____ of all time. He was a child genius. He started writing music at a very young age. He wrote all kinds of music. His 7._____ *The Marriage of Figaro* is still famous. So is his *Great Mass in* 8._____. Beethoven was a great 9._____ and composer. His *Moonlight Sonata* was very famous. He 10._____ later in his life. But he still 11._____ orchestras. His *9th Symphony* is one of the greatest of all pieces of 12._____ music.

B Read the passage above and answer the following questions.

_____ 13. Bach "wrote tunes for orchestras, choirs, and **solo** instruments." A "solo" instrument is one that is played _____.
   a quickly   b well   c loudly   d alone

_____ 14. Which piece is described as "one of the greatest of all pieces of classical music"?
   a Beethoven's *Moonlight Sonata*.
   b Beethoven's *9th Symphony*.
   c Mozart's *The Marriage of Figaro*.
   d Mozart's *Great Mass in C Minor*.

_____ 15. Which statement best summarizes the passage?
   a Bach, Mozart, and Beethoven worked together to write their music.
   b Bach, Mozart, and Beethoven were three of the best classical composers.
   c Many classical composers started writing music when they were young.
   d Anyone can become a successful composer if he or she works hard enough.

Unit 30

150 **The Nutcracker**

Every Christmas season, people all around the world go to the 1._____.
And many of them see *The Nutcracker*. It is one of the most famous and popular
ballets in the world. It was 2._____ by Peter Tchaikovsky. In the story, it is
Christmas Eve. Clara receives a 3._____ as a present. She falls asleep
in a room with the nutcracker. Suddenly, the nutcracker and the toys grow big,
and they 4._____. Then, they 5._____ an army of mice and defeat
them. The nutcracker becomes a 6._____, and he and Clara go to his
castle. They watch many 7._____ there. Then, Clara wakes up and learns
it was only a dream. The music and dances in *The Nutcracker* are very famous.
The music is beautiful, and the dances 8._____ great skill. Along with the
story, they have made *The Nutcracker* an important part of Christmas for many
people.

B Read the passage above and answer the following questions.

_____ 9. What is closest to the main point the author wants to make?
- [a] *The Nutcracker* was the first ballet ever produced.
- [b] *The Nutcracker* is the most difficult ballet to perform.
- [c] *The Nutcracker* is a popular toy among children and adults.
- [d] *The Nutcracker* is an important part of Christmas for many.

_____ 10. The main character in *The Nutcracker* is named _____.
- [a] Nutty
- [b] Mouse
- [c] Clara
- [d] Peter

_____ 11. "Every Christmas season, people all around the world go to the **ballet**."
A "ballet" is _____.
- [a] a type of colorful toy
- [b] a type of holiday tree
- [c] a type of dance performance
- [d] a type of musical instrument

Answer Key

Unit 01
1 jury 2 justice 3 citizens 4 grand 5 petit
6 prosecutor 7 evidence 8 trial 9 court 10 defendant
11 innocent 12 guilty 13 a 14 c 15 b

Unit 02
1 earnings 2 save 3 spend 4 insurance 5 transportation
6 entertainment 7 invest 8 debt 9 budget 10 income
11 spending 12 savings 13 manage 14 b 15 a 16 c

Unit 03
1 resources 2 renewable 3 nonrenewable 4 human
5 energy 6 waste 7 in supply 8 gas 9 skills
10 knowledge 11 produce 12 capital 13 c 14 b 15 a

Unit 04
1 advanced 2 inventions 3 communicate 4 cell phones
5 the Internet 6 distances 7 airplanes 8 medical
treatment 9 vaccines 10 discoveries 11 a 12 c 13 d

Unit 05
1 seasons 2 conditions 3 extreme 4 streams 5 drought
6 levels 7 floods 8 tropical storms 9 d 10 a 11 c

Unit 06
1 dividing 2 hemispheres 3 imaginary 4 runs 5 equator
6 Northern 7 Southern 8 Antarctica 9 Eastern 10 Western
11 prime meridian 12 Greenwich 13 a 14 b 15 a

Unit 07
1 branches 2 executive 3 legislative 4 judicial 5 enforce
6 Congress 7 bills 8 votes 9 signs 10 carried out
11 court system 12 break the law 13 d 14 c 15 c

Unit 08
1 Egyptian 2 Nile River 3 flooded 4 rich 5 pharaohs
6 god-kings 7 slaves 8 huge 9 constructed
10 pyramids 11 Sphinx 12 hieroglyphics 13 b 14 c 15 a

Unit 09
1 city-states 2 Athens 3 Sparta 4 birthplace
5 democracy 6 free 7 warlike 8 trained 9 fought
10 thinkers 11 philosophers 12 thoughts 13 a 14 d 15 b

Unit 10
1 enormous 2 covered 3 stretched 4 ruled
5 Middle East 6 lead 7 emperors 8 capital 9 powerful
10 weak 11 defeated 12 invaders 13 b 14 a 15 d

Unit 11
1 survive 2 photosynthesis 3 sunlight 4 chlorophyll
5 captures 6 carbon dioxide 7 take place 8 chemical
9 feeds off 10 produces 11 releases 12 breathe 13 a
14 c 15 b

Unit 12
1 warm-blooded 2 cold-blooded 3 body temperature
4 regulate 5 produce 6 rely upon 7 internal
8 soak up 9 amphibians 10 c 11 d 12 a

Unit 13
1 a variety of 2 vegetation 3 plant eaters 4 herbivores
5 rhinoceroses 6 meat eaters 7 hunters 8 predators
9 prey 10 carnivores 11 omnivores 12 chickens 13 b
14 b 15 a

Unit 14
1 organisms 2 extinct 3 alive 4 become extinct
5 disasters 6 habitats 7 hunted 8 harmful 9 ecosystems
10 surviving 11 endangered 12 protect 13 c 14 c 15 c

Unit 15
1 bones 2 fossils 3 form 4 petrified 5 buried
6 remained 7 minerals 8 rock 9 study 10 c 11 b 12 c

Unit 16
1 resources 2 replaced 3 used up 4 conserve
5 waste 6 off 7 electricity 8 turn on 9 save
10 energy 11 c 12 b 13 d

Unit 17
1 constantly 2 hills 3 erosion 4 break down
5 weathered 6 canyons 7 sand 8 erode 9 topsoil
10 volcanoes 11 violent storms 12 lava 13 a 14 a 15 c

Unit 18
1 weather 2 rainy 3 thermometer 4 temperature
5 barometer 6 air pressure 7 drops 8 rain gauge
9 anemometer 10 blowing 11 weather vanes
12 direction 13 c 14 a 15 d

Unit 19
1 planets 2 inner 3 outer 4 Mercury 5 Mars 6 solid
7 moons 8 farther 9 Saturn 10 Neptune
11 made up of 12 at least 13 c 14 d 15 b

Unit 20
1 hearing 2 tasting 3 feeling 4 seeing 5 eyesight
6 dim 7 directly 8 clean 9 nose 10 smell 11 blowing
12 sunburns 13 b 14 d 15 a

Unit 21
1 $\frac{1}{5}$ 2 $\frac{1}{3}$ 3 $\frac{2}{3}$ 4 $\frac{1}{4}$ 5 $\frac{1}{2}$ 6 $\frac{2}{8}$ 7 $5\frac{1}{2}$ 8 $5\frac{2}{3}$ 9 $\frac{1}{2}$
10 c 11 b 12 a

Unit 22
1 polygons 2 line segments 3 closed 4 meet
5 triangle 6 rectangles 7 rhombuses 8 pentagon
9 octagon 10 congruent figures 11 squares
12 identical 13 c 14 b 15 a

Unit 23
1 giving a test 2 sheets 3 × 4 go on a picnic 5 pieces
6 share 7 plus 8 ÷ 9 coins 10 count 11 d 12 c 13 c

Unit 24
1 pints 2 measuring cup 3 cup 4 meters 5 kilometers
6 measures 7 inches 8 feet 9 scale 10 weighs
11 kilograms 12 grams 13 b 14 a 15 c

Unit 25
1 heroes 2 monsters 3 gods and goddesses 4 mythology
5 Mount Olympus 6 Zeus 7 underworld 8 marriage
9 wisdom 10 light 11 hunt 12 war 13 d 14 d 15 b

Unit 26
1 declarative 2 interrogative 3 exclamatory
4 imperative 5 facts 6 period 7 paragraph 8 question
9 question mark 10 emotion 11 exclamation point
12 order 13 c 14 b 15 a

Unit 27
1 masterworks 2 elements 3 lines and shapes
4 imitate 5 abstract 6 go well with 7 shadows
8 contrast 9 dark and light 10 space 11 crowded
12 balance 13 c 14 c 15 c

Unit 28
1 drawing 2 ice sculptures 3 blocks 4 artwork
5 bed covers 6 quilts 7 simple 8 folk art 9 rocks
10 wood 11 sand 12 pieces 13 a 14 c 15 c

Unit 29
1 composers 2 composed 3 tunes 4 choirs 5 solo
6 musicians 7 opera 8 C Minor 9 pianist 10 went deaf
11 conducted 12 classical 13 d 14 b 15 b

Unit 30
1 ballet 2 composed 3 nutcracker 4 come to life
5 battle 6 prince 7 dances 8 require 9 d 10 c 11 c